He had been well trai~~~
crucial moment: he be~~~
her absolutely. At la~~~
slowness, she took off ~~~
she never so much as t~~~
awaiting her command.

'Put your tongue in my navel!'

Pub near Church
St Mary's Platt

24.3.00

John Collings
Funeral

By the same author

XAVIERA HOLLANDER

Yours Fatally!

Book One of the
Golden Phallus of Osiris **trilogy**

This edition published 1995
by Diamond Books
77–85 Fulham Palace Road
Hammersmith, London W6 8JB

First published by Grafton Books 1987

ISBN 0 261 66643 6

Printed and bound in Great Britain

Set in Times

Preface

As soon as I finished writing my trilogy of Lucinda novels (*Lucinda My Lovely*, *Hot Nights on Xanthos* and *Erotic Enterprises Inc*), I was asked to do a similar series on the theme of Doña Juan. I liked the idea and wrote some preliminary notes. But then, I got hooked (not Happily Hooked – that's the latest instalment of my autobiography for which my man, John Drummond, shares the blame!) but intensely excited by some of the marvellous Egyptian exhibits in the British Museum and the myth of the lost phallus of the god, Osiris. My imagination caught fire; Doña Juan was put aside and I lost no time in recording the chronicle of *The Golden Phallus of Osiris* of which this is the first volume.

Maybe, when this series is completed, Doña Juan will steal back into my thoughts. And those of my readers who were amused by Lucinda and her entourage will surely welcome the fleeting appearance of Jennifer Maxwell, though in rather unfortunate circumstances, in *Yours Fatally!* That's the trouble with fiction, the characters come to life and haunt their creator.

Contents

Part I

1

I Think I've Found What You Are Looking For

Anna glanced at her gold Cartier watch, the latest present from Chuck, and judged that it was time for her to change into the slinky white dress which she liked to be wearing when he got home. Its creamy texture set off perfectly the delicate coffee colour of her skin, and she knew it. She was beautiful, very beautiful, and that, together with the fact that she was intelligent in a shrewd, cunning way, had caused her to be chosen to live with Chuck Hughes by Asi Moriba.

People did not refer to Salamba as a police state: diplomats classed it as 'one of the emergent countries of Africa'. Asi Moriba, boss of Salamba's secret police, would have smiled: he knew better. Now that the foreign mining companies had moved into the country, Moriba considered it a wise precaution to plant his agents where they could gather useful information. Americans merited special attention. While the United States remained friendly to the bizarre regime in Salamba, they were a source of revenue, technology and luxuries. If things changed, and in politics nothing is impossible, they could make good, juicy hostages.

So Anna went to live with Chuck Hughes shortly after he arrived in the country. Chuck, fresh from a campus in Wisconsin and a few months in the Chicago offices of the mining company, fondly believed that he had picked her up at a chance meeting in the bar of the Hilton.

She had been wearing that same white dress, a tigress waiting patiently for its prey. He had come to the bar, still blinking from the intense sunlight, and ordered a

11

long, cold drink. She came from out of the shadows, accidentally brushing against his arm, apologizing and smiling at her unintentional intrusion. Chuck looked up and what he saw took his breath away.

Anna's mother was Salamban but her father was a Swedish archaeologist who had left Egypt in a hurry but had lingered in Salamba before taking off for Cape Town. Their daughter was tall and slender, her flesh temptingly dusky, with soft brown hair which flowed down to her shoulders, and unexpectedly vivid blue eyes. Her lips pouted slightly as though she were perpetually on the point of kissing. Chuck gazed, fascinated, at the long, tapering fingers which had fluttered against the bare skin of his arm, the wrist, fragile as porcelain and the velvet smoothness of her arm.

'Do you mind?' she asked, as she perched on the stool next to his.

'No, please,' he assented, eager and confused.

She crossed her legs: they were sheer perfection. 'Can you tell me the time, please?' Her voice was throaty and sensual. 'I've been waiting for ages for a friend. I guess it's so late now that he won't show up.'

'It's almost eight,' replied Chuck.

'Damn him! That's my whole evening wasted.'

Chuck was not at all a pushy fellow but this was an opening that even he could not miss. Very diffidently, he suggested that, as she had been stood up, she might care to have dinner with him. From that moment, his downfall was a certainty.

After dinner, she had been in no hurry to leave and they had taken a couple more drinks before Chuck had braced himself to ask if he could see her again. It had all been surprisingly easy. There had been two or three more dates before she stayed the night. And two or three

nights together before she _____ in. Which was exactly
as Asi Moriba had intended _____

The very first time they m____ ___e, Anna had displayed
an imperiousness which l__ ___rly overwhelmed her
guileless victim. She had st____ and stood before him,
haughty in the glory of he____ flesh. He had never
seen such breasts, as brea____ ly lovely as the tear
drops of the gods. He knel____ her and she accepted
his tribute as a queen does _____.

She knew how to tantali____ ____ntil he was insane with
desire for her. Merely ru____ ___er finger nails down his
spine made him tremble and she would bite him all over
his body, just hard enough to make him wince and
want more. By degrees, she would dominate him, only
permitting him to do what she desired, and some nights
denying him the joy of her body. On such evenings, he
accepted any humiliation which she cared to inflict on
him in the hope that, in the end, she might relent. There
were times when she was so willing, so compliant, that he
convinced himself that she had fallen in love with him.
But, more often, she treated him with just that touch of
scorn that lashed him into a desperate attempt to win
her. There was nothing that he would not do for her, if it
gave her pleasure or satisfied the whim of the moment.
To Chuck, Anna was the most exotic creature in the
whole world and, while he might persuade himself that
she was his, in fact he had become so completely besotted
by her that she really possessed him, body and soul.
Which was also exactly as Asi Moriba had intended.

She finished her toilet, slipped into that certain dress,
ran a brush through her hair and walked through to the
verandah to wait for Chuck to drive up in the Range
Rover. She checked the time again and smiled as she
recalled how he had bought her the fanciest watch he

could find because her first words to him had been about the time. He was late: that was unusual.

It was perhaps another half an hour before he drove up, tyres squealing as he swung the vehicle off the road onto the dirt track which led to their house. He leaped down and ran over to take her in his arms but she shook him off.

'Where on earth have you been?' she demanded petulantly. 'You are so late; you know how much I worry in case something has happened to you!'

'I'm sorry, darling, really I am,' he pleaded. 'Just as I was about to leave the mine, something turned up to delay me.'

'What was so important that you could not come home to me?' She was obdurate: he was not to be forgiven so easily.

'Nothing to interest you, dearest. Merely routine.'

She looked hard at him and he simpered like a schoolboy who had been caught with his hand in the cookie jar.

Anna said nothing but went inside to fix a drink for each of them. She could read him so easily. She did not allow him to have secrets from her and she resolved that she would know all about whatever had occurred at the mine before the morning. She had her own ways of finding out these things and they were highly effective. She could take her time.

So the subject was dropped while Chuck relaxed over his scotch and soda and their Salamban cook prepared a meal of curried chicken. When they were sitting in the gathering dusk, she was able to slip into his coffee a little of the white powder which she found worked like a charm, sapping his will as it stimulated his libido.

'In a little while, we'll see who is the boss,' she murmured to herself. Chuck sipped his coffee contentedly.

There were tiny beads of sweat on his forehead: they always appeared when his sexuality was starting to drive him. He was shifting uncomfortably in his armchair and she could sense his growing need.

'How about going into the house?' His voice was hoarse.

'I like it out here on the verandah, now that it's cool,' she answered. 'Let's stay for a little while.'

He snorted impatiently. 'You'll be bitten by the mosquitoes.'

'Five minutes,' she said and he acquiesced sullenly.

She let him suffer, bringing him to the boil. Eventually she cocked her head provocatively and favoured him with a faint, mocking smile.

'I suppose what you mean is, let's go to bed. Why aren't you man enough to ask straight out?'

He knew that she was challenging him to argue so that they could have a row and then she would sulk and tell him that she did not feel like it tonight. So he swallowed his shame, accepted her rebuke.

With an arrogant toss of her head, she led the way. He followed her into the bedroom and locked the door. He wanted her so badly: without a word, he tore off his clothes but she merely stood there, watching him. Her disdain fuelled his frenzy.

Very deliberately, she shook her head. 'I don't think you deserve me tonight.'

Her voice was so calm and controlled he was plunged into despair.

'Please,' he begged, 'please, Anna, darling!'

'Aren't you pathetic.' She flaunted her strength and his abject weakness. 'You can't exist without me, can you, my little Chuck?'

He shook his head miserably. Resist now, and she would dismiss him to unbearable solitude.

15

'You want to play one of our games, Chuck, do you?' Her smile was hard and sadistic. 'Maybe, just maybe, I might be kind to you. But you have to beg. Grovel!'

He was on his knees before her. She slapped him playfully but with enough of a sting to keep him in his place.

'Take off my shoes! Kiss my feet!'

He lay there before her on the dusty floor, adoring her, sucking her toes. She spurned him with her foot as if he were a dog which was making itself a nuisance to its mistress.

'Do you want more?' she teased. 'Or shall I keep you down there, where you belong?'

He had been well trained and he knew that this was the crucial moment: he begged, he cringed, he submitted to her absolutely. At last, she relented. With awesome slowness, she took off her clothes and lay on the bed, but she never so much as touched him and he stood in agony, awaiting her command.

'Put your tongue in my navel!'

She reckoned that this was about as far as she could drive him without risking a collapse of his sexual tension and she was not ready to release him yet. With his face pressed against her belly, he was drugged by that musky scent of her. Every cell of his body ached for her, every muscle was taut as a bowstring, screwed up to breaking point with lust.

She grabbed his hair and yanked his head up. 'I really am annoyed with you. Do you know why?'

He shook his head and tried to move down again onto her body, but she pulled him away roughly.

'I am talking to you. Behave – or I'll make you sorry!'

She meant it. He mumbled an apology and waited.

'I want you to tell me what it was that was so important this evening that you didn't want to come home to me.'

16

'Anna, it was nothing like that. Honestly.'

'Tell me!' There was a ring to her voice which told him that he had to obey. He was completely in her power.

With a sigh, he said, 'One of the boys brought me a strange object which they had found in the mine. I needed time to examine it and to find out how he had come across it. You know how they make a long story over the simplest thing. That's all it was.'

'A strange object? Where is it?'

'It's in my pocket.'

'Show me!'

'Please, darling, can't it wait?'

'Now!'

He climbed off the bed and slouched over to where he had tossed his jacket. From a pocket, he took a long, chunky piece of metal. She held it in the palm of her hand.

'It's heavy.'

'It should be. I believe that it is solid gold.'

'Gold? What is it?'

'I'm not sure, but I have a suspicion that it is a fantastic object from ancient Egypt that I was once told about.'

'Tell me!'

'That would take a bit of time, darling. Please. Look at the state I'm in!'

She smiled derisively. 'A little self-control will do you good, my dear. Now, you tell me all about this mystery of yours and don't try cutting it short. I want to hear the whole story. Then, if you have been good and obedient, I shall be pleased with you, and you know what you can expect if I am pleased, don't you, Chuck?'

'You promise?'

She nodded, 'I'm waiting.'

Now he ached for her, but her will was stronger than his and, as always happened, she prevailed. With an effort, he pulled himself together sufficiently to narrate what had occurred.

It had begun a year before Chuck had come to Salamba. He had completed his degree in mining engineering and he was attending a conference at Columbia University in New York. It was an unusual meeting, bringing together academics from many different countries, experts in a wide range of subjects. During a break between sessions, Chuck had come across a man called Louis Halevy and they had got talking. Halevy was a Professor of Egyptology at the Sorbonne. It was a subject for which the great Paris university was renowned and Halevy's reputation was so extraordinary that, although he was a Jew, he had been free to work inside Egypt even during the most difficult times.

'And what's your speciality?' Halevy had asked.

Chuck had explained how he had just obtained an appointment with one of the biggest international mining concerns and that shortly he was being sent to Salamba.

'It's exciting,' he enthused. 'You see, Salamba was typical of so many of the newly formed countries of Central Africa; lots of people and ghastly poverty. Then, almost out of the blue, they discovered an enormous deposit of rare earths.'

'Rare earths?'

'They're strange substances and it is a miracle to come across them in this sort of quantity. They are used in many industries but the big companies are very secretive about all their properties. However, they are prepared to pay almost anything for some of them and Salamba is being transformed by the wealth which is pouring in.'

'Like the oil boom?' asked Halevy.

'It's ten times, maybe a hundred times more important. But they are not easy to work, so you can imagine what

18

an opportunity it is for me – my first job outside the States.'

Halevy nodded. 'As a matter of fact, if there is anything in a legend that goes the rounds, Salamba could be interesting to me, also.'

'I thought that you worked exclusively in Egypt.'

'Have you ever heard the myth of the death of Osiris?'

'Wasn't he cut up, or something?' Chuck was vague.

'That's right. Osiris was the great god of Upper Egypt, and he represented the power of good, along with Isis, his wife. But Osiris was captured by Seth, the evil god, who killed Osiris and cut his body into thirteen parts which he scattered throughout the world. But Isis travelled through many lands until she had found the parts and she brought them together and Osiris lived again. It's all tied up with fertility rites, of course, but Isis only recovered twelve of the parts of her husband's body. The phallus of Osiris was never discovered and it remained buried in the earth, which explains why the soil is fruitful, you see.'

'I follow. But what has that to do with Salamba?'

'Well, there is a tale that an image of Osiris was made for the priests of ancient Egypt, a figure in solid gold, and that the myth of Osiris was reenacted with the statue.'

'You mean that this figure was cut into thirteen parts?'

'That's right. And what is intriguing is that the golden phallus was also buried and never found. Or, at least, it was not found until a few years ago when, so they say, a Swedish archaeologist, digging in Egypt, came across it. Up to that moment, nobody believed that the thing ever existed; it was just one of those tales, and we still don't know. What is certain is that the Swede quit Egypt without a word of warning and headed south, eventually ending up in South Africa. He certainly passed through Salamba and the story is that he had made off with the golden phallus and that he hid it somewhere, in case the Egyptian authorities caught up with him. So, perhaps, it's in Salamba, who knows?'

'Do you believe this story?'

'Mr Hughes, I have seen many strange things, and I've learned to keep an open mind, no matter how unlikely a yarn may appear. Behind most myths, there is some real event. Let's say that the history of the golden phallus of Osiris is not supported by one scrap of evidence so there is no university or foundation which would finance an expedition to try to recover it. And that means that if it does exist, the chances of finding it are remote.'

'I suppose it is believed to possess all sorts of magic properties?'

'Of course. It is the most potent fertility symbol in the world. That is, it would be, if it were to be found.'

'If it were to exist,' amended Chuck.

Halevy nodded. 'Keep your eyes open,' he chuckled. 'You never know your luck.'

'If I come across a solid gold phallus, I promise, you will be the first to know.'

'And that is the whole story,' Chuck told Anna.

She looked curiously at the object which she still had in her hand. 'And you think that this is what your boy has found in the mine?'

'I don't know, I'm not an Egyptologist. But from what I do know about metals, I'm fairly certain that this thing is solid gold and it looks like a penis, don't you think? Maybe it is a coincidence, but it's strange.'

Anna was more convinced than she showed but she had never told Chuck about her Swedish father who had come so mysteriously out of Egypt and voyaged on into South Africa.

'Anna, darling, you did promise.'

He looked so dejected, standing naked before her.

'I would have thought that after all that, the feeling would have worn off,' she taunted.

'Please. You did promise,' he repeated.

'Well, I've changed my mind. I have the right to change my mind, haven't I, Chuck?'

It was another of her traps. He had been taught that he must never contradict her. So, he nodded.

'Say it, Chuck, say that I have the right to change my mind.'

He gulped. 'You have the right to change your mind or do anything you please,' he whispered.

She smiled contentedly, 'That's a good boy. I think you deserve a reward.'

He looked up at her expectantly but she shook her head.

'No, you haven't been that good. But I'll tell you what I shall permit you to do. This golden phallus of yours, it's clean isn't it?'

'Yes. When it was brought to me, the first thing I did was to wash off the dirt.'

'Good. Well, I've had men, but I've never been given the works by a god. So, my little Chuck, you may masturbate me with the golden phallus.'

He stared in disbelief. 'And me?'

'You can do whatever you fancy. I should have thought that the sight of me coming over this divine dildo in your hand should be enough to bring you to a climax.'

So, they made love, the three of them, Chuck, Anna and Osiris. She was excited by this thing. How many women, priestesses and princesses, had eased it inside them, praying that it might help them to quicken life within their wombs? Maybe it had a magic of its own or perhaps she was seized by the superstitions of her mother but she had a wonderful, glowing sensation which spread from her loins until her whole body seemed to pulse with a great, golden throbbing. There was an aura of potency; she had never experienced anything like this with Chuck himself. She struck him sharply around the head.

'Faster, damn you, work!'

His arm ached and she was pressing down painfully on his wrist but he was conscious that his sole purpose was to bring her satisfaction. She was gasping and groaning, lugging his head to and fro, as though she could communicate to his plunging hand the commands of her crotch. Her grip grew tighter and his eyes watered as she wrenched his hair until, with a shrill scream, she came, pulsating like a wild animal on that golden phallus. And such was the compulsion that she exercised over him, that he too was a sticky, soaking mess, grovelling at her feet. And that also would have met with the approval of Asi Moriba. Asi was the only man who had taken Anna and subjugated her.

Next day, Chuck Hughes passed by the Central Post Office and sent a cable to Louis Halevy. He did not want to be too specific since he feared that the Salamban authorities might take some action against him if they were aware of his discovery. I THINK I'VE FOUND WHAT YOU ARE LOOKING FOR. COME URGENTLY – HUGHES, ran the text of his message.

He need not have bothered with his precautions. While he was sending his cable, Anna was reporting to her boss and lover, Asi Moriba.

2
Sing a Song of Soccer

The sentry snapped smartly to attention and presented arms as Asi Moriba strode into the presidential palace in Ibari. Moriba, a rugged giant of a man, scowled and the sentry shuddered. Some men thought that the president, Daniel Lomo, was the most powerful man in the country but nobody would argue about who was the most feared. To fall into disfavour with the chief of police qualified any citizen of Salamba for a one way ticket to the notorious prison camp outside the capital at Lake Oswonde or to the cemetery.

The palace was a sumptuous building, a proud affirmation of the country's independence of the colonial powers. Nevertheless, it had been lavishly furnished with English and French pieces of the eighteenth century – tables, chairs, sideboards and bureaux, along with a number of fakes which had been slipped in by unscrupulous dealers, and the President of the United States, in person, had presented the head of the Salamban government with a table-top replica of the Statue of Liberty as a symbol of the friendship which bound their two countries together for as long as the dollars continued to flow.

Asi Moriba crossed the enormous expanse of the lobby where mere ambassadors might loiter for days before being granted an audience with the president. None of the palace ushers dared to interfere as he thrust open the door and entered what was already being termed the throne room.

Daniel Lomo was waiting for him and the two men

immediately went into conference. According to the newly-written constitution, the president should have called a cabinet meeting, but since Lomo had confined all the other members of the cabinet to the Lake Oswonde camp, he and Moriba had to hold their meeting without the benefit of the counsel of their colleagues.

'What's all this nonsense about some pagan relic being found in the mining camp?' demanded Lomo.

He was a wizened dwarf of a man, barely reaching up to Moriba's elbow, with crinkly, grey hair and a squashed nose like that of an unsuccessful prize fighter. But, in his fifty-five years, Daniel Lomo had got the better of some of the best brains in international politics and revealed himself to be a ruthless, cunning, tough autocrat.

'I've been checking up,' replied Moriba. 'If the thing is genuine, it could be worth a fortune.'

'If!' snarled Lomo.

'The American has sent a cable urging a Louis Halevy to come here. This Halevy is a world authority. We should do nothing until he has arrived. If he says that this is the real thing, then we go into action.'

'And how will we know?'

'I can rely on my agent to be fully informed.'

'I suppose that your agent is another of your cast off mistresses, some whore who will sleep with anybody.'

'I have my own methods of ensuring loyalty.' Moriba growled. 'That's not a matter which need concern you.'

The two men glared at each other but it was the president who backed down. His views on women were extreme and well publicized. Any woman who was guilty of immorality should be stripped of her civil rights and sent to one of the state nunneries for spiritual and mental retraining.

As in most other black African states, when Salamba had become independent there had been a tussle for

24

power between various tribal and political groups. A Moslem fundamentalist faction had seized control and persecuted its opponents with fanatical ferocity. Men were branded or mutilated and women accused of adultery were stoned to death. The genius of Lomo was that he had realized the possibility of fighting terror with terror. With some undercover help from the CIA and some right-wing groups in Europe, he had preached a new doctrine of Christian fundamentalism. Portraying himself as the champion of the church militant, he had swept the Moslems from power with the aid of such divine agents as St Peter and poison gas, St Paul and car bombs. The only words of Jesus that Lomo ever quoted were, 'I come with a sword.' So, once he was installed as president, all the repressions of the Moslem fundamentalists were retained, only the names were changed.

'Very well. I'll leave you to keep this American mining manager and whatever it is that he has dug up under observation. We have to talk about other things which are a great deal more serious.'

The president's tone was urgent but Moriba remained cool and detached. Daniel Lomo found his manner irritating and he launched into an offensive.

'This tour by the Scottish football team. There must be no hitch!'

Moriba smiled ironically. 'Of course not. We know, don't we, that the real religion of our country is football, whatever the Moslems or the Christians might pretend. A bomb in this palace wouldn't worry anybody, except you, if you were to survive. A bomb in the Daniel Lomo Stadium at our first important home international – that would be serious. The government would lose control, the regime would fall and the anarchists take over.'

'I am touched by your concern for my safety,' Lomo

25

sneered. 'Since you are not doing your job, I have taken steps to protect myself.'

'I'm sure you have,' Moriba grinned, 'but you need not have worried. I have the situation well in hand.'

'Like hell you have!' shouted the enraged president. 'Do you know what that Milos is planning?'

At the name of the leader of the anarchist opposition, Moriba's smile broadened. 'Ah, Milos, your bogey man!' he chuckled. 'Of course, I know. He intends to kill you – preferably at the football match where he would get maximum publicity.'

'You know? And you never warned me?'

'Come now, Mr President,' mocked Asi Moriba. 'I have told you that everything is under control. I saw no reason to alarm you. However, you had better tell me what you have done. I don't want my men shooting some stooge, planted by you, when all their efforts will be needed to deal with Milos and his terrorists.'

Daniel Lomo suppressed his indignation. 'You remember that German free-lance, Kurt Loewe, who worked with us during the revolution? I kept in contact with him and he is flying to Ibari on the same plane as the Scots. I've told him to stick close by them and watch for any attempt by Milos to infiltrate the team and its supporters.'

'And what's his cover? He hardly looks like a brawny centre-half from Aberdeen, does he?'

'Don't be ridiculous! He is travelling as a Dr Gerstein, my personal dentist. Try not to shoot him by mistake, Moriba.'

'When my men shoot somebody, it is never a mistake,' Moriba assured him. 'Now, if you have recovered from your attack of nerves, I have a lot to do and can't afford to waste time, sitting around here and holding your hand.'

He rose to go.

'One of these days, Moriba, you'll go too far,' Lomo hissed.

'Maybe,' the police chief assented. 'Meanwhile, you should worry less about your personal safety. People dislike you but they hate me and they won't murder you if they think that I would succeed you. That should be some comfort to you!'

And Asi Moriba strutted out of the presidential presence, leaving Lomo little consoled by his bland statement.

On Saturday, 11 July, Africavia flight 101 from London, Heathrow, to Ibari stood on the tarmac, its four jet engines raising a miniature dust storm, while the captain waited for clearance to take off. The Salamba flight was never full. The fact that the line flew a Jumbo was more a concession to national prestige than realistic scheduling. On this morning, there were more passengers than was usual. The Scottish football eleven, together with their reserves, their manager and his staff and a small core of devoted fans, took a solid wedge of seats amidships. Immediately behind them sat Kurt Loewe, a thickset, bulky man, nursing an attaché case, with his nose stuck into a medical journal in German. Nearby, also reading a learned journal, but with considerably more understanding, was Louis Halevy. As there was no direct flight from Paris to Salamba, he had taken the early Air France airbus from Charles de Gaulle which connected with Africavia 101. Kurt Loewe paid little attention to the Frenchman: he was more concerned with a party of a dozen Germans who occupied seats in front of him.

They were all men in their thirties, sober-faced but with powerful physiques. They spoke little, but their eyes were watchful. Casually, Loewe asked the pretty black Salamban air hostess if she knew who they were.

'I heard one of them speaking German, and I am also

German,' he explained. 'I wondered whether they would be going to the same conference that I am attending.'

'I guess not,' she giggled. 'They are a deputation of military advisers, invited by President Lomo to help in training the Salamban army.'

Loewe digested this information and found it suspicious that Lomo had never mentioned to him that a group of his men would be flying in the same plane. They looked tough customers and Loewe resolved to keep an eye on them.

As for the rest, there was merely a nondescript scattering of the sort of men and women that one finds on almost any long flight, wives going to join their husbands, businessmen nursing their ulcers, employees of the airline.

One passenger did catch Loewe's attention; an outstandingly pretty girl, sitting incongruously among the muscular Scottish footballers. Sandra Mitchell was not yet twenty and this was her first trip abroad. She was the girlfriend of one of the team's stars, Donald McFee, who was in the next seat and feeling rather self-conscious since nobody else had a wife or girl-friend travelling with them.

But Sandra was not simply coming along for the ride, to give her man encouragement and a touch of home comfort. She was a singer and had managed to get herself engagements in Africa.

Time dragged as they waited for clearance to take off.

'Excited?' asked Donald, squeezing her hand.

She nodded. 'I don't know much about this Salamba place, but I bet it will be a hell of a lot different from Inverclyde.'

They had met at Inverclyde three months earlier. She had been singing in a club called The Blue Siren which was the one bright spot in the dingy little town amid the closed-down collieries and abandoned steel works of the Clyde valley. Perhaps because there had been a lot of unemployment and times were hard, people more than ever needed somewhere to relax, where the lights would be brighter, there would be music and folk could have a bit of fun. So Bill Auburn had taken over a rundown pub from the local brewery and turned it into The Blue Siren. It wasn't Las Vegas, but while the outer bar served mild and bitter and bacon sandwiches and retained much of the old cloth cap image, inside you could get a decent dinner with French wine, dance on the disco floor and watch the cabaret in a surprisingly trendy setting. The Blue Siren had become the 'in place' – not that there was much competition in Inverclyde. The only other form of live entertainment was the local football club. Although Inverclyde Rangers were a side to be taken seriously, at least in the eyes of their own supporters, since the team functioned during the day and The Blue Siren at night, there was no clash between them.

Sandra remembered vividly that night. The act was billed as Sandra and Sax. It had been drizzling and she unbuttoned her raincoat as she pushed open the door and peeped into the disco. It looked like being a quiet night: not more than a dozen people were eating at the tables and there was nobody on the floor. She went upstairs to what was flatteringly called her dressing room and took down the shiny, black, nylon gown, decorated with sequins, from a plastic hook. It was a deliberate throwback to the fifties, as were her silver shoes, tucked under the wash basin where she fixed her make-up.

Not that Sandra was old fashioned. She was a sprightly, violet-eyed blonde who was into roller skating and hard rock, but not when it came to earning a living. She had that delicate Dresden china look which definitely did not go with baggy trousers and belting out the latest hit from *Top of the Pops* while brandishing an electric guitar. Too many kids were trying to do the same thing and Sandra was not stupid. She could never be a second Annie Lennox, so she cashed in on her looks and worked up an act of sentimental songs and blues numbers which she could coo enticingly.

That night when Bill had knocked on the door and told her she was due on stage, she had slung over her shoulder her partner, Sax, a battered saxophone, patted her hair into place, glanced in the mirror and, satisfied with her appearance, hurried out of the dressing room and downstairs.

She pushed open the door leading into the disco-diner. The place had filled up quite a bit since her arrival; there was a blue haze of cigarette smoke, something which annoyed her when she sang, and a buzz of conversation. The two overworked waiters bustled between the tables and never even gave her a glance. At the back of the room stood a baby grand piano and beside it, her microphone. Freddie Hawkins, the club pianist, was watching for her entrance and he struck up a few introductory chords. As she walked into the spotlight, she surveyed her audience. There were the regulars, businessmen dining out on the expense account, a scattering of salesmen from out of town and one group that might have been a birthday party. At one table, there sat four young men who seemed out of place and fidgety. I wonder what they are doing here, thought Sandra, as she started her first number.

The spot dimmed to a misty blue and Freddie filled the air with his soft, blue chords.

> 'Tired old moon, lazy old moon,
> Bring back my lover, my man, real soon,'

She murmured the words into her mike, fondling it as if, by some magic, she could turn it into her dream lover.

30

The noise died away at the tables: all heads were turned towards her. Music is love, she sensed. Just for this moment, all of them, out there, are in love with me while the spell lasts.

> 'Oh, let it be,
> Just him and me
> And the lazy old moon – together.'

She let her glance fall on the table with the four boys. One of them, a small, wiry teenager, was staring at her, wide eyed, as if he could devour her. My God, she thought, he's really smitten and he must be in his first pair of long pants. At the end of the chorus, Freddie played an extended version of the verse to give her time to ready her saxophone and join in the final chorus.

There was the normal ripple of applause, little more than a polite acknowledgement of her existence from the serious eaters and drinkers, more enthusiastic from the younger folk who had been captivated by her husky voice or the charm of her personality. The dark young man was clapping as though his hands were on fire. She gave him a smile and then turned to Freddie for her next song. This was a more light-hearted number but she ended, as always, with a couple more soulful lyrics.

> 'My man's gone away,
> Left me oh so blue!
> My world's all in pieces,
> Don't know what I can do.'

Her voice was little more than a moan. Freddie's piano echoed her despair and the last sob was from her saxophone.

It was good. The complete silence at the end was more of a tribute than the applause which followed. She bowed

31

and, as the spot came on bright again, walked between the tables to the exit. The dark boy was still clapping after she had left the room.

Upstairs, she put away her saxophone and freshened herself up at the basin. She was about to change her clothes when there was a tap on the door.

'It's me, Bill. Can I come in?'

'Sure. I'm decent.'

He walked in and gave her an approving look.

'You were good tonight. The whole act went well.'

'Thanks, Bill. So, was there something you wanted to say to me?'

'There's a young lad down there who wants you to join him in a bottle of champagne.'

'Oh, come on, Bill, I'm tired. Do I have to?'

'Sandy, we don't sell champagne here every night, do we?'

He was right, of course. She shrugged her shoulders, straightened her dress and followed him downstairs to join her admirer.

They were waiting for her, all four of the men at the table, but it was the dark boy who pulled a chair out for her and greeted her.

'You are sensational, Sandy. May I call you Sandy?'

She nodded and smiled her gratitude but before she had a chance to answer, he went on, his words coming in a torrent.

'My name is Donald McFee and me and the lads are here on a celebration. And your singing, well it's made the evening for us, isn't that so, boys?'

The others nodded self-consciously. Sandy looked at her host. He was like a coiled spring, short but tense and with some immense inner power, ready to explode. His eyes darted and flashed as though his body could never be at rest.

'And who are your friends?'

'Oh, they're my mates from the factory.' Donald dismissed them with a wave of his hand.

'I see,' smiled Sandra. 'I've never seen you here before, so what are you celebrating that's so special?'

A waiter brought over a bottle of non-vintage champagne in an ice bucket. Donald regarded it with suspicion.

'Is that the best you have?' he asked.

'We do have a vintage champagne, but that is very expensive.' The waiter gave him the smile of one who knows, guiding one who doesn't.

'Flaming hell, man, did I ask you the price?' Donald shouted. 'Whatever it is, bring it!'

'Hold on, Donald,' protested Sandra, 'he warned you for your own good. It really does cost an arm and a leg.'

'Well, you're worth it,' asserted Donald, and he dismissed the waiter who had been hovering near the table in case Donald should change his mind and listen to reason.

'And the celebration?' Sandra reminded him.

'Today,' Donald announced proudly, 'I signed up for Inverclyde.'

'The Rangers? You're a footballer?'

'Yes, as from today. Of course, I've played a lot of amateur soccer, for the factory side and for Auchtergillie.'

'Auchtergillie?'

'That's the village where I was born. Do you not know it, it's not very far?'

Sandra shook her head. There were so many tiny villages in the valley of the Clyde whose men and women were, sooner or later, sucked into the great black hole of Glasgow.

'I had a trial for Inverclyde Rangers today, and they signed me up straight away,' he explained. 'They're only in the Lowland League, that is, they're not in one of the professional Scottish League Divisions, but they may get promotion and for me, well, it's the first step of the ladder. I tell you, Sandy, in no time, you'll see me in the blue shirt of Glasgow Rangers. So, drink up, lassie.'

It all sounded so easy when Donald said it but Sandra knew that in professional football, like the arena of pop music, the vast majority of the young hopefuls never made it. However, tonight was Donald's. He was on top of the world; disillusionment would come soon enough, so she accepted the glass of champagne and drank to his success.

Donald could not take his eyes off her; the lads from the factory might not have existed for all he knew or cared. He talked incessantly – about his parents, his pals, Auchtergillie and the school and the factory and, above all else, about football. He never mentioned going out with girls nor did he ask Sandra about her own life. She realized that inviting her to join him had been a tremendous step for him: underneath all the chatter and the boasts, there lurked a very young, very inexperienced and very nervous person.

The cabaret ended with Freddie playing a couple of arrangements. Bill started the disco music again and a few people drifted onto the floor.

'Do you want to dance?' Sandra asked.

He hesitated for a fraction as if he were afraid of making an exhibition of himself then, grinning widely, he led her to join the other dancers.

To Sandra, dancing was second nature. She moved naturally, smoothly, as the music pulsed through her. With him, it was different. He was agile and his body responded to rhythm, but whereas she was relaxed, he was tense, as though he was worried that he might touch her and interfere with her own private ritual. His self-consciousness irritated her and after some five minutes, she returned to the table.

'You've been very sweet,' she told him, 'but I am tired. It's been a long day and I am singing again tomorrow night, so please excuse me.'

'What, are you away home, then?' Donald asked.

Sandra nodded and kissed him lightly on the cheek.

'Shall I walk you home? Or get you a taxi?'

'No, thank you, there's no need. I really am going straight back to bed. Alone!' she added, just in case he had the wrong idea.

'I wasn't thinking of anything like that,' he was pathetically apologetic. 'But I would like to see you again. I mean, not just here.'

'That would be nice. I suppose if you are going to be the star of Rangers, I'll see you round the place.' She had no desire to make a firm date with him, or anyone else. If only he would let her escape so that she could get back home and go to sleep.

'I tell you what, why don't you come to the match on Saturday? It'll be the first time I'll be turning out for the Rangers and it ought to be a hell of a good game. Please, say you'll come?'

'I might.' She had no intention at all of standing about in the cold for an hour and a half on a Saturday afternoon.

'That'd be marvellous. You know, I'm sure I'll play better if you are there to watch. I can get you a ticket for the covered stand. I'll drop it in here tomorrow.'

She told him not to bother but he refused to be put off. She wished him luck and he said how much he was looking forward to her seeing him play. At last, she was free of her persistent fan.

For the next few days, she tried to dismiss Donald from her mind, but the thought of him kept popping up at all sorts of odd moments. There was something about his enthusiasm, and that strange combination of his self-assurance in his role as a footballer and his awkward

35

shyness as a man that she found intriguing. Oddly enough, at that time, she had never considered him as a potential lover.

And now they were sitting side by side in a Jumbo jet, their destination Africa. For both of them, it was a miraculous escape from the cold, grey world in which they had lived all their lives up to then. They were tense with excitement. Loewe, scrutinizing his fellow passengers over the pages of his journal, was tense with apprehension.

The great machine started to taxi along the runway. The loudspeakers crackled and their captain welcomed them aboard and wished them a good flight. Bored stewardesses demonstrated oxygen equipment and pointed out the emergency doors and where the life rafts were stowed. They checked that everybody was securely strapped into their seats and that nobody was surreptitiously smoking a last cigarette. The Boeing pointed its nose into the wind, the captain opened the throttle full and with a triumphant scream of farewell, the aircraft rose majestically, shaking itself free of the soil of England and tore its way into the sky.

Taking off is a moment of stress in any flight, but once aloft, the members of the Scottish party relaxed. Chatting among themselves and sipping cold drinks, they found nothing to interest them in their fellow passengers. Not so, Kurt Loewe: he watched incessantly the bunch of German military advisers – or whatever they really were.

There was one person, however, who commanded the attention of all the passengers. The stewardess who walked down the aisles and checked that everybody had their safety belts properly fastened, was attired in Salamban national dress, or rather the lack of it, and was exhibiting, to universal admiration, a lavish expanse of ebony-tinted thigh. Sandra noted without enthusiasm the lively gleam in Donald's eye, as the helpful, dusky siren fumbled with his belt. Sandra could have sworn it had been correctly secured and required no attention.

She called out to the girl. 'Please, could you bring a rug or a blanket? My husband,' she stressed the word and glared menacingly at the stewardess, 'has a touch of fever and needs to be kept warm.'

'What's all this about a fever?' Donald demanded as the young African hurried away, swinging her hips to the delight of the footballers.

'You may not have one now, but you soon will have,' Sandra assured him.

She took the blanket from the stewardess and with a nod of her head, indicated that Donald and she would be able to cope without any further assistance. Under the cover of the blanket, she proceeded to unzip his fly.

'Sandy, we can't make love here,' Donald whispered anxiously.

'We won't be able to do everything I would like,' she assented, 'but I think we can manage enough to take your mind off that little black bombshell.'

Seated side by side, as they were, contact had to be confined to a little judicious groping and massaging. Under the gentle but persistent coaxing of her fingers, Donald was soon the embarrassed possessor of a fine, firm erection. If only they would show an inflight movie! Sandra nestled closer and started to play with her tongue in his ear, licking and gently chewing, something which never failed to excite him, and he began to move up and down in his seat in time with the silent music which she was performing on his most sensitive instrument. Well, if you can't beat 'em, join 'em, thought Donald, as he slipped his hand under the blanket and undid the zipper on Sandra's jeans. Her crotch was deliciously moist and Donald was completely absorbed in his labour of love.

'Oh, it's that sort of fever,' commented the stewardess who had approached unnoticed. 'Can I be of any assistance?'

Sandra glared at her balefully and informed her tersely that her services were not required. The effect on Donald, whose fever was close to boiling point, of the unexpected proximity of yet more delectable female flesh was dramatic. He made a wild grab at the tantalizing houri but he was yanked back into his seat by Sandra. With the other hand, she pulled a wad of tissues from her pocket and applied it, in the nick of time, to the spurting fountain in Donald's groin. He relapsed with a moan and the stewardess tittered at the spectacle.

But there were others who were not amused. Kurt Loewe had observed the episode. The sight of the young couple and their mutual masturbation fascinated him, although he was certain that he disapproved. But he could not tear his eyes away and as their rhythm accelerated, involuntarily he got to his feet and, as if in a trance, crept across to the scene of the action. It was disgusting, he told himself, but was guiltily aware of his own growing erection. The spell was broken by the sight of Donald's ejaculation. Loewe tapped the grinning stewardess on her shoulder.

'What the hell do you have to do to get any service on this plane?' he demanded. 'Where is that gin and tonic I asked for hours ago?'

With a glittering smile of absolute hatred, she hurried off to carry out her errand. Loewe stared at the panting couple before him and strode back to his own seat with a warm feeling of virtue vindicated.

'Now you ought to be able to behave yourself for the rest of the flight,' Sandra informed Donald.

He protested weakly and then relapsed into silence.

The stewardess took Loewe his drink and on her way back, without saying a word, took the blanket away.

For perhaps half an hour, Sandra looked at a couple of magazines and pointed out some of the articles to her companion.

Donald was in the mood for reminiscing. 'Do you remember that first game, Sandy?' he asked.

Of course she remembered. And she remembered the days before the game when, every now and again, she would think of Donald as an arrogant kid who hadn't yet grown up.

Saturday came. It was one of those days when the sky is a sullen grey, threatening but never delivering rain. In the morning, Sandra was busy, shopping, but back in her room, knocking up a quick snack, she was haunted by the sight of that blue ticket, standing on the mantelpiece. It was as if her conscience was scolding her for deserting her eager champion. She had decided to stay at home and watch TV but her eyes could not avoid that ticket, a silent rebuke.

'Oh, what the hell, I must be crazy,' she grumbled as she pulled on her old, thick, duffle-coat, wound a scarf around her throat and jammed a woolly tammy firmly on her head. She scowled at the ticket, as if it were an enemy, put it in her pocket and went out to catch a bus to the stadium.

From her seat in the covered stand, she had a perfect view of the pitch. Inverclyde never attracted the vast crowds who followed the giants of the Premier Division. But, by local standards, there was a reasonable turn-out, somewhere between two and three thousand people. On her right, there was a solid pack of regular supporters, muffled in the blue and white colours of their team, sporting huge rosettes and flashy tam-o'-shanters, all of blue and white. Some carried heavy wooden rattles,

39

others hand-bells. They were in high spirits and were making a lot of noise, but seemed peaceable and good humoured. Sandra hoped they would stay that way.

There was a group of fans of the visiting team on the other side of the ground, quiet and on the defensive, an outnumbered force in enemy territory. They only came from Melrose, no more than forty miles away, but on the terraces of Inverclyde Rangers, they were as much aliens as if they had arrived from Siberia. The crowd was waiting, like a slumbering beast, its noise a confused hubbub. To her amazement, Sandra realized that she was looking forward to the game with a suppressed excitement.

The two teams and the referee and linesmen filed onto the field to a savage roar of applause, Melrose Athletic in an all-red trim, the home team wearing their blue shorts and white shirts. They were trotting and jigging up and down to limber up. Inverclyde clustered around the goal to Sandra's left, passing a ball between themselves and shooting at the keeper, while Melrose indulged in a similar routine at the other end. The referee called the two captains together. She watched him spin a coin into the air. The Melrose captain pointed towards the goal on her left and the two teams took up their positions.

She had no difficulty in picking out Donald. He was so much smaller than the great, lumbering men around him, a pigmy among giants. Yet he was stationed in the centre of the attack, the classic striker's position, and it was he who flicked the ball to his right to start the game.

Rangers went straight into the attack, moving purposefully into their opponents' half of the field. The roar of the home crowd swelled to encourage them, but a hefty fullback, wearing his red shirt like a symbol of defiance, took the ball from the Rangers' winger by brute force and punted it up the field.

At first, the two sides seemed to be fairly evenly matched. Rangers were quicker on the ball and altogether more stylish, but the Melrose eleven were heavier and they played a tough, spoiling game. There were a few desultory raids by both teams, as they played themselves in, but there was not yet any real rhythm and no menace to the attacks.

And then, Donald took control. There had been a typical Rangers move, swinging the ball between the forwards until they had run into the solid wall of the Melrose defence. Their long clearance reached their own striker, only fifteen yards from the Rangers' goal. The ball was at his toes – and then, it wasn't. Donald had skimmed in and robbed him, before the Melrose forward was even aware of his presence. He was away, careering up the centre of the field, dodging and swerving his way around the outpaced defenders. It was so sudden that, for a moment, the home crowd was absolutely silent, caught unawares like their team's opponents.

Then there was a huge, delighted roar; the fans were on their feet, jumping up and down, willing their man to smash his way through. But that was not Donald's way. It was magic. He was a bird of prey, swooping in for the kill, a ballet dancer, tripping, leaping, skipping his way through the dull throng. And always, at his feet, as if drawn to him by some magnetic force, was the ball, bouncing away from the men of Melrose, obeying his will like a live thing. He was past one, two, three defenders and then, straight ahead, stood the Melrose goal, the keeper crouching apprehensively for the shot which was to come. Donald's right foot was drawn back, the keeper was advancing to cut off the shot and the tension in the howling, screaming crowd could almost be felt physically. Sandra found that she was clutching the arm of a stranger standing next to her, but he was oblivious to her and

41

everybody else, except the white shirt bobbing across the pitch in front of him.

What happened next was apparently an impossibility. Donald connected with the ball which should have gone straight into the goal-keeper's arms. Instead, it swung away, fast, low and wide to Donald's right where, unmarked, the Rangers' winger was tearing upfield to take the pass and place the ball effortlessly into the net. At that moment, Sandra knew that when Donald had said that he would play for Glasgow Rangers, this was not an idle boast: it was a simple statement of fact. To have renounced the chance of scoring his first goal for Inverclyde, after having beaten the defence of Melrose in a solo run of blinding brilliance, to have known that his partner would be in place for the shot, these were the marks of a football genius.

The crowd went crazy. In a matter of seconds, Donald had become their idol. A star had been born!

It was only a few minutes before Donald was rewarded for his self-denial. He collected a loose ball midfield and, with that incredible turn of speed, was through between the Melrose backs and, with a high, swinging shot, crashed the ball into the back of the net, past the hands of the desperately diving keeper.

Sandra was no longer merely watching. She was with him every time he ran onto the ball, straining with him, thrusting with him to penetrate the hostile defence, flexing her own muscles for his shots. Melrose held on until half-time, but only luck prevented Donald from scoring twice more.

In the second half, Melrose adopted a simple policy of concentrating all their efforts in smothering Donald. This made things easier for the other Rangers forwards, who were able to put away a header from a long corner for their third goal. Still the pressure was on Donald.

Whenever he came near the ball, there was a man in a red shirt, poised to push him off it, even before he reached it. The mood of the Rangers supporters grew angry. Already there had been three fouls on Donald. Now, once more, he was off on one of his runs, the man who had been marking him sprawling on the ground after he had charged the empty space where, a fraction of a second earlier, Donald had been standing.

'Jesus Christ,' exclaimed the man next to Sandra, 'You'd swear that the ball was tied to the laddie's boot laces!'

This time, the two Melrose backs were waiting for him. As he ran up the field, they converged on him. They had it all worked out beforehand. They were massive, iron-muscled men and they were going to charge him simultaneously from either side. Sandra was sick with fear: Donald had so slight a physique, the sandwich technique could cripple him. Already, the fans were howling their hatred before the tackle came. Donald lingered for a trice, as though he was giving his adversaries a chance to get into position. Then, as they slammed with all their force at his body, he sprang forward like a bullet from a gun. They connected, not with his quicksilver body, but with each other as he tore through the gap. They lay, groaning in agony on the grass, but nobody paid any attention to them. All eyes were on Rangers' new-found hero. In front of the goal he checked his rush and took deliberate aim at the top left hand corner of the net. The keeper watched and leaped to catch the ball. But as he jumped high to his left, the ball thundered past at no more than knee height to his right.

Melrose were able to pull back one goal shortly before the end of the match but, by then, the result was assured. And, to complete the Inverclyde rejoicings, in the very last minute of the game, Donald scored again, this time a

43

simple shot against a tired and dispirited defence. With a hat trick in his first match, there could be no doubt that Donald had arrived.

At the final whistle, some of the crowd rushed onto the pitch as if to mob their hero, but Donald, with the rest of the players, was soon safely in the changing rooms and the spectators began to straggle away from the stadium. Sandra took her time. On the back of her ticket, Donald had written, 'Meet me after the game at the café on the corner of Irvine Road.' So she walked slowly to the café, about a hundred yards from the ground, found a table, and ordered a coffee while she settled down to wait for Donald.

She had been there for perhaps ten minutes when he hurried in. He looked around anxiously but when he saw her, his face relaxed into a broad smile.

'Sandy! I'm so glad that you made it. I thought that perhaps you wouldn't bother to come. I mean, you being a cabaret star and all that. You must be very busy.'

'I would have said that as from today, you are the star,' she told him.

He sat down beside her and smiled contentedly. 'It didn't go so badly, did it?'

'Don't be so damned modest. You were brilliant.'

He squeezed her hand and then got down to ordering some sickly, cream pastries for them both and a tea for himself. For some reason, he was immediately at his ease with her and all his little-boy nervousness had vanished. By the time they parted, Sandra had agreed to go roller skating with him the following Wednesday evening, the first free night she would have after the end of her cabaret contract at The Blue Siren.

'And this evening,' he asked, as they walked towards the bus stop, 'Do you have something special?'

She smiled. 'It's Saturday, remember? That means that

The Blue Siren will be full and I'll be there until late. You'll have to wait till Wednesday, I'm afraid.'

He nodded moodily. 'And I ought to be with the lads, after my first match.'

He picked her up from her room on Wednesday. She was wearing sawn-off jeans and blue and white sneakers. She watched him closely, as he looked at her.

'Not like the outfit for the cabaret, is it? Are you disappointed?'

He shook his head. 'No. I think that you would be great whatever you wore, Sandy. It's just different.'

Roller skating was still something of a novelty at Inverclyde. One of the old cinemas had been converted into a rink and Sandra had been there a few times but it was new to Donald. She had her own skates: he hired a pair at the rink. At first, they sat beside the floor, watching the other skaters and sipping soft drinks. Hard rock blared from giant loudspeakers suspended over the arena, drowning all sound of the skaters. The music spoke to Sandra; she needed to let herself go, to move her limbs, to be free. She pointed towards the floor and Donald got to his feet. They adjusted their skates and slid into the melée.

He was good. Although he was not a practised skater, with his control and co-ordination he was able to follow her moves and, in no time, he was performing fancy arabesques. They linked arms, gliding faster and faster, oblivious to the mere mortals around them. Their movements were in perfect harmony: they had become one person, swift as Mercury, strong as Jove, driven forward by the vitality of the hard rock in their ears and the ecstasy of speed.

With a pang of guilt, Sandra realized that she was enjoying herself in a way she never had with her first lover, Rex. For the first time in her life, she was with a

45

man with whom she could share; they were doing their thing together. Rex had taken advantage of her adoration: he had taken, she had given. But with Donald, it was quite different; he would never treat her as a passive object, somebody to give him the pleasure he sought and whom he could then abandon. It was marvellous, exhilarating, she was free, free, wonderfully free! The thought flashed into her mind – would they fly, like this, if they were to make love together?

Afterwards, they went for a meal at a pleasant country hotel, a few miles out of town. Again, she was struck by the contrast between the way she had been treated by Rex and the attention which Donald lavished on her. He hung on her every word and nothing was too much trouble if he believed it would give her pleasure. To Rex, she had been a slave; in the eyes of Donald, she was a queen.

She learned a lot about him, as they talked over their food. How his father had been a seafaring man, always away on some voyage and finding entertainment and consolation in every port, until the time when he found the charms of Valparaiso greater than those of Auchtergillie and his current señorita more attractive than Annie McFee, his lawfully wedded wife. Sandra's own father had died while she was still a child, so she knew what it was to grow up under the wing of a protective but dominating mother. Her affair with Rex had been her liberation: Donald had found his freedom on the soccer pitch.

'That game, last Saturday, could be very important,' he told her. 'You see, both Inverclyde and Melrose are trying to get into the Scottish League, as soon as there is a vacant place. That result could make all the difference.'

'And if the Rangers were in the League?'

'Then we would play against the other fully professional

46

clubs and we would have the opportunity to get promotion each year. Think of it! Instead of having to find fixtures against the half-hearted teams from round here, we could be at home to the greatest – Rangers, Celtic, Hearts, Aberdeen. We might even be in the European Cup, playing the cream of the continental sides, Real Madrid, Benfica in Lisbon, Juventus of Turin, or Ajax in Rotterdam, and God knows who else. Wouldn't that be terrific?'

His eyes shone and Sandra could not avoid being infected by his fervour.

'But, there I go, always on about myself,' Donald apologized. 'What will you be doing, now that you have finished at The Blue Siren?'

'Don't you worry about me,' Sandra laughed. 'I have a few engagements lined up, and next month I'll be singing in a club in Glasgow.'

'Does that mean I won't be seeing you?'

She smiled at his alarm. 'It'll only be for a week, and I'll probably be back here most afternoons anyway.'

It was getting late and Sandra wondered whether he was going to suggest that they stay the night at the hotel, but Donald's strict presbyterian upbringing must have been too strong an influence, and he escorted her back to her lodgings with blameless propriety.

They had been flying for about two hours when they were served a meal. The attempt by the airline to combine British and African cuisine was not an outstanding success and there was a threat of mutiny among the Scots. Loewe watched attentively. Could it be that Milos and his men had somehow infiltrated the team? But they quietened down when they were given some canned bacon and beans which had been carried in the galley in case of an emergency and the feast was washed down with a few bottles of beer.

Louis Halevy was a seasoned traveller and he found

this flight as boring as all the others he had been obliged to endure. He was looking forward to the stop at Cairo and the chance to get out for a short while into the open air. Loewe, on the other hand, knew that more passengers would join the plane at Cairo and he would have to be more vigilant than ever.

Donald and Sandra had some misgivings over their food but they did not join in the demonstration of the rest of the team.

'My mother would have a fit if she saw me eating this stuff,' Sandra confessed with a grin.

'Your mother!' Donald exclaimed. 'What did she say when you told her that you were going to Salamba?'

'She said that I would be better going with her to the kirk to ask God to forgive me for all my wickedness instead of venturing into the land of the heathens,' chuckled Sandra.

Sandra's mother, that pillar of righteousness, had really brought them together. Donald had never slept with Sandra and although he was obviously in love with her, the subject of sex never crossed the chaste young man's lips.

Then came that Sunday afternoon, when Sandra took him to meet her mother. She had stayed away as long as she could, but she knew that the longer she put off her visit, the more sullen would be Mrs Mitchell's mood of resentment. So she resigned herself to the inevitable and reckoned that if she brought Donald home with her, since he was a serious minded and presentable young man, she would be spared the worst of her mother's displeasure.

She was wrong. Mrs Mitchell opened the door to her erring daughter with the solemn air of one of God's elect, obliged to entertain a soul condemned to eternal damnation but one to whom she was willing, as a sign of the mercy of the Lord, to offer a cup of weak tea and a chocolate biscuit. She gazed at Donald, carefully washed and shaved and wearing his best suit, with mistrust and instant dislike. Any young man who would consort with a fallen woman, for so Mrs Mitchell considered her daughter, must himself be evil, an emissary of the devil, a commercial traveller, or even the ultimate horror, an Englishman. She ushered them into the drawing room and viewed them with gloom. There was a long silence until her mother frowned at Donald and addressed Sandra.

'So, what became of your other friend? There's talk in the town that he's been arrested in England – for stealing, so they say.' Mrs Mitchell spoke with smug satisfaction.

'Rex? I've really no idea.' Sandra's tone was brusque. 'And how have you been keeping?'

Mrs Mitchell shrugged her shoulders. 'I don't get any younger and it's not easy for a widow, living on her own these days.'

Sandra had introduced Donald but Mrs Mitchell made no attempt to include him in the conversation. She told her mother what a splendid footballer, Donald was.

'Ah, football,' her mother complained. 'Just a lot of thugs, running about and maiming one another. And what with all the violence in the crowds these days, I shouldn't be surprised if it were to be banned.'

The emphatic nod of Mrs Mitchell's head left Donald in no doubt that if the matter were to be left to her, the ban would be total and instituted without delay. The conversation dried up and Mrs Mitchell moodily sipped her tea and grimly surveyed the brace of lost souls.

'We can't stay, Ma,' Sandra said, as she gulped down her scalding hot tea, 'Donald has to get back for a training session. We only looked in to see how you were getting along.'

'Training on the Lord's day! I've never heard the like of it,' exclaimed the indignant widow.

'Well, that's the way it is,' snapped her daughter. 'If you've finished, Donald, we'd better be on our way.'

Donald sprang to his feet gratefully and hurried after Sandra to the door.

'It's been a great pleasure, meeting you, Mrs Mitchell,' Donald called over his shoulder, as they scuttled out.

They went back to his lodgings, a converted studio which he had taken after joining Rangers. Donald hardly said a word while they walked through the quiet streets. In his room, without asking, he brought her a drink and took one himself.

'I'm sorry, love,' Sandra comforted him. 'I would never have asked you to come along if I'd known that she was going to be such a misery.'

Donald did not answer. He put down his glass, looked her squarely in the eyes and asked in a low voice, 'Who is this Rex?'

'I was going to tell you, but I hadn't got round to it. I somehow did not feel that I was ready.'

So Sandra told him of her affair, of what it meant to waste love on a man who was not fit to receive it and how it felt to be tossed aside, to be treated as no more than a convenience. She spoke frankly, not glossing over anything to spare his feelings or her own and, as she talked, she found that she could at last see the whole episode in perspective and objectively, as if it were something which had happened to somebody else or she had witnessed in a movie.

'And you say that it is over?'

'For getting on for two years,' she assured him, 'But it went on hurting for a long, long time.'

She had no idea how he would take it and, unexpectedly, she found that she cared very much.

'I'm glad, I'm so glad.' His voice was subdued. 'I mean, I'm glad that it's over, of course. I'm sorry that you were hurt but I don't think I could bear the idea that you belonged to some other man.'

'I don't belong to any man, Donald. I learned my lesson.' She glared at him defiantly, 'I was just a daft, moonstruck kid, but now I live my own life and nobody is ever going to use me again.'

'No, that's not what I meant,' Donald replied apologetically. 'But, Sandy, you are such a lovely woman, I can't tell you how frightened I have been that, after we have been out together, you have been away to some other man, a lover who was more to you than I could be. I could not believe that I was the first fellow that you had been with and I would wake up at night, wondering where you were and who you were with.'

Sandra smiled. 'You had no reason to worry. I've had plenty of boyfriends since Rex, but I've never had anyone serious. That is, not until now.'

'Really, you mean that? There's nobody else?'

By way of answer, she kissed him gently and he held her fast in his arms as he had never dared to do before. That they made love then seemed the most natural thing in the world, the obvious conclusion to which their lives had been leading.

His body was perfect. She adored the smooth, rippling muscles, his athlete's lean, spare torso. And as he took her, there was a softness which suffused his features, a wonderful expression which she had never seen previously. Everything about him was just right. That, more than anything else, was what made their coming together such a terrible disappointment.

He was so tense, so unsure of what she wanted. And before she had the chance to show him, to lead him and use her experience to guide him, his desperate need for

51

her overpowered all his attempts at self-control and he exploded agonizingly when he had done little more than touch her. She was left, frustrated and angry, while he lay beside her, panting for breath.

But he had amazing powers of recuperation. She could not believe how soon he was ready to take her again and, with the dispelling of his initial anxiety, all his natural grace and agility began to assert itself. Just as when they were skating, his body began to move to hers, the rhythm of her body became his, they even were breathing together, and now they made the sweetest music.

It was pure bliss and each time, unbelievably better. She loved the way he smiled when she made little groans and grunts of delight, the subtle slowing and quickening of his thrusts in response to her ache for him and the way he seemed to be able to hit exactly the right spot. Her body was arched, her legs gripping him like scissors of sensuality, pushing him deeper while his hands played over her flesh in a wild act of worship. She pulled his head onto her breast and suckled him as if he were her helpless baby, at the very moment that their bodies shook, as each of them was seized by the wild, sweet, life-death of orgasm. She was throbbing, screaming, completely manic, possessed utterly. All her capacity for loving welled up within her as if to engulf her man and weld the two of them together for ever.

That night, their lovemaking was so uncomplicated, a wordless acknowledgement that they belonged to each other. As they came to know each other more profoundly, they acquired a new subtlety, new foreplay to heighten their delight by the long crescendo of anticipation. They learned to make love with their mouths, their hands, their feet, every part of their bodies could contribute its own special wonder. They knew that feel, that odour, that taste which was unique to each of them. They loved with all their senses and with the whole of their bodies.

The week that Sandra was performing in Glasgow, she was conscious of each minute that she was away from him. But worse was to follow. There was a week's engagement in Edinburgh, too far for her to get back during the day, but after three days, Donald broke training to come to her.

However, while her career as a singer was slowly blossoming, that of Donald was developing at a fantastic rate. His first ambition had been fulfilled. Talent scouts for Glasgow Rangers, hearing of his sensational first game for Inverclyde, were at the later fixtures and snapped up the prodigy. As a sop to Inverclyde, it was agreed that he would play for the non-league side for the rest of the season. After that, he would don the blue shirt of Glasgow Rangers.

But an even greater honour was in store for him and an even more coveted blue shirt. During the summer months, a Scottish team had been invited to tour a number of African countries, preparatory to their matches in the opening rounds of the World Cup. The opposition would not be of the calibre of the great sides of Latin America or the stronger European countries, and the selectors took the opportunity to give some of their young players a taste of international experience. Even so, it was a tremendous triumph for Donald when he was included in the touring team. Nobody could remember the last occasion when a man who had not yet played for a League club was chosen to play for his country.

Sandra was almost as happy as Donald himself but she had an indefinable premonition. Suddenly, the roles had been reversed: she was the one who was unsure of herself. She knew that she needed him. The tour did not worry her: she would miss him but he would come back to her.

53

One evening, on impulse, she turned to him and suggested that they get married before he left. Donald thought about it before answering.

'I love you, Sandy, and I want to marry you. There never has been and there never will be another woman in my life. But don't you think that we should wait a wee while? You have your singing to get on with and, as for me, at this moment, I don't think I could cope with a distraction.'

A distraction, that was how he considered her! She was indignant but she did not argue. He was not throwing her over like Rex, but she knew that as from now, she took second place in his life – and it hurt.

'OK, if that's the way you want it.'

He looked at her hard, but said nothing to soften the blow.

Perhaps as a form of reprisal, Sandra started to look for bookings farther afield. And, in a very small way, she had her revenge.

'I'm off next week,' she told him, only a few days later. 'I have this chance to sing in a club in Liverpool.'

'You're going to sing in England?'

He looked put out and she was glad.

'It's not the end of the earth,' she smiled. 'Not like Africa. But, you know, ever since the Beatles, Liverpool has been special in English pop music. It's like being asked to perform in a shrine – if you know what I mean.'

He nodded. 'I suppose you're right to go.'

'Well, you won't be leaving for your tour yet awhile. Why don't you come with me?'

'I don't think I could get away. The whole side is in strict training. There's a lot of us who haven't ever played together, so we are putting in a month's intensive practice at Ibrox Park. Then we are off to Salamba.'

'Where the hell is that?'

54

Donald wrinkled his nose into a wry smile. 'To tell you the truth, I have only the vaguest idea. I just kick the ball, you know, somebody else has to fly the plane. It's one of those new countries in Central Africa with a wild, black dictator and screwy politics. All I know is that they are mad about football and we have a couple of matches there before we move on.'

'I think I'll stick to Liverpool,' Sandra said.

'But you'll be back before we leave?'

'Don't fret yourself, Donald. I'll be there, waving my handkerchief when you board that plane.'

Smokey Tavern, in Liverpool, lived up to its name. It was a great cavern of a place with none of the intimacy of The Blue Siren, but there was a professional show biz atmosphere and Sandra took her engagement there seriously. Perhaps if Donald had been there to give her moral support, she would have been less nervous, as she made her way onto the stage which had been erected at the back of the club. The room was packed, but all those men and women sitting at their tables, talking, laughing and drinking, were remote strangers who did not send out the warm vibrations of the folk back home. She needed all her courage to face them with an air of self-confidence which she did not really feel. What she feared was not so much hostility as indifference.

She had splashed out on a new dress for the occasion, a sheath of electric blue which clung to her body's contours and gave her a sleeker, more sophisticated presence, and she moved her hands seductively over her hips as she sighed a new blues number.

'Chinatown baby, waiting all the night;
Her man never comes: he just don't treat her right,
Little lady from Chinatown.'

55

Her chant, half-spoken, half-sung, wove its spell and she could sense that she was getting through to them. The cold English thawed and when the last, plaintive lament of her saxophone died away, they gave her a big hand. She sang another couple of quicker songs, took her bow and, with a surge of relief, left the stage.

She was sitting at the bar, enjoying a gin and tonic with the compliments of the management, when she was joined by a heavy-jowled, baldish man in his mid-forties. He looked her up and down appreciatively, like a butcher assessing a carcass of prime beef.

'That's a nice act you've got together,' he told her. 'I think, handled right, you could go a long way.'

Here it comes, she thought, he's about to make me one of those offers that a poor, stagestruck girl cannot refuse. Like hell!

'Now, I have a proposition for you,' he droned on. 'Here, let me get you another drink, your glass is almost empty.'

She was tired and irritable. 'Thank you, but I buy my own drinks. And, for your information, mister, I don't hop into bed with generous strangers.'

His smile broadened and he fished out of his pocket a card which he handed to her.

'Let's get this discussion off on the right foot. If I took you for some slut off the street, I wouldn't be wasting my time talking to you.'

She read the inscription on the card – 'Jacobus van der Bijl, Impressario,' and an address in Johannesburg.

'I need an act to go on tour in six weeks' time and I think that you can fill the bill. The money's good and you can do with the experience. Interested?'

'On tour where?'

'You would start in Cape Town, then Durban and Johannesburg.'

'South Africa! I don't want to get involved in any sort of political trouble. There are a lot of black folk in show business over here.'

He nodded. 'Quite right! But there need be no problem. As far as I am concerned, you can sing to blacks, whites and every colour of the rainbow, as long as you fulfil your contract with the halls where I will book you. Some idiot who should have known better, a famous American singer, ran foul of the apartheid issue and then had to cancel at short notice. That's why I am looking out for a replacement now. What you should do, is not go direct to South Africa, but stop off at Ibari, that's the capital of Salamba. It's the one state in Black Africa on good terms with the Union of South Africa, so it would be a handy half-way house.'

Salamba! And about the same time as Donald and the Scottish team would be going there! Fate or coincidence? It was an opportunity which she could not resist.

'Very well, Mr van der Bijl, I could be interested. When can we talk?'

He told her the name of his hotel and they arranged to meet there the following morning.

She said nothing to Donald until she was back at Inverclyde the following week. He was relaxing after an arduous day at Ibrox Park, at the end of which the team had been given their detailed travel plan. Only then had the full impact registered with Donald.

'Think of it, Sandy,' he enthused. 'Bloody Africa, and there's me who hasn't even been as far as London!'

'So when are you off to Salamba?'

Donald consulted the typed itinerary. 'We fly to this place, Ibari, on Saturday week from Heathrow.'

'That's the Africavia flight 101,' Sandra commented.

'That's right. How did you know that?'

She laughed at his astonishment. 'It's not too difficult

to work out, since there is only one flight a week direct to Ibari. And I have a seat on the same plane.'

'You what?' he gasped.

She told him about the South African tour and how the timing was such that she would be able to stay in Ibari long enough to see the first match of the Scottish side's programme. She was not sure how he would take the news, but once he had got over the initial shock, Donald was his old self, kissing and cuddling her with delight. What more could a man want? He would have his girl and his game – and whatever else there might be waiting for them in Africa.

They felt that they had something to celebrate and what was more natural for lovers than to celebrate by making love? Sandra had bought some slinky gowns for her tour, which she displayed to Donald with the swagger and self-assurance of a professional mannequin. He nodded approval but she sensed that he was only mildly interested: footballers are rarely devotees of fashion. So she slipped off her dress and stood before him, wearing only a couple of wisps of gauzy nylon, masquerading as bra and panties. She thrust out her hip provocatively and with a wink and a toss of her head, invited him to take her.

The effect on her man was electrifying. With a whoop of joy, he clutched at her, but she eluded his grasp.

'There's steam coming out of your ears,' she laughed. 'Man, have you no manners, seizing a lady with all your clothes on?'

He peeled off the offending garments in a fever of anticipation and ran towards her. Clasped in his arms, she could feel the tense eagerness of his body. His lips were pressed against hers and his tongue explored the warmth of her mouth as if to prepare for a deeper, more intimate penetration of her. They let themselves fall onto

58

the sofa in the corner of the room. Donald went to mount her, but she pushed him onto his back and took his long, straining penis into her mouth. He gasped in surprise and pleasure. Nothing like this had ever happened to him before: oral sex was not a speciality of villages like Auchtergillie. Her tongue darted like a firefly, teasing him and thrilling him and he squirmed in ecstasy.

'Where did you learn to do that?' Donald's voice was hoarse.

Sandra did not reply. She had been taught that it was rude to talk with her mouth full. And she had learned a lot of other things as well since her first sexual experience with Rex. Now, she was the teacher and Donald her pupil and both of them were enjoying the lesson. The scent of his body was pungent in her nostrils, exciting her with its masculinity, undiluted by any cosmetic. She licked and nuzzled his fine, upright penis, while his fingers caressed her head and played with the delicate folds of her ears. She flicked her tongue over his balls: they were taut and she knew that he could not hold back much longer. But, just as he was on the point of coming, she pulled back, leaving him in agonizing suspense; while she slid upwards until her mouth was level with his. As she kissed him, the taste of his own sweat was heavy in his mouth. She grasped his penis, smooth as satin and soaked with her saliva, and plunged it deep into her own hot, wet vagina. After the tension as he had approached his climax and then been denied, the relief was exquisite and their bodies were locked together in the glory of their mutual and simultaneous orgasm.

'Africa can't be hotter than that,' said Donald, when he had got his breath back.

3

Bungle in the Jungle

It was mid-afternoon when Africavia 101 started its approach to Cairo. The flight had been uneventful, deceptively so, Loewe suspected. There was some low cloud so Sandra saw nothing of the fabulous country of the pyramids and the sphinx, apart from a glimpse of the sprawling, brown expanse of Cairo which filled the whole landscape. The plane seemed to skim over a clump of palm trees and a few seconds later they were streaking along the runway towards the terminal buildings.

During the stop-over, the plane was refuelled and everybody had to wait in the transit lounge, a bare, miserable room which, despite the air conditioning, was stuffy and oppressive. Loewe sipped a cup of coffee and tried to look like a dentist. The group of Germans paced up and down restlessly as though they were on sentry duty. Halevy found himself a quiet corner and settled down with a paperback.

But for Sandra, life was marvellous. Whatever was wrong with Cairo, she was away from Inverclyde, from the cold, from the damp, from her mother, from the memory of Rex. She cuddled Donald as if she could somehow communicate to him what it felt like to be free. He smiled back at her but she sensed that he was feeling the strain of being on his first international tour after so few professional appearances. Was he ready yet to walk the tight-rope of success?

Everybody was impatient to be on their way once more. A group of Scotsmen were attempting to coax an Egyptian fruit machine to accept and function on British coins. A young mother was comforting a whimpering child. Halevy could not concentrate and put away his book. Kurt Loewe realized with a start that he had smoked the best part of a packet of cigarettes. Distant loudspeakers announced the comings and goings of other flights while they remained, apparently ignored by all of Egypt except for the flies.

At last, they were called back to the plane. The airport bus bumped its way over the apron until they were alongside the Boeing in its gaudy yellow, green and purple livery. They went back to the seats that they had vacated and Loewe checked that there were no interlopers, especially among the Germans and the Scots. They were all there, nobody missing and no strange faces.

They had been seated for five minutes when a second bus drew up and a handful of passengers who were joining the flight at Cairo came aboard. Loewe was alert. He had put on a pair of spectacles. He felt that they gave him an inoffensively academic appearance. A couple of girls went past his row and sat down, whispering to each other. Their intimacy, the way they gazed at each other and kept touching convinced Loewe that they were lesbians – not what he was on his guard against. Two young men pushed their way along the aisle and sat in the bank of seats directly to his left. They were athletic-looking, bronzed, loose-limbed youths, probably from the Midwest. Loewe strained his ears and caught snatches of their conversation. They were speaking in English and it sounded as though they were working for a relief organization active in Africa. They sounded genuine and Loewe thought they need not bother him. Then every nerve tensed: some sixth sense was hammering at his brain as a thickset man sat down in the same row as him. Milos! He knew it was Milos although he had never set eyes on the notorious anarchist. The newcomer had

61

the heavy, square features characteristic of the Balkan people.

The man smiled at Loewe as he took his seat and the German feigned recognition.

'Why,' he cried, 'it's Herr Last! You are Herr Last, aren't you, from Bremen?'

The man shook his head. 'Sorry to disappoint you,' he replied in flawless German, 'but you are mistaken. My name is Antonescu. I am from Bucharest.'

'I do apologize,' Loewe chattered on, 'you are so like Herr Last. The resemblance is incredible, and how well you speak German! Are you a professor, perhaps at the university, a specialist in German?'

The man laughed. 'Nothing so distinguished, sir. I work for the Rumanian Trade Delegation. We have to be fluent in languages, you understand, since nobody we do business with its going to take the trouble to learn Rumanian.'

Loewe nodded sympathetically, but he was watching the last of the new passengers to board the plane. Although he was sure that he had located Milos, it was likely that he would have accomplices with him. However, the only people to follow the self-styled Rumanian were three tall boys, students by the look of them, pale and fair with cold, blue eyes, and the language they were speaking sounded like Swedish. After them, the door was closed, the ventilation system broke into noisy, hissing activity and the plane began to vibrate as the engines were restarted. The rigmarole of the oxygen masks and life rafts was repeated for the benefit of the travellers who had come aboard at Cairo and who paid not the slightest attention to the pantomime. Then, after a brief salutation from the captain, they were off on the last leg of the flight to Ibari.

'What have you got in that odd looking case of yours,

lassie?' Roddie MacEwen, the Scottish centre-half asked Sandra.

'It's my saxophone,' she answered.

Loewe sat tensed in his seat, ready to pounce. Ever since the bootlegging days in the States, the cases of musical instruments had been the classic receptacles for hidden weapons. Was it possible that this fragile-looking slip of a girl was one of the terrorist gang? As Sandra took down the case from the rack over her seat, Loewe's hand moved towards his shoulder holster.

'Ay, well, give us a tune,' called MacEwen.

'Not here,' Sandra answered. 'If I can get an engagement in Ibari, you and the lads can come and give me a bit of support. God knows, I might need it.'

'Excuse me.'

Sandra stared up at the chunky man who had left his seat and was now standing, looking down at her through his heavy, metal-framed glasses, his right hand tucked inside his jacket, his wary expression belying the polite smile on his lips.

'I heard you say that you play a saxophone,' Loewe explained, 'May I see it?'

'But it's just ordinary,' Sandra laughed.

'Please, I must insist.' His tone was harsher.

'Who the hell do you think you are?' Donald flared up.

'Don't get excited, darling,' Sandra said. 'Well, are you satisfied?' she demanded, opening the case and thrusting the saxophone under Loewe's nose.

He pretended to examine it as if he were a connoisseur, nodded affably and slunk back to his seat.

'Where the hell did you get that thing?' MacEwen asked.

'That's a long story,' she replied.

She had no intention of telling him of that day, two years before, when she went to Rex's lodgings and found

63

that he had taken off. It was as if the world had come to an end. She had been out with boys before, but this was different, the real thing, not a schoolgirl grope in the back row at the cinema.

She had first met Rex when her mother had sent her to the supermarket in the high street. He was a stranger, wandering among the unfamiliar shelves. As she reached for a can of peas, he asked if she could show him where to find instant coffee. She led him to the display, helped him to choose the bargain offer of the week and suddenly found that they were chatting like old friends. He did not try to ask her out as they parted at the check-out. And that was that, or so Sandra thought.

But two days later, she saw him again. He was climbing out of a large, oldish car, parked in front of Mrs Macdonald's front door. He was tall and he had a man-of-the-world air, the aura of the wide world outside Inverclyde. She knew that he must be a gentleman from a big city and that he would not remember her. But, as she was passing, he looked up and said hello to her. She blushed and was so confused that she could hardly answer. He told her that he was staying at Mrs Macdonald's since he had business to do in a lot of towns around Inverclyde. Then, just like in the movies, he had invited her for a coffee. She had sat, gazing into his eyes, while he told her about the wonderful, glittering life in London. And soon he would be going to New York. Her boyfriends in Inverclyde had tried to affect a swagger, but with them it was a sham. Rex was the genuine article.

After that, she would drop in at Mrs Macdonald's on her way home from school. He was always pleased to see her and although she was certain that he must be a very important executive, he never once turned her away. Soon, she was coming round during the evening, making any excuse to her mother to get out. Then came the evening when she stayed the night.

She had arrived at Mrs Macdonald's, breathless and tearful. Rex leaped to his feet and she stumbled into his arms.

'Why, sweetheart, whatever is the matter?'

She could not answer. Her sobs choked in her throat, she shook her head and pressed herself hard against his chest. His arms were strong, protective; they would keep her safe from everyone who wanted to hurt her.

'Here, I'll get you a glass of water. Or would you rather we went out for something stronger?'

'No, I'll be all right now,' her voice quavered. 'Water's just fine.'

While he was away, fetching the water, she dabbed her eyes and quickly smeared on some fresh lipstick. She drank a few mouthfuls and then told Rex of the furious row she had had with her mother. Mrs Mitchell was nobody's fool. Her daughter's newly acquired habit of slipping out every evening could only have one explanation. And Mrs Mitchell made it clear that she violently disapproved.

'She told me that if I went out again tonight, I needn't bother to come home,' Sandra told Rex. 'And she meant it.'

'And still you came.'

'The devil himself couldn't keep me away from you, Rex.'

Then he kissed her. Not like the other times, but long and passionately, as if he could draw her very soul from her through her burning lips. He did not have to say a word; she knew that they would sleep together that night.

Ever so gently, he led her to the bed and started to take off her clothes; her pretty blouse with blue flowers,

65

her simple tartan skirt. She was still wearing her school-girl's white cotton bra and panties as Rex undressed. Somehow, she had not expected him to be so hairy; the thick, matted tufts on his chest excited yet frightened her. They seemed to be warning her that all men were animals. Her eyes fell to his very brief pants, which seemed as if they were about to burst. Her cheeks were flushed and Rex read fear, doubt and shame in her timid glance. He turned out the light before pulling off his pants and drawing her to him.

She trembled but clung to him desperately. She let him place her between the crisp sheets and she felt his hands exploring her body, caressing her firm young breasts and then slipping off her panties. He was in no way rough or violent, but he had about him the masterful manner of a man who had long experience of taking what he wanted from women. She was wildly anxious to please him and she lay there, open to him, ready for anything just as long as it was what he wanted and the way he wanted it. She gasped with pleasure as his lips closed around her nipples, drawing first one then the other to a stiff, taut surrender to his greedy mouth. Then she felt him, huge, rock hard and urgent, sliding up between her thighs, his hand gently opening her lips and she knew that she was soaking wet with anticipation.

He was big. It hurt but she would not draw back. She had to belong to Rex: this was the ultimate declaration of love. After this, everything would be different, this would bind them together for ever. He was pushing, probing and then he was inside her, moving slowly but remorse-lessly. The pain subsided and her muscles tightened around him; an embrace within an embrace, as he held her tight in his arms. Did all men have that strong, heavy scent, she wondered, or was it personal to Rex. Now he was kissing her again, filling her mouth with his thick, moist tongue. She welcomed his weight, pressing down on her body, holding her captive. She could only move as he moved, her body and her will subservient to his.

He seemed to sense his power over her and his thrusts became longer, faster, more insistent. She was fighting for breath, her body filled by her lover. She could hear his breathing, gasping and ragged, and he was not kissing but biting her. Then, with a choked cry, he raised himself on his elbows and rammed himself so deep inside her that it was as if he were about to split her yielding body in two. She felt his awesome tremor, shaking the whole of his body. He had possessed her: now she possessed him. Again, again and again she sensed those wild spurts and then felt the sudden calm. It was all over but he lay there so still that she was alarmed.

'Are you all right?'

There was a pause and then he said, 'Fine, dear.'

'And me,' she faltered, 'Was I – was it how you like it?'

He answered her with a quiet, satisfied kiss.

'You're lovely, just lovely, my Sandy.'

Despite her mother's bluster, Sandra did go home, but things had changed. There was a barrier between them and she could not settle down to the old routine. Every evening, she went to Rex but she did not usually stay the whole night. She wanted to move in with him but he said that Mrs Macdonald would raise problems. When she did stay the night, they were discreet: they made little noise and Sandra left early in the morning, letting herself out by the back door. But if she were to be there all the time, Rex warned, there would be trouble.

He was away during the days in his car, and sometimes she arrived before he was back. It was on one of those evenings that she noticed the odd-shaped, scuffed, plastic case. She opened it and saw the saxophone. At that moment, Rex came into the room. He frowned, as if displeased that she should be prying, but kissed her as usual.

'What's this, then?' she demanded. 'Are you some sort of musician?'

He laughed. 'Not at all. But I used to play a bit, just to amuse myself, you know.'

'Go on, play me a tune,' she pleaded.

But he refused, saying it would disturb the other lodgers. He appeared impatient and ill at ease and the saxophone was never mentioned again as long as she knew him.

Their love affair, which Sandra believed was destined to last as long as they lived, came to an abrupt end after a little more than six weeks. There had been nothing the previous night to forewarn her. They had made love. She had satisfied his physical need: she never stopped to consider whether she had been fulfilled. All that mattered was that Rex was happy. At half-past eleven, he had kissed her goodnight and she had walked home; people went to bed early in Inverclyde.

So, the following evening, she was round at Mrs Macdonald's. She had purposely put on a new, see-through nylon blouse which she knew Rex would like, in his favourite shade of mauve. She went to run upstairs to his room, but the way was blocked by the formidable presence of his landlady, her arms crossed over her substantial bosom, her chin jutting aggressively at the intruder and the light of battle gleaming in her eyes.

'If it's your fancy man that you've come to visit, you're in for a disappointment. He's gone.'

'You mean he's not yet back from his work,' Sandra corrected her.

Mrs Macdonald gave a mocking laugh. 'Work do you call it? He never did a day's work in his life. That is apart from stealing from honest folk like myself. Yes, and taking advantage of silly wee lassies who ought to know better!'

'You must be wrong. Let me in, please.' Sandra's heart was pounding. Fear was creeping through her body like some invisible fog, spreading chill doubt. Surely it was impossible.

'See for yourself!'

Mrs Macdonald led the way into the room which had been so cozy and comforting when she lay there with Rex. Already it had the cold, abandoned air of a place where nobody lived. All Rex's things had disappeared; his clothes, the little radio-cassette player, all his expensive toiletries, every trace of his existence, with a solitary exception. In the middle of the room, on the rickety table, stood the saxophone in its case.

Sandra shook her head, stunned by the shock. 'Are you telling me that he's away in his car, then?'

Mrs Macdonald gave her a look which would have withered a woman far less sensitive than Sandra.

'His car? What sort of blather is that supposed to be? How would he be having a car? It was on hire purchase and the man came round this morning to repossess it. Your fellow got it with some sort of stolen credit card for a deposit. Seems there was some reason why the card hadn't been reported stolen until now. I suppose that he must have found out about it and that's why he took off. As for that,' Mrs Macdonald nodded contemptuously at the saxophone, 'his hands must have been so full with all his things, and him without his car, he couldn't manage to carry it. Not that it's worth very much.'

Sandra went home. She did not say a word to her mother but went straight up to her room. She was there when the police came round to interview her. The young sergeant was sympathetic. It was obvious that the girl was a victim and not an accomplice. She was not able to give them much information. She had been so blinded by her love for Rex that she had accepted everything he did without ever asking questions, except on the occasion of the saxophone. She learned that Rex was a small-time crook, specializing in burgling houses when the occupants were at work. Doubtless this was how he had acquired his musical instrument. The police had a list of articles which had been taken from houses in the area and which they suspected had been stolen by Rex. But the saxophone was not claimed by anybody. Since, legally therefore, it had to be considered as Rex's own property, the police made no objection when Sandra took it away with her.

Of course, she had got over it. That is, as far as one ever gets over a broken heart from one's first love affair. But she could not stand the silent triumph in her mother's eyes and, shortly afterwards, she moved out and found a room of her own. She had just left school and had to find some work. As she had already done a little singing with some local groups, she began to look around and pick up a few bookings. At school, she had acquired a smattering of music and, playing about with the saxophone, she had found how easy it was to get a tune out of it. That is how she came to adopt it as her gimmick and it went well with the half-whispered, half-crooned love songs which she made her thing. She had just about got her act together when Bill Auburn heard her perform and booked her for the cabaret at The Blue Siren.

It all seemed so long ago. When she was reminded of what had happened by somebody like MacEwen asking her how she had acquired her saxophone, she knew that she was not the same person as the wide-eyed little kid, straight out of school, who had doted on the mysterious stranger in the supermarket. She looked at Donald, who

70

was leafing idly through the glossy magazine which the airline, like all the others, produced to inform and divert their passengers. I wonder whether he has really grown up, she thought, or is he still as confused and immature as I was when I was with Rex. He was something of an enigma. She was certain that he loved her but he was so nervous and highly strung that she found it difficult to cope with his sudden changes of mood. He had become something of a celebrity; his name had been in all the British newspapers and he had been compared with the greatest virtuosi of the football pitch from the past. It had been so rapid a change in his life-style that it had knocked him off balance. She had never had to adjust to that sort of fame but she judged that he had the strength of character to see him through.

They had been in the air for about half an hour when she was disturbed from her reverie by the announcement over the address system.

'This is your captain. I have to tell you that this aircraft has been taken over by armed men, one of whom is holding a pistol to my head. He assures me that if there is the slightest resistance, the co-pilot and myself will be shot and the plane destroyed. I must say that I don't think that he is bluffing.'

There was a pause and then another voice. 'Now, please be sensible, no heroics. We have no interest in killing anybody but we won't have the slightest hesitation if you try anything stupid. Stay in your seats and fasten your safety belts and you won't be harmed. OK. Commando, take up your positions. Zuleika come forward and relieve me.'

While he was talking, the students and relief workers had got up from their seats and begun to patrol the aisles, making sure that their leader's instructions were being obeyed. Loewe was taken completely off balance and

71

watched as one of the 'lesbians' joined the men walking purposefully along the aisles. The other, presumably Zuleika, went forward through the first class compartment.

The leader of the hijack team was standing, a heavy automatic pistol in his hand, covering the captain. The two co-pilots were sitting at their controls, rigid, looking straight ahead of them with their hands resting palms down in front of them, while the Boeing flew on automatic pilot. Zuleika passed quickly into the cabin, took a cursory glance at the radar screen and the charts and then gave the captain his orders in a hard, clipped accent which gave no clue to her nationality.

'Change course. Bearing one nine five degrees. Then revert to automatic. Don't try to play any clever tricks. I am a qualified pilot and I shall be right behind you, watching every move and I am quite prepared to blow your brains out.'

She let the co-pilots see that she was holding an ugly, squat-nosed pistol.

'Do you people know what you are doing?' exclaimed the captain. He was a burly man in his late forties who'd had years of experience with British Airways before he became the senior pilot of Africavia. He took the hijack as though it was a personal insult.

The new master of flight 101 patted him on the shoulder. 'You get on with your flying and leave the thinking to us. Now, before you ask or figure it out for yourselves, we are heading for Kampala. OK?'

'Kampala!' snorted the captain. 'Entebbe airport! What makes you think that the Ugandans will give you clearance to land? They won't want to get mixed up in Salamban politics or whatever else you are involved in.'

'Our landing at Entebbe will be an embarrassment to them,' agreed the hijacker, 'but they would be even more

72

embarrassed if we were to splatter this great big bird, with all its passengers, over their runway.'

'You wouldn't dare!' the captain exploded.

'Are you willing to take the chance?'

The captain glared in impotent fury. The two guns were trained on him.

'We're waiting,' Zuleika told him.

His hatred was almost tangible as he very deliberately lifted his hands, switched to manual and eased the plane onto the new bearing.

The other man waited until the change of course had been completed and the aircraft was once more on automatic. 'Watch them,' he ordered Zuleika. 'Don't take your eyes off them for a second. I am going to see how things are back there.'

In the tourist class cabin, the young men and the girl strode along the aisles, checking the seat belts of the passengers. The huge cabin had become strangely silent. Frozen in shock and fear, what could the passengers say that would mean anything? A child whimpered; it could be heard all over the compartment. The passengers felt the slight banking of the plane and the sun seemed to move along the cabin, as they changed course.

Loewe's first reaction was to turn to the man beside him who was sitting without stirring a muscle, doubt and horror in his eyes.

'So you are not Milos,' Loewe was rebuking himself, but the other heard and shook his head, confused and uncomprehending.

'I told you, my name is Antonescu! What's the matter with you? First you call me Last, now Milos?'

But Loewe ignored him. His attention was focused on the man who had just entered from the first class compartment. He was stocky, with close-cropped black hair streaked with grey, and a long scar ran down his left

73

cheek. There was an authority about his bearing which marked him out as the leader.

Sandra, along with everybody else, also watched this man. There was something about him which set her flesh tingling. His mere presence among them was like an electric shock.

'Any trouble?' he asked.

His voice was deep and vibrant. Although his movements were purposeful and calculated, when he spoke Sandra sensed that this was no cold, unemotional machine, trained to kill without compunction, but an intelligent, vital man, smouldering with passions which he kept under an iron control. She glanced at Donald, sitting beside her. He was bolt upright, absolutely still, his face pale. He might have been a figure in a waxworks.

The sound of his question seemed to jerk Alan Chalmers, the hefty Scottish right back, out of the trance-like state into which they had all been plunged.

'Who the hell do you think you are to treat me and the lads like some sort of dumb animals?' he roared.

He was clambering to his feet when the other 'lesbian' hit him. She did not bother to use the machine pistol which she had pulled out of her canvas shoulder bag when the plane was seized. As quick as a panther, she crashed the side of her right hand in a wicked karate chop into the throat of the burly footballer. He clawed the air, fighting for breath, and his limbs jerked wildly as he collapsed into his seat.

'You'll live,' the girl spat the words, 'The bruise will hurt for a few days. That is, unless you have another go.'

Sandra was trembling with pent up energy. Why didn't Donald make some sort of move? The leader turned his grey eyes on her in a steady gaze as though he could divine the thoughts which were racing through her brain.

'Better a live lover than a dead hero, don't you think, little lady?'

She had no need for words to answer his challenge. Her face spoke defiance and her adversary smiled at her approvingly, as if in tribute to her spirit.

Kurt Loewe had witnessed the sudden violence and had sized up the man who had taken them all prisoner. The suspect Germans, like the rest of the Scottish footballers, had offered no resistance, but they were clearly not members of the hijacking force. That one man was the key to the situation. He was more than simply the leader. He was the source of all their strength. Without him, the others would be just kids, easily managed by the combination of the military advisers and the Scots. It had to be done at once. Every minute's delay reinforced the authority of this brigand of the air. Imperceptibly, Loewe inched his hands towards the buckle of the belt which kept him in his seat.

He was in luck. The man – it had to be Milos – was distracted by one of the Germans.

'Where in God's name did you come from? I never saw you board the plane?' the German called out.

There was a mischievous twinkle in Milos's eyes as he replied.

'Naturally. First class passengers always embark after everybody else, and I always travel first class.'

He was walking slowly along the aisle and was almost abreast of Loewe's row. The German's fingers had reached the metal buckle. Gingerly, he eased it out of the clasp and let the smooth nylon slither free. He kept his eyes resolutely to the front, holding his breath and tensing his muscles for the spring. His brain was calculating the precise distance between him and the 7.5 mm Ceska in Milos's right hand. The gun was hanging quite loosely, almost dangling from his fingers, not trained

75

on any one person. One swift pounce, and with Milos disarmed, the others would not dare to shoot. He was certain: that was the way it had to be.

Milos was alongside him, as near as he would get. It had to be now. Loewe dived, uncoiling himself from the awkward seat with the agility of a man who has been trained to think with his body in order to survive. He moved like lightning, hurling his own right arm forward to grab Milos's wrist, counting on the element of surprise.

But Milos must have been waiting for him. Perhaps he had heard the barely audible click of the belt fastener. As Loewe came at him, the hijacker brought the muzzle of the pistol up in a vicious jab and rammed it hard into his face. Loewe screamed in agony. The glass of his spectacles shattered and jagged splinters tore into his eye. Blood streamed from the broken flesh and the lacerated socket of his right eye. As his body slumped across the seat, Milos reversed his grip and hit him hard with the butt of the gun on his left temple. Loewe gave an incongruous gurgle as he lost consciousness.

'I guess that in future you'll have to make do with one eye,' commented Milos laconically. 'Nelson managed and Moshe Dayan didn't do too badly.'

Antonescu moved to go to the help of the bleeding man but Milos motioned him back to his place.

'Leave him,' he commanded. 'You!' he called to a cowering Salamban stewardess. 'Take care of him. The rest of you, stay where you are.'

The stewardess ran to the galley and brought a basin of water and a towel. She started to mop up the mess of Loewe's face. Nobody else stirred except the other members of the hijack team. One of them laughed sadistically, but Milos silenced him with a frown.

Sandra had watched the drama. It was as unreal as a movie scene and yet she felt totally involved. What was

76

more, she found that she had experienced something like the thrill which she had known when she had made love with Donald on those really good nights. She had no feeling for the prostrate Loewe, the martyr. In spite of herself, she was attracted by the power, the violence, the passion, in the man who had struck him down with such savagery. His presence made her feel that Donald, sitting mute and motionless, was but a shadow of a real man. She suffered a qualm of conscience at her emotional disturbance and the dampness she felt in her crotch. What was happening to her that she found sexual satisfaction in such brutality?

Milos glanced across at her and it was as if he knew. She found that she was trembling, but it was not from fear.

'Weren't you about to serve a meal?' he asked a stewardess.

'Snacks or afternoon tea,' she answered.

'Well, you had better get on with it. We'll be in the air for another couple of hours or more and we don't want the customers complaining to the airline, do we?'

The girl smiled nervously and scampered into the galley.

At the control tower of Ibari's new international airport, President Daniel Lomo had just driven up in his golden Rolls Royce with his motorcycle escort. Without waiting for any formal welcome, he scurried into the building and found himself among a dozen or so officials, huddled over a display of large-scale maps. Asi Moriba was already there and he gave Lomo a patronizing smile.

'What the devil is going on?' demanded Lomo.

'It's the plane bringing the Scottish team, Your Excellency,' answered an air traffic controller. 'It's been hijacked. One of the crew managed to smuggle out a

77

radio message while the terrorists were preoccupied. It appears that they are making for Entebbe.'

'The Ugandans won't let them land,' snapped Lomo.

'Oh yes they will,' interjected Moriba. 'I've sent them an urgent message, asking them to co-operate.'

Lomo spun on him. 'What sort of a mess have you and your men made of this? I suppose it is Milos?'

'Of course it's Milos,' Moriba answered. 'Don't let things get you down. It is all going according to plan.'

'You expected this?'

'Something along these lines.' Moriba was unperturbed. 'I hoped that they would show their hand early.'

'And who gave you the authority to contact the Ugandan government?' Lomo shouted.

'Nobody – I took it.'

Before Lomo could reply, one of the officials pushed forward, a paper in his hand. 'Excuse me, Your Excellency,' he stammered, 'but we have this minute received a radio message from the plane. It's from the hijackers; a list of their demands.'

Lomo seized the paper and started to read it.

'Wait a decent time and then call them up and say that we agree,' said Moriba.

'What are you talking about?' cried Lomo. 'How can you say we agree when you haven't even seen what they are asking?'

'What they are asking is not of the slightest importance,' grinned the chief of police. 'Just tell them that we agree and leave the rest to me.'

'There's a list of detainees they want released,' scowled Lomo. 'They would have us empty Lake Oswonde, here, you look!'

He thrust the paper into Moriba's hand but the latter did not even spare it a glance.

'I told you, we agree,' he said.

Lomo shook his head in annoyance. To release his detested enemies was the last thing he wanted to do, but he had no wish to contradict the head of the police force, who had God knows how many spies and informers in Salamba and outside. If only Moriba would confide in him, but he insisted in playing a lone hand. Lomo wheeled on him.

'You realize that if I go along with your scheme, whatever it may be, that the responsibility for what happens is yours, a hundred per cent!'

'It always is,' laughed Moriba. 'Now, let's get ready to extend a hearty welcome to Milos and to the gallant Scottish footballers who are probably wetting their pants.'

On Zuleika's instructions, Africavia 101 was gradually losing height. It had passed Kampala to the west and Sandra could see below them the vast expanse of Lake Victoria, its still green waters stretching beyond the horizon. For the third time, the co-pilot called up Entebbe Control and requested permission to land.

The strain was beginning to tell on the plane's captors. Sandra watched one of the young Swedes as he stalked the aisle. The way he kept biting his lip, the dark stains of sweat under the armpits of his olive green shirt, the jerky way he turned his head at the slightest movement among the passengers and the way his finger twitched on the trigger of his machine pistol made her wonder how long he could keep his cool. Milos alone appeared untroubled.

She could not keep her eyes off him. He had been forward, checking up in the pilots' cabin. As he strode past her, she cried out to him, 'Why don't you tell us what this is all about?'

He turned and gazed at her but was on the point of continuing down the aisle. His detachment nettled her.

79

'What are you trying to achieve?' she called. 'Or are you in it for the kicks?'

The smile faded from his face. 'Don't be childish! If you are interested, we have sent a message, demanding the release of fifty political prisoners who are being held in conditions which would disgust you.'

'What the hell have your Salamban politics to do with us?' she shouted.

'Nothing at all, little girl! But Lomo, blood-thirsty old devil that he is, dare not risk having anything happen to a visiting international football team. If they were to be harmed because of his obstinacy, the people would lynch him. That's why he'll give us what we demand.'

'But you, whoever you are, what's all this to you? You're not a Salamban.'

'I'm paid,' he retorted.

'And that's it, is it? You'd do anything as long as the money was right?'

'I have my price,' he agreed, 'but I wouldn't allow myself to become involved with any movement if I disapproved of its ideals.'

'Is that so! What are you, a mercenary?'

'I'm an anarchist, a leader of the movement in Salamba. When I feel that my work is finished there, I'll move on to somewhere else. Or, just maybe, I might stay on,' he added, as though a new thought had entered his head.

Even while she was arguing with him, Sandra was aware of the attraction which this man had for her. It had nothing at all to do with his politics or his morality: it was that inner strength of his that awed her.

Kurt Loewe had been stretched out on the seats across the aisle from her. He had recovered consciousness and was groaning and tossing about feverishly. He could see little of what was going on around him but he listened attentively to their conversation. She's fascinated by that thug, he thought bitterly.

Sandra had no chance to speak further with Milos because he was called to the pilots' cabin. He strode away from her and disappeared through the first class compartment.

'It's Entebbe.' Zuleika told him jubilantly. 'We're going in.'

Even as she spoke, they heard the radio operator calling them up from Entebbe control.

'Come in on runway twelve, I repeat, runway twelve. Taxi to the far end of the field. Do not, I repeat, do not attempt to approach the tower or the terminal buildings. After you have landed, remain in the aircraft. We will contact you with instructions.'

'Entebbe is an unlucky airfield for hijackers,' the captain remarked grimly.

'You are thinking of the way the Israelis raided the place. That's years ago,' Milos answered. 'Things have changed.'

'We'll see.'

'You just concentrate on putting this heap of junk on the floor in one piece,' Milos ordered. Turning to Zuleika, he told her to make an announcement, instructing the passengers to remain seated when the plane was down.

They were coming in very low. Sandra could see the ripples on the surface of the lake and then the swampy land was rushing past them, vivid green in the late afternoon sunshine. The white concrete of the control tower loomed up from nowhere and a tremor ran through the plane as the wheels kissed the bumpy runway and then they were speeding along the ground towards the terminal. A couple of fire tenders were running towards them, as if to head them off, but when they reached the apron the pilot pulled the big plane onto a lane to the left and taxied right the way across the width of the field until he brought the plane to a halt in the far corner. He switched off the engines and, all at once, there was complete silence in the huge plane. Even Loewe ceased moaning.

'Everybody stay seated,' Milos warned.

It was eerie. They sat, facing forward as if they were waiting to watch a movie on some invisible screen. The lights flickered and then went out but there was still sufficient daylight for the hijackers to keep them under observation and, after a few seconds, the emergency power supply started up and the compartment was brilliantly lit.

Outside the plane there was scarcely any activity as far as they could see. The two fire tenders had taken up positions a couple of hundred yards from the Boeing. Nothing stirred.

'Now what?' called an elderly woman.

'We wait,' answered Milos.

'Can't you let this man be taken off?' asked Antonescu, pointing to the semi-conscious Loewe. 'You can see he is badly hurt; he ought to be rushed to a hospital.'

'Nobody leaves the plane. Not yet.'

Sandra looked at the injured man. His face was haggard, he was deathly pale and the bandage which had been bound over his wound was already tinged a dirty reddish-brown as the blood oozed through the soggy dressing. She felt sick but strangely unmoved. Maybe he is dying, she thought. I've never seen a dead person; perhaps he will die, sitting there, before my eyes. She knew that she ought to be horrified; didn't girls get hysterical at times like these? She felt a pressure on her hand and turned her head. Donald was staring at her anxiously.

'Are you all right, love?'

He sounded so ineffectual that she wanted to laugh. She nodded, she could not be bothered to reply. Looking up, she caught the eye of Milos as he went past. There was the ghost of a smile on his lips, sardonic, mocking, perhaps even pitying those who did not possess his unwavering strength of will. The more she told herself that he was hard, cruel and hateful, the more she found herself drawn to him. And that frightened her more than all the violence.

One of the Swedish boys who had been in the forward cabin came over to Milos.

'Zuleika sent me to find you. There's been a message from the control tower offering us food and water.'

'Tell them that until we receive an answer to the demands which we sent to Salamba, nobody approaches this plane.'

'A doctor?'

'Nobody. That's final.'

The hours passed. Night came quickly with hardly any twilight. There was a dramatic moment when powerful flood lights were switched on all around them turning the darkened airport into a stage on which the immobile Boeing was the sole actor.

The news of the hijacking filtered through the censorship in Salamba but the fact that the Scottish team was on board was suppressed. Anna heard about it on TV at home in their bungalow. She told Chuck when he got back from the mining camp.

'Isn't that the flight that your friend was taking?'

'Halevy? Yes, you're right. I hope nothing happens to him.'

'They say that it is Milos,' Anna said. 'I would not give much for the chances of anybody who was a hostage in his hands. If they kill him, what are you going to do with your Golden Phallus?'

'Anna, don't be so cold blooded! The poor guy's out there but he's still alive.'

'All you Americans are so sentimental, you make me sick. Listen, Chuck, that thing could be worth a fortune, couldn't it?'

'Honestly, I have no idea. Halevy would know.'

'Halevy's half way to being dead,' Anna retorted. 'If they murder him, we should take our chance on this relic being genuine.'

'What are you saying?'

'That we should get the hell out of this country and take your golden phallus with us. Think, Chuck, you will be the only man with two penises!'

'I'm not sure that would be right,' Chuck cautioned. 'And it would mean my throwing up my job.'

'You'll do as I tell you,' asserted Anna. 'Where have you put the damned thing? I looked for it this morning in my dressing table. It wasn't there and the maids have not touched it.'

'It wasn't safe, lying around the house. I took it back to my office and locked it in the safe.'

'You what?' cried Anna. 'You should have asked me first. Now you bring it back here tomorrow. Understood?'

Chuck stared at her coolly. 'It stays in the safe.'

Anna could not believe her ears. This little man had the nerve to defy her. She went to strike him but he caught her wrist and threw her aside.

'This is too important for one of your tantrums. I'm holding on to that thing. I owe it to Halevy. I called him to this godforsaken country and the least I can do is to make sure that the golden phallus, if that is what it is, will be waiting for him, when he gets here.'

'If he gets here,' sneered Anna. 'I'll make you sorry for this, Chuck.'

But he had walked out of the room, leaving her alone with her rage.

It was shortly before eleven that night when the radio in the Boeing crackled into life. Milos pushed his way into the cabin where the other girl had relieved Zuleika.

'It's Ibari,' she cried. 'They're coming through.'

'We have a link to Ibari through Entebbe control,' explained the co-pilot. 'Take the microphone, they are asking you to acknowledge the message personally.'

'This is Milos,' he spoke slowly and clearly into the microphone. 'Who is there?'

Silence. Then, over the hiss of static, a muffled voice. 'Hold on, Milos. You are speaking with Ibari. I have President Lomo for you.'

Another pause, then a different voice. 'Milos, this is Lomo. Can you hear me?'

'That's him,' muttered Milos, 'I'd recognize the old fox anywhere.' He spoke into the microphone. 'I can hear you well. So, tell me, Lomo, have we a deal?'

'Listen carefully,' Lomo's words grated through the mesh of the loudspeaker. 'We are concerned with the safety of all passengers, I repeat, all, but especially with our guests from Scotland. Under the circumstances, we have decided to accept your conditions for their release. We propose that you fly to Ibari – '

'No way!' interrupted Milos. 'The exchange takes place in Entebbe.'

For fully five minutes, the only sound in the cabin was the incessant crackling of the static. Nobody moved, waiting, listening.

There was a click and Lomo was back on the circuit. 'Very well; Entebbe. We shall release your accomplices, the full list which you transmitted, tomorrow morning. They will be conveyed to Ibari International Airport and then flown in one aircraft to Entebbe. There, they will be escorted to your plane. When you can see them safely on the tarmac, we shall require you to release half of your hostages. Your accomplices will then board your plane and you will let go the remaining passengers. You will be free to fly to the destination of your choice but we shall hold you responsible for the safe return of the aircraft and its crew. Is that fully understood?'

'I agree to those arrangements. Please note that we have one wounded man on board. Don't worry, Lomo, it's not one of the footballers.'

'Any further casualties among the passengers or crew, and the exchange will be cancelled and you will be hunted down for the pirates that you are.'

'The situation is now calm.'

'Good. Keep it that way. We cannot yet forecast the exact time of arrival of the flight from here but zero hour for the exchange will be midday.'

'Very well. But when my men are on the tarmac, there will be nobody else out there with them. No police, no soldiers. Your men are to keep their distance.'

'Nobody would want to risk being contaminated.'

'That's the authentic Daniel Lomo,' grinned Milos. 'Call us in the morning to confirm that everything is on schedule.'

There was a grunt which Milos assumed signified assent and then the contact was cut.

'I'll go and spread the glad news,' said Milos to the others.

'No need,' the girl told him. 'When we heard that they were going to play, I switched your conversation into the internal circuit. Everything that Lomo said was heard in the passenger compartment.'

'So much the better,' Milos commented. 'They could hear that it was genuine and not some invention of mine.'

Back among the passengers, there was an air of relief, almost a holiday atmosphere. But there were a few sullen faces.

'So you murderous bastards have got your own way,' growled Alan Chalmers when Milos came past.

'I'll tell the lady to hit you a bit harder next time,' Milos told him with a friendly smile. He was carrying a portable microphone and he addressed all the hostages.

'You've heard the good news. At midday tomorrow, you will be free. But, until then, you will have to put up with a few minor inconveniences. First of all, you will have to make do with whatever food there is left in the galley. I don't suppose you will complain if you feel a bit hungry. Next, the toilets and washing arrangements will leave something to be desired. You can go, one by one, the men amidships, the women to those at the rear. You will have to wait until tomorrow afternoon before you will be able to have a proper wash. You will smell a little in this tropical heat but consider how much worse it is for the freedom fighters in the jungle. Lastly, we all need some sleep. Your guards will take turns and we don't want any of you causing trouble during the night. So, each of you will be given a sleeping pill. Nothing serious, I assure you, but strong enough to keep you out of mischief until the morning.'

The two girl hijackers were already walking along the aisles, giving everybody a pill and a glass of water.

'What if we won't take your damned dope?'

'Then I regret that your sleep will be permanent,' Milos answered the disgruntled questioner.

'But I have a weak heart,' protested a woman.

'Madam, in this life, we all have to take risks sometimes. Swallow it like a good girl, it's in a worthy cause.'

His eyes were on Sandra when she was given the white capsule. He nodded genially as she gulped it down. Donald took his pill without a word and put his arm around her protectively as they waited for the drug to take effect.

Whatever it was that the anarchists had dispensed to them, it was strong and worked rapidly. Sandra had a soothing sensation of detachment, as if she had been wrapped in cotton wool and her consciousness seemed to dissolve into a heavy, death-like sleep.

Milos made sure that nobody had got away without swallowing a sleeping pill and he stood, keen-eyed and alert, until he was certain that all the passengers and crew were insensible. Only then did he relax and divide his forces into two watches.

Sandra had no idea what the time was when she opened her eyes. Bright sunlight streamed through the windows and the temperature in the cabin was already uncomfortably high. Donald stirred restlessly, his head upon her shoulder. Several of the Germans were awake and were being escorted to the diminutive lavatories. The guards were back to a full complement and they still refused to let the passengers out of their seats except to be taken to the toilets. Somehow the stewardesses had managed to heat up some abominable coffee and Sandra gratefully drank a cupful. Around her, the other men and women slowly returned to life.

Milos strode down the aisle, checking that everything was in order. Zuleika's voice floated out from a loudspeaker.

'Ibari has just called to confirm that our comrades embarked without any hitch. They are now airborne and we estimate that they should arrive at Entebbe in an hour and a half.'

Sandra's empty stomach was rumbling but the stench

in the overheated compartment was so intense that she had no appetite. Donald shook his head groggily, clambered to his feet and was led by one of the Swedes to the toilets. He returned, wrinkling his nose in disgust.

'You can't stay in there,' he complained, 'there's no water for flushing the loos. If I'd been there one minute longer, I would have passed out. Some poor devil has been sick. I hope to God that plane is on time and we can get away from here before we are all ill!'

Sandra decided to hang on as long as she could without facing the ordeal. She looked at Loewe. He was lying perfectly still and not making a sound. Sleeping? Nobody paid him the slightest attention. As time went by, every one of them was straining their ears for the first throb of an approaching aircraft.

Louis Halevy had coped with the eternity of suspense and fear better than many of his fellow passengers. He had the Jewish talent for enduring and he watched what went on around him with the self-discipline of a scholar. He observed the indignation which the Scots were barely able to restrain, the wild panic of some other travellers and the quiet defiance of Sandra to which Milos himself responded. What he found peculiar was the behaviour of the group of German military advisers. It was not that they did anything strange, rather it was the complete absence of any positive action. They were quiet, passive, but it was not merely an acceptance of their predicament. Could they be waiting, conserving their forces for some trial of strength which was to come? They were so controlled that Halevy could have believed that they were carrying out a military manoeuvre.

The time dragged by. The guards were pacing up and down, glancing repeatedly through the windows at the empty blue sky. Sandra began to fear that something had gone wrong: perhaps the other aircraft had crashed in the jungle where it would never be discovered and they would be condemned to go on sitting and waiting until Milos had them all shot.

Then Zuleika, who had rejoined the pilots, announced that Entebbe control was in contact with the plane from Ibari which had started its approach to the airport. Hardly had she finished, when the distant hum of its engines could be heard. It was another eternity before one of the passengers in a window seat pointed to a tiny black dot, like a speck of dirt in the clear heavens. The droning echoed in the cavern of the Boeing until Sandra had the impression that the other aircraft was going to fly right inside the fuselage of the jumbo. It passed above them and then it disappeared behind the terminal buildings.

'What the hell?' Donald was howling in fearful bewilderment as their prospect of deliverance died away.

Sandra had no idea what was going on but she remarked how calm and unconcerned Milos was. It must be all right.

The plane completed its circuit and was once more closing in, its massive undercarriage projecting, its nose drooping, as the pilot brought it into line with the runway. There was a cloud of dust as its wheels touched and the roar of its engines became a deafening scream. It passed the jumbo and then taxied away until it appeared no larger than a toy, parked in front of the control tower.

At once, there was a flurry of activity around it. Steps were in position almost before the plane had rolled to a halt and two long, articulated buses pulled in beside it. One pair of eyes was not watching the line of ant-like figures disembarking. Milos was looking at his hostages, vigilant even at the eleventh hour. They remained obediently in their seats, suppressing their mounting excitement.

It could not have taken much more than five minutes

for the men from Salamba to have left the aircraft and taken their places in the buses which, at once, began to move off towards the corner of the airfield where the big Boeing was standing. They were being driven much faster than when they were in normal service, swerving and swaying over the grass and concrete until they were within a couple of hundred yards. They braked violently and waited. For near the main terminal building, a jeep raced towards them, a huge red cross painted on its flat bonnet. At the same time, one of the tall mobile stairways was moving in their direction.

Milos had gone into the pilots' cabin to pass orders over the radio. Zuleika had taken his place, keeping the passengers under observation. Louis Halevy had a perfect view of what was happening outside. The medical jeep was standing near the buses and eventually the convoy was joined by the mobile stairs. They formed a rough semi-circle, standing well clear of the Boeing. At last, the new arrivals filed out of the buses and stood in the open. Among them were a dozen or so armed soldiers in the uniform of the Salamban army. They remounted the buses which then were driven off. Halevy followed them right the way to the terminal. The released prisoners walked towards the Boeing. They were strung out so that they could easily be recognized by their comrades on board.

'All passengers in Rows one to twenty-five, prepare to leave the aircraft.' Milos ordered. 'Keep in your places until you are told to move.'

There was a stirring among the Germans and some other travellers as they gathered up their belongings.

'What about our luggage in the hold?' asked a fussy, grey haired woman.

'You will have to wait for it until we have finished with the plane,' Zuleika called.

'It's a disgrace. I shall complain to the company,' protested the woman.

Halevy burst out laughing. A few hours ago, she was praying that she might get away with her life: now, she was seething with indignation at being deprived of her cases for a few days. How quickly people get over their fears. She had dismissed her ordeal before it was even over.

Milos had ordered the crew of the jeep to get out of their vehicle and stand well away where they could be watched. Now, he came back into the passengers' compartment.

'We are going to use the rear exit,' he told them. 'When you are given the command, those of you who are in the party to disembark will walk to the door and file out, one at a time. You two,' he pointed at Antonescu and Halevy, 'will carry the wounded man. At the foot of the stairs, you will hand him over to the Red Cross personnel. All clear?'

There was a rumble of assent. Milos went to the rear door. Slowly, the stairway began to move towards the Boeing. It was beneath them and they felt the tiny shock as it engaged by the rear door.

Sandra had sat through all this performance. She had not been to the loo since the previous afternoon and she was bursting. The stink had been so awful that she had put off going until now the pain was unbearable. She wanted to see the final scene in this drama, but she could not control her bladder any longer. She had stumbled to her feet and was hurried away by the other 'lesbian' just before the stairs reached the fuselage of the Boeing. The relief was exquisite: the hijack forgotten for that blissful moment.

When she emerged from the privy, the stairs were in place and Milos had at that instant opened the heavy rear

92

door. There was the marvellous odour of fresh air and the sunshine poured into the plane through the doorway, as if to welcome them back to life.

That was the moment when the first shot rang out. The girl who had been escorting Sandra was driven back against her by the force of the bullet which had smashed into her head. Sandra was too shocked to realize that the warm, sticky liquid on her face and arms was the dying girl's blood, which was gushing all over her. Immediately a whole volley of shots echoed through the plane.

The first bullet had whizzed past Halevy's ear and he had ducked in his seat. Now he knew what the Germans had been waiting for. Of course, it was for them that zero hour was fixed for midday. They had held their fire until the very last moment when all the hijackers would be concentrating on what was happening outside the plane, watching for the attack which never came, the ambush from the men on the ground.

No less than three of the gunmen had picked Milos as their target but, at the moment that they were about to shoot, Sandra walked across their line of fire. In that fraction of a second, they checked, their weapons aimed, their fingers on the point of squeezing their triggers. But the man who was covering Sandra's escort had already tightened his grip and sent a bullet thudding into the girl and, at once, the rest of the men opened up on the other hijackers.

Before Sandra's brain had a chance to register what was going on, Milos had leaped forward and grabbed her arm from behind. He fired twice at where the Germans were bunched together, the bullets screaming past Sandra's ear. Then he darted to the open door, clasping her before him so that her body screened him from his attackers. For perhaps a second, the drama in the Boeing was played out in front of her. She saw the corpse of the girl hijacker slide to the floor. One of the Swedes uttered an unearthly shriek as his chest seemed to explode, flesh, bone and muscle hammered apart from the torrent of lead from two machine pistols. A German staggered and clutched his right arm, his gun falling to the carpet. Sandra saw his lips moving: she knew that he was swearing although she could not hear his words. A stewardess was howling hysterically. Halevy seized her and dragged her into the comparative safety of the padded seats. She saw Zuleika drop to the ground but she had no idea whether she had been hit or was taking cover. As if by magic, a couple of tiny holes appeared in the side of the plane above one of the windows.

Then she was out of the plane, half dragged, half pushed by Milos. She had no opportunity to recover her balance: she was hurled down the long, metal staircase. She stumbled, cracking her knee against the wall of the stairs, but Milos, still gripping her wrist, lugged her after him.

Spread out in front of them was the line of released prisoners. At the sound of gunfire, they scattered and began to run for the perimeter fence of the airfield. At the same time, Sandra caught sight of a posse of jeeps and armoured cars emerging from behind the terminal buildings and small groups of soldiers appeared at various points along the fence near where the Boeing was standing. Milos did not hesitate. He sprinted to the Red Cross jeep. He was pulling her along, but Sandra realized that she was running with him and not making any attempt to hold back or hinder her abductor. The crew of the jeep had started to run back towards their vehicle but Milos let fly a couple of shots in their direction and they flung themselves to the ground.

By now the first of the Germans in the Boeing had got to the open door and was aiming his automatic at them.

His first shot was well wide but he was being joined by more of his comrades. With a frantic dive, Milos reached the driving seat of the jeep. As he jumped, he let go of Sandra's wrist, but she leaped into the jeep beside him. The engine was still warm and it roared into life and Milos crashed the jeep into gear. As it sprang forward, Sandra heard a wild, singing noise: a bullet had ricochetted off the side of the vehicle.

Inside the plane, the last of the hijackers had been overpowered and the commander of the Germans had taken charge. However, Louis Halevy was watching, fascinated, through the window at the runaway jeep as it tore towards the boundary fence. The leading trucks of their pursuers were nearly half-way across the airfield and were, if anything, gaining on them. Milos did not let up. He and Sandra ducked in their seats as the jeep hurtled into the stout wire fence. The windshield disintegrated into a shower of fragments, the fence buckled and then strands of metal were flying in all directions as the jeep tore its way through the yawning gap it had made.

Sandra was gasping for breath, the wind whipping her hair and skin, her body bruised from the mad, leaping, plunging progress of the jeep. Suddenly, they had reached a road and Milos swung the jeep onto the carriageway. They had made it: they were free.

But for how long? There were not a lot of roads around Entebbe airport and the armoured cars and army jeeps would be in hot pursuit. Milos drove for about ten minutes along the highway. Then, right in the middle of nowhere, he pulled up.

He turned to Sandra. 'Out!' he ordered.

'But if I'm with you, they won't shoot,' she protested.

He shook his head. 'Don't count on it. You've probably saved my life in the plane. Now it's too dangerous for you to stay. This isn't your struggle. Out!'

Before she could argue further, he had pushed her bodily out of the jeep. 'Somebody will be along soon to rescue you,' he called.

'Good luck,' she shouted, but he was already on his way and he could not have heard her.

Why did she want him to get away? She had seen his ruthlessness and she knew that he had used her in making his escape. As he had said, it was not her struggle. What the hell did she care about what went on in Salamba? Yet she had thrilled to his daring and she felt as if she were swamped by his total masculinity. Sharing his dangers had been like a sort of weird love affair. And now what?

She watched the cloud of dust move towards the horizon. After the frenzy of the battle in the plane and their flight, the calm all around her was unnatural. The wind was singing in the long grass and distant trees nodded their heads peacefully. She was amazed at the extent to which her emotions had been captured by Milos. She had not spared a thought for Donald. He was her boyfriend, after all, and she had no way of knowing what had happened to him during the melée in the Boeing. He might be dead, or perhaps he was horribly wounded and was calling for her. God, she thought, what a heartless bitch I must have become!

She began to trudge back the way they had come. It was not as hot as she had anticipated and the breeze was refreshing after the ghastly stench of the aircraft.

She had walked a hundred yards or so past a fork in the road when she saw the first of the police jeeps. It was approaching fast but when the driver caught sight of her, he flashed his headlights and the vehicle screeched to a halt. A young police sergeant called to her.

'You were the girl who was taken hostage, yes?'

She nodded. 'I'm all right,' she assured him, 'but can

96

you take me back to the airport? My boyfriend will be dreadfully worried.'

The sergeant consulted the two other men who were in the jeep. One must have been a superior officer of some kind: he was wearing scarlet shoulder bars. He was the one who replied.

'I'm sorry, but our job is to chase this bandit. Another car will be along soon. Did he hurt you?'

'No. But you know he is armed and dangerous.'

The sergeant cast a doubting glance at the officer.

'She's right,' he growled. 'Why don't the bloody Salambans do their own dirty work?'

Sandra had only the sketchiest ideas of African politics, but she could see that these Ugandans had no affection for the regime of Daniel Lomo or his countrymen.

The officer hesitated but his dilemma was resolved for him. Trundling along the road came an armoured car. It stopped beside them and a Ugandan army officer jumped out. The policemen saluted respectfully.

'Well,' shouted the officer, 'why are you hanging about here? You're supposed to be hunting down a criminal, not chatting up pretty girls on the road!'

'Begging your pardon,' the police officer replied, 'This lady was the bandit's hostage. We have just this minute found her and she is in a very distressed state. I have my orders, sir, and our first consideration is the safety of the hijacked victims. I, and my men, are going to take the lady back to Entebbe where she can receive medical attention.'

The army officer snorted. 'She looks fit enough to me. Very well, put her into your jeep and get out of my way!' He glared at Sandra and called out to her. 'You were with this man. Which way did he go?'

'It's been such a shock,' Sandra sobbed, 'and I was very confused, but I remember he drove off down that road.' She pointed to the fork behind them and indicated the road which Milos had not taken. 'I think,' she added, as if to placate her conscience.

The army officer climbed back into the armoured car which made off at high speed.

'OK, miss, shall we be on our way?' asked the police officer.

She climbed into the jeep. The sergeant turned it round and they drove back along the road to Entebbe. She was sitting beside the officer who smiled at her and said, 'Funny that a hunted criminal should choose the road you pointed out. It comes to a dead end in about five miles.'

'I don't suppose he knew,' she answered. 'After all, he is a foreigner. And I might have been mistaken,' she added.

'Of course,' the officer agreed affably.

When they got back to Entebbe, they found that the passengers had disembarked from the jumbo, which had been damaged by some of the bullets, and were about to be taken aboard the Boeing 727 which had flown in from Ibari with the prisoners. Donald broke away from the group and rushed to Sandra, seizing her in his arms as if she had been brought back from the dead.

'Sandy, my Sandy, thank God you're safe!'

'I'm just fine.' She kissed him tenderly but without emotion.

There was an ambulance nearby. Loewe, lying on a stretcher, was being carried to the rear doors and lifted inside. Three wounded hijackers, including Zuleika, were also being brought into the ambulance. Sandra saw the German with the shattered arm impatiently shake off the nurse who went to help him and climb, unaided, into the vehicle. Lying on the dusty ground there were four corpses, their frightfulness hidden by the coarse army

98

blankets which had been thrown over them. She shuddered.

'You're lucky, young lady,' Louis Halevy called to her. 'One of those could so easily have been you.'

Or Milos, she thought guiltily.

The articulated buses had come back to carry them to the terminal building. Wearily, they climbed on board.

Outside the terminal, there was already a crowd of excited reporters and TV cameramen. They swarmed around Sandra, shouting questions, begging her to pose for pictures, pushing and jostling each other to get as close as possible to the heroine of the getaway saga. She felt tired all of a sudden and these chattering, gesticulating men and women were getting on her nerves.

'No, he didn't hurt me,' she answered as they fired questions at her. 'It all happened so quickly: there's really nothing I can tell you.'

They were pleading with her to give an interview, each one of them endeavouring to get an exclusive. She shook her head, wearily fighting her way to the asylum of the terminal.

'Can't you see that she is exhausted?' Donald shouted. 'Leave her alone. If she feels up to it, she may give you a statement before we leave.'

But she didn't.

In Ibari, Daniel Lomo was taunting Asi Moriba.

'Seems that Milos has given your boys the slip.'

Moriba scowled. 'We'll catch up with him. And you should be happy that all your Scottish footballers are in one piece. I understand that your Kurt Loewe nearly messed everything up. It's what I would have expected from him. The doctor says that he is going to survive, worse luck!'

'I thought that you said that Milos and his men were

going to attack at the football match?' queried the president.

'Don't worry, Daniel, they will, now that their hijack has failed. They mean business,' smiled Moriba, 'and this time, you will be their prime target.'

But the last word on the episode came from the captain of Africavia flight 101. Concluding his entry in the aircraft's log, he wrote, 'I warned them that Entebbe was unlucky for hijackers.'

Part II

4

Cat and Mouse

Later that evening, the Boeing 727, which had brought the prisoners from Salamba to Entebbe, flew into Ibari International Airport with the passengers of Africavia 101. The television cameras were out in force but the hijack episode was, as far as possible, played down. The story of the day was the formal greeting by President Daniel Lomo, in person, extended in a speech of great eloquence, to the Scottish touring football team.

Flashlights popped and the cameras whirred while the captain of the visiting side said how much he and his men would enjoy their stay in Africa and were looking forward to experiencing more of the sporting spirit of their hosts both on and off the pitch. With all the fuss concentrated on the footballers, Louis Halevy was able to retrieve his case and pass through immigration control with much less delay than he had anticipated. As he emerged into the main concourse, Chuck Hughes hurried over to him.

'Say, Professor, am I glad to see you! When we heard the news about the hijack, I can tell you, we really were worried that you might not make it.'

'And I can tell you,' rejoined Halevy, 'that the same prospect had me worried too.'

Chuck grabbed his case and led the way to where the Range Rover was parked outside the terminal. 'So how bad was it?' he asked.

'Bad enough. I'll tell you all about it later. Right now, all I want is a shower and a shave.'

'Sure,' Chuck answered. 'We're going straight back to my place where we can fix you up. It's not far, about fifteen minutes from here, just out of town. I guess you could do with a decent meal, too, couldn't you?'

'First, my friend, a good, stiff drink!'

Anna was watching out for them and she ran out of the bungalow to welcome the weary traveller. She had decided to impress the Frenchman: after all, he might turn out to be useful. She certainly succeeded. Her short dress was of vivid scarlet silk and she wore an exquisite hibiscus flower of the same hue in her hair. It was as though her lovely body was wreathed in flame. Louis Halevy, relaxing in an easy chair on the verandah, feasted his eyes on his hostess, so gracious and ready to please and so glamorous. But he thought it wiser not to raise the subject of the extraordinary object which had lured him to Salamba and Anna was too wily to mention it before Halevy had had an opportunity to examine it. His time would come.

Another passenger who left the airport with the minimum of attention from onlookers was Kurt Loewe. He was carried to a waiting ambulance and rushed to Ibari General Hospital where he underwent an operation on what had once been his eye.

Sandra, on the other hand, had been photographed by a number of newsmen and she appeared on the TV news programme. However, this was not because of her fame as an artiste, nor because of her dramatic role in the hijack. She was the girlfriend of the dashing young Scottish striker, and that was enough for the football crazy Salambans to accept her as a sort of second-hand celebrity. But when she got to the hotel, she found that Christian fundamentalism, as expounded by Daniel Lomo, was no respecter of persons.

'A double room, please,' said Donald to the receptionist, a young black man who peered at them through horn rimmed spectacles.

'You are married, of course,' he queried.

'Well, not exactly,' was Donald's evasive answer.

'I regret that we are unable to provide double rooms to couples who cannot produce a valid marriage certificate,' the receptionist told them. And the way he glared at them convinced them that he meant what he said.

A little judicious swapping later with other members of the team enabled them to have adjoining rooms with a connecting door. That night, Donald stealthily slipped into Sandra's room as if he were a mischievous schoolboy venturing into a neighbouring girls' school. The situation was so absurd that they both burst out laughing.

'Be quiet!' warned Sandra. 'If anyone catches you in here, you'll probably be sentenced to be castrated by one of their peoples' courts or whatever they call the damned things.'

They undressed in silence and made sure that the door was locked before they got into bed. They had been through so much since they last shared a bed that they lay quietly in each other's arms for perhaps five minutes, simply wallowing in the joy of being alone and once more between clean sheets. It was marvellous to return to sanity.

'It's so good to be back, Sandy!'

Donald was holding her close and he kissed her gently on her bare shoulder. She closed her eyes as he stroked her hair and felt herself being lulled by the warmth of his body and his old, sweet tenderness.

And yet something had changed. His hands caressing her breasts, his lips pressed against hers, his aroma, the feel of his skin, his soft words of love and his hard, hard cock, everything was just the way it used to be. So, what was wrong? On other nights like this in Inverclyde she had been wild with desire for him; when they had made love, the stars had danced in ecstasy. He kissed her, he

105

fondled her, his lips paid homage to every part of her. He did all the right things, but – . But what? It was agreeable and it felt good: it used to be pure magic.

When he penetrated her, she so much wanted it to be how she remembered it. She ran her fingers over his lithe body and she felt him respond immediately to her sensual movements, but she was left strangely, frighteningly unmoved. She closed her eyes; there flashed into her mind the vision of a man's face and it was not that of Donald. A strong face, square-jawed with a scar down the left cheek and the light of defiance in cool, grey eyes.

All her sexuality was stirred by that recollection. She could sense his strength, his energy flowing into her, setting her juices flowing and inflaming her with an animal lust. Donald was murmuring words of passion in her ear but she consciously shut out his voice and heard instead that of her fantasy lover, a man whom she had never known except at the wrong end of a gun.

Every second that she fucked Donald, she was being unfaithful to him. She was ashamed, and at the very same time she revelled in the glorious sensation. Her orgasm was tremendous, a mind-shattering experience which swept Donald along with it. The whole universe was engulfed in that uncontrollable throbbing, pulsing rhythm of which she was the centre. She was screaming and sobbing and weeping, her hands tearing at Donald. She had raised herself until she was erect, her man prone before her, scissored between her thighs, seized by the violence of her passion.

'God, Sandy, what came over you?' gasped Donald when he had got his breath back. 'You've never been like that before. It was as though you wanted to murder me. And so fast! I thought that you liked to take it nice and easy.'

She said nothing until that other face had faded away. Unwillingly, she opened her eyes.

'I don't know, darling,' she lied. 'For some reason, that's the way it happened tonight.'

'But it was so different.' Donald was troubled. 'Is everything all right? I mean, there's nothing changed between us, is there, Sandy?'

She answered him with a kiss. 'It's nothing, dear. I suppose that it was all the excitement and the strain of what we've been through. And now, I am tired. With all the noise we made, you ought to be getting back to your own room before the cops raid us.'

'Oh, can't I stay with you?' He looked so anxious that Sandra was moved.

'Yes, of course you can. But I do want to get some sleep now.'

Donald also had been worn out by their exertions and in a very short time he had dozed off. He lay quiet and unmoving, breathing evenly like a little boy without a care in the world.

Sandra too was soon asleep, but she was not at rest. She cuddled up to the back of the man sleeping so peacefully beside her. Eventually, soothed by the warmth of his body, she drifted into a dream-wracked sleep of a sort. It was Milos who was sharing her bed, but a Milos strangely transformed. He was no longer the active, dominating partner, but lay submissive to her, unable to move as though he were in a trance. Her hands were pulling and pinching his flesh which had become as soft as that of a new-born baby. She knew that he had to accept whatever she wanted to do to him, just as she had once had no will of her own to resist Rex's using her body.

The sensation of her strength and his weakness gave

Sandra a glow of pleasure. It was as though her unconscious mind was revolting against the way it had been
dominated by the real life Milos and was having its
revenge. Their roles had been reversed. It was she who
had the long, thrusting penis and, mysteriously, he who
had a vagina into which she was driving. She was aware
that she was hurting him but that added to her satisfaction. She was rubbing her body against his back sinuously
and with growing urgency but he still lay, open to her as
if spellbound. Her hands grasped his cock while, to the
rest of her, he had become a woman.

The illusion was erotic and she was aroused by it. Yet
it gave no sense of sexual fulfilment: indeed, as she
continued to make use of the unresisting body, her feeling
of frustration grew. There was no way her phantom penis
could reach an orgasm and what had been a sensuous
massage had changed into mere friction which chafed and
left her angry and sore.

She had no impression of suddenly waking up, merely
an imperceptible slipping out of her sleep. She realized
that she was gripping tightly Donald's erect penis and
was masturbating her sleeping lover while her own clitoris
was hot and swollen from her persistent pressing of
herself against his buttocks. Yet, so strong had been her
dream or nightmare, that she had to pass her hands over
Donald's face to assure herself that there was no scar on
his left cheek. Her sex life had always been so straight
and uncomplicated, she felt disturbed and distressed by
the vividness of her experience and by its weirdness.

Donald moaned faintly in his sleep and she clutched
him tighter, desperately holding on to reality and the
world, peopled by men and women of flesh and blood,
not phantoms.

In the Ibari General Hospital, another bedside scene of quite a different character had been played out that night. Kurt Loewe had come out of the anaesthetic to find himself in the neat, white-painted private ward. He was not alone. Seated beside his bed, stern faced and impatient, was Daniel Lomo. A nurse who had been fussing over his pillow and straightening his sheets was dismissed by the president's peremptory nod.

'Oh, you're awake at last. You've taken your time!'

The injured man wearily blinked his one eye and tried to take in his surroundings and what had been happening to him.

'Come along, man,' scolded Lomo. 'I've been here for hours and I haven't time to waste. Tell me what you saw: anything which might help us to catch Milos.'

Loewe made an indistinct croaking noise.

'Drink this and pull yourself together, man!'

Lomo handed Loewe a glass of water and he gulped down a few mouthfuls. It helped: he gazed owlishly at the ugly little man at his bedside.

'We were hijacked,' he mouthed the words clumsily as he tried to clear the fuzziness of his mind.

'We know all about that,' interrupted Lomo. 'Moriba's men rounded up the gang who were on board the plane: they're all in prison or dead – except Milos. He got away.'

'The girl,' mumbled Loewe.

'What girl? The one who went with him? She was a hostage. He used her body as a shield. I suppose you were not in any state to see.'

Loewe shook his head vigorously.

'I couldn't see, but I heard enough. Before the shoot out, they talked, Milos and that girl. I was in the next seat. He was bragging about freedom fighters and the usual nonsense but she – I tell you, it wasn't what she

109

said but the way she spoke. She was fascinated by him. Watch that girl: sooner or later, she'll lead you to Milos.'

'You mean the one who was a hostage? Are we talking about the same girl?' snapped Lomo.

'I mean the girlfriend of the young Scottish footballer. The bitch is in league with Milos. I heard. She's in love with that man.'

'You are probably raving, but I'll look into what you say.'

With a farewell glare at the stricken man, the president strode out of the room.

A few hours later, he recounted Loewe's story to Asi Moriba. The police chief listened attentively and gave a grim smile.

'Loewe is not a reliable witness. In fact, like most of your very special friends, he's not much good at anything. However, it would not be the first time that an impressionable girl had fallen in love with her kidnapper. There was only one girl travelling with the party from Scotland and she was the one who was carried off at Entebbe by Milos. I'll get a detailed report from the Ugandan police and I'll take the matter up myself, if the story sounds interesting.'

'You mean if the girl looks interesting,' retorted Lomo.

Moriba did not bother to contradict him. Ignoring the president, he was ordering the girl on his switchboard to put in a call to the chief of police at Entebbe.

At about the same time as Lomo was with Moriba, Chuck Hughes was driving, with Louis Halevy at his side, out of Ibari towards the enormous open cast mine. Although it was not far from the capital, there was soon a dramatic change in the countryside. The scrub-covered plain gave way to a landscape of jagged, broken rocks which rose in fierce majesty from the marshy banks of the wide, sluggish river which flowed through Salamba, dividing the country in two.

'If this find of yours is genuine,' Halevy said, 'what could that Swedish archaeologist be doing in such a remote spot as this?'

'That's easy,' answered Chuck. 'Before this highway was built out to the mine, this was the line of an ancient track which crossed the country from north to south.'

'And the spot where your boy actually made the discovery?'

'That was on the site of an old mine working. This part of the world is fantastically rich in minerals and men have scratched ores out of the ground here since primitive times. Of course, they were not looking for the rare earths, but there was plenty of copper and silver.'

They crossed the river by a long stone bridge on which the road narrowed to a single lane.

'This is the only bridge in the whole of this part of the country,' Chuck explained. 'It was here before we opened up the big deposits in the mine and we must get it widened or build a second bridge: it's a dreadful bottleneck for the heavy trucks.'

The mine workings were surrounded by a stout stockade and to get in they had to pass through a barricaded gateway.

'Why all this security?' asked Halevy.

'Do you need to ask after what happened to you on the plane?'

Inside Chuck's office, Halevy waited while the American opened the safe and extracted the object which had so excited Chuck that he had summoned Halevy so urgently.

'Gee, Professor, I do hope that I haven't been wasting your time,' Chuck said anxiously, as he passed the heavy chunk of metal to his guest.

'I can only decide that after I have examined this thing more closely,' replied Halevy. 'Whatever it is, we can say definitely that it is man made and it is certainly an unusual object.'

'I'll leave you to it. Please, use my office. I have to go to the work face but I'll be back in time to take you home for lunch.'

Chuck left and Halevy settled down behind his desk with some reference books which he had brought with him.

There were other former passengers from Africavia 101 who were working that morning. The Scottish team were due for a practice session at the Daniel Lomo Stadium. Sandra was still in bed while Donald bustled about, shaving and showering, before going to meet the other players downstairs in the hotel lobby.

'Are you feeling all right?' he asked.

'I'm fine, darling. I just feel a bit lazy. Off you go. I'll get up after you have left and probably go out and look at the shops. I'll see you back here for lunch.'

After her restless night, she wanted to take things easy. She soaped herself with a rich, creamy lather in the hot bath and let herself relax in the scented water. Refreshed, she swathed her limbs in the thick, white towel and began to forget her bad night. She had put on a simple, cotton dress when the two, hefty policemen arrived to take her away.

They stood there, their features absolutely impassive, heavy revolvers at their sides, in their olive green uniforms.

She was gripped by panic. 'You must be mistaken. What have I done or what am I supposed to have done?'

'You are Sandra Mitchell?'

'Yes, but – '

112

'You are to come with us, miss.'

'Let me leave a note for my boyfriend.'

'Please, now!'

They escorted her to a waiting car and refused to answer her questions or to tell her where they were going.

They drove through the centre of the city with a siren blaring and other vehicles pulled in to the side to let them pass. Her two guards and the driver never said a word during the whole of their journey, which ended when they stopped outside an imposing, tall block of dazzling white stone and glass. Taking her by the arm, they pushed her through the door, across a lobby and into a lift. They rose swiftly to the very top of the building. When they emerged, it was into a vestibule in which stood four or five white leather armchairs of modern design. Their feet sank into the thick pile of the carpet which was also snow white. Above their heads, a couple of closed circuit television cameras scanned the whole of the space. They approached a door which slid open and the policemen thrust Sandra inside. The door closed silently behind her and she was alone with the sole occupant of the room.

Sandra gasped. Asi Moriba was seated behind an enormous desk, an expanse of thick glass supported on pedestals of glowing rosewood. Behind him was a lifelike painting of a lion in the act of tearing apart and devouring a gazelle. But Sandra's eyes were fixed on the man himself. He was grinning at her, as massive as a mountain, or rather a volcano, for she was aware that she was in the presence of a veritable force of nature, a man who exuded power and brute strength, yet who possessed an awesome degree of cunning and intelligence. He had not uttered a word but she felt her flesh cringing before him. He had the same vitality, the inner fire which had impressed her in Milos but this man was dominant in quite another manner. He was not imbued with Milos's ruthless idealism, but what was immediately apparent to her was that he was someone who bent men's minds or broke their bodies, and who enjoyed it.

However, when he spoke, his manner was mild and courteous.

'Please take a seat, Miss Mitchell.'

'Who are you and why am I here?' she demanded.

He was cool, detached and amused; with a contemptuous gesture, he pointed to a chair. She obeyed. He was the sort of man who was always obeyed. Only then, he answered.

'My name is Asi Moriba and I am the Minister of National Security in Salamba. You are here because I wanted to talk to you.'

His manner made it clear that no further reason was needed. She was terrified; her inquisitor's personality seemed to be crushing her, destroying her spirit.

'Why are you afraid?' he asked. 'Have you a bad conscience – something you have done which you should not have done?'

She could not speak but mutely shook her head.

'I hope not,' Moriba continued smoothly. 'I would regret having to take any action which could be considered inhospitable to a tourist. Especially one who had so recently been through so distressing an experience. You did find the hijacking at Entebbe distressing, didn't you, Miss Mitchell?'

It took all her willpower to find her voice. 'Yes, of course, it was horrible.'

Moriba smiled and nodded his agreement. 'I am sure it was. But what did you find so horrifying; the terrorist crimes of this Milos and his gang, or the severity with which they were overcome by my men?'

114

'It was all ghastly.'

'Yes? And what about when Milos carried you off in the jeep? Was that ghastly too? Or did you find it a thrilling adventure, Miss Mitchell?'

Sandra could feel her courage ebbing away before this remorseless tyrant. His icy control was terrifying. If only he would scream and shout or pound the desk, he would have shrunk to mere human proportions and the tension would have been bearable. She was bathed in sweat and had the sensation that she was caught like a fly in a web and that she would never be able to escape from the gigantic, black spider who was smiling down at her so enticingly.

She gritted her teeth and called on her last reserves of strength. 'Mister, if you think that I enjoyed being fired on by your goons, or Ugandan cops or, for all I knew, other terrorists, you must be out of your mind.'

'I am delighted to hear it,' beamed Moriba. 'You see, there have been some suggestions that you were not entirely the innocent victim everybody took you to be. If you had aided Milos to get away, that would have been a serious matter, I am sure that you agree. However, you say that you did not and I am more than happy to accept your word. That is, until such time as we capture Milos and we interrogate him. I am certain that I can rely on you to keep out of trouble during your stay in Salamba. The conditions in our prisons are not intended to appeal to European sensibilities, so please, Miss Mitchell, don't get yourself involved in anything which should not concern you. And now, let us turn to more pleasant topics. I understand that you are hoping to perform in one or two cabarets here before you go on to fulfil your engagements in South Africa.'

'How did you know that?' gasped Sandra.

'Please, Miss Mitchell, do not be stupid. I am the chief

115

of all the police forces of the country, what you might call the Top Cop. It is my job to know everything that goes on. I know all about your contract with Jacobus van der Bijl. But, please, do not get so agitated. I assure you that the arrangements which you intend to make meet with my complete approval.'

'But I don't even know yet where I shall perform in your country,' Sandra protested.

'Of course you don't,' purred Moriba. 'But I do. For the whole of next week, you will be starring at The New Jerusalem.'

'The what?' Sandra was dumbfounded. 'I think that whoever has been telling you about my act could not have given you a very clear idea of what I do.'

'Nonsense! You sing rather sexy, sentimental songs. It is you, Miss Mitchell, who are under a misapprehension. You see, our president, the good Daniel Lomo, is, in his own peculiar way, a religious man, which is another way of saying that he makes life hell for a lot of people. He is absolutely against sins of the flesh, if I might use a rather old-fashioned phrase, and all other sorts of popular entertainment. That is why all our bars and discos and even brothels have been nationalized and given these high-sounding names. I, however, am responsible for what goes on inside them and, under my protection, there are a number of quite reasonable night spots in Ibari. One of these is The New Jerusalem. And now, Miss Mitchell, tonight, you will have dinner with me.'

Sandra blinked. 'What? Minister, I am dreadfully sorry but you see I am here with my boyfriend and – '

'Miss Mitchell,' interrupted Moriba, 'You do not understand. That was not an invitation but an instruction. I have never been refused by a woman and I have no intention of allowing you to be an exception. I do appreciate that you will need to give some plausible explanation

116

to the young man who, in violation of Salamban law, spent last night in your room.'

'In my room?' Sandra repeated.

'You would not want me, as head of the police, to follow that up, would you? President Lomo himself takes a keen personal interest in pursuing all crimes of immorality and sentences are always severe. So, as I was saying, you can tell this friend of yours that you are obliged to have a business dinner to clinch an agreement with the owner of the club where you will be singing.'

'Your ideas on morality don't exclude lying, then?' Sandra asked, with a flicker of her old spirit.

'Don't be ridiculous,' snapped Moriba. 'We shall indeed dine at the New Jerusalem in my private room and, while we are there, I shall introduce you to the gentleman who runs the place and who will give you a contract. As the state owns the club, he is not strictly speaking the owner but I don't suppose that a dashing, young footballer from a village in darkest Scotland would be concerned with the difference. Now, I think that we understand each other and you should be getting back to your hotel. I shall send a car to pick you up at eight. Please be ready: I do not like to be kept waiting.'

Sandra got to her feet. She was not sure what she should say to her imperious host but Moriba had already turned away and picked up some papers. She had been dismissed; the door had been opened silently and her escorts were waiting for her outside.

Back at the hotel, Donald was frantic with anxiety after he had been told by the righteous receptionist who had refused them a double room that Sandra had been taken away by the police. He had tried without success to contact the British embassy and was on the point of going himself to the offices of the Ministry of National Security

117

to find her. He clutched her to him and struggled for words to express his relief.

'So, what was it all about then?' he demanded when she had assured him that she was safe and had not been harmed.

'It was a lot of fuss about nothing very much. They wanted to ask me some questions about what went on during my safari with that Milos character.'

'Then why the hell did they have to come and drag you off as if you were a hit man with the Mafia? Some bloody cop who thinks he can play at being the big boss! He is going to be in a lot of trouble when I find out who he is. I'll have him torn into little pieces.'

Sandra shook her head slowly. 'No, Donald, darling, that's not a very good idea.'

But when she had explained that her interview had been with Asi Moriba himself and that she was obliged to have dinner with him that night, Donald's anger was diverted from some anonymous policeman to Sandra.

'What's this that you are telling me, then? Instead of being with me, you are off with one of the savages from here after you have only met him for five minutes?'

'Be sensible, Donald! He's not a savage but the most powerful man in the country. And the dinner is purely business. I'm meeting the guy who runs a club where I shall be singing.'

'I'll bet!' Donald retorted scornfully. 'And what is the name of this fantastic club?'

'It's called The New Jerusalem,' faltered Sandra. 'I know it sounds phoney, but I promise you, Donald, it's absolutely on the level.'

'And am I invited to your jolly dinner party?'

'Don't be difficult, darling. You are in training, aren't you.'

'That's neither here nor there,' he growled. 'Are you

118

saying that this guy who happens to be the chief of the police is fixing you up in a club out of the goodness of his heart? Or have you already arranged to go to bed with him? And, tell me, why is this booking with this particular club so important?'

'Singing happens to be my career,' hissed Sandra. 'If you remember, when I suggested that we get married, you put your career first. Well, as that was the case, I had to start thinking about my own.'

'Are you trying to trap me into marriage then?' he flared up.

Sandra was close to tears. After the ordeal at the hands of Asi Moriba, this senseless quarrel with Donald was too much. She grabbed her handbag, pushed her way past him and ran out of the hotel. She found a café nearby and sobbed quietly over a cup of coffee. Donald made as if to follow her and then changed his mind. Turning on his heel, he strode into the hotel bar where he sulked over a soft drink.

Louis Halevy spent a morning undistracted by emotional upheavals. When Chuck had returned to take him to lunch, the Frenchman was in a thoughtful mood. Very methodically, he placed markers in the books he had been using and watched Chuck as the young man discarded the clip-board he had carried during his visit to the work face.

'Well, Professor, what do you think? Is this the real thing?'

The two men gazed at the heavy chunk of metal lying on the desk. It seemed to have some strange quality, a kind of life of its own and a power to affect human beings. Chuck remembered Anna's savage behaviour in the presence of this object. Even now, he felt a tightness in his chest which did not seem to be simply due to the

119

stuffy atmosphere in the office. He was strangely aware of his own body and it was as though his flesh was crying out to touch somebody.

Louis Halevy was a man with a strong scientific bent and had no time for superstitious nonsense. But there was something about that piece of inert matter which got through to him as well. His sex life had been as straight as a Roman road and he was so square that he practically had sharp corners. Yet, for the first time in his life, he experienced a desire to touch another man. Casually, he picked up the lump of gold and he felt a thrill run through his hand and arm as if it were alive. He passed it to Chuck and put his arm around the young man's shoulders. There was an uneasy stirring in his loins and the crazy notion came into his head that he would enjoy pressing his lips to those of Chuck.

'I think that you had better put this thing away somewhere safe, don't you?' he murmured.

Chuck held it for a few seconds and then reluctantly returned it to the safe. When it was stowed away and the safe door closed, the weird emotional tension which both men had experienced vanished.

Chuck said again, 'What do you say? Is this the genuine article or not?'

'Can we come back here this afternoon?' Halevy asked. 'There are a few things that I would like to think over before I give you a definite answer and we might then have quite a lot to discuss.'

He sounded so serious that Chuck refrained from pursuing the matter and the two men drove back to the bungalow in almost total silence. Anna was waiting impatiently, but she read the warning in Chuck's face and confined her conversation to small talk about the forthcoming football match, which was already monopolising Salamban radio and television programmes.

They returned to the mine and, once more, Halevy shut himself in Chuck's office, leaving the manager to wander around the plant for a couple of hours before he asked Chuck to join him.

'I must apologize,' Halevy began. 'I have treated you with gross discourtesy after you have entertained me with such hospitality. Please forgive me.'

Chuck shrugged his shoulders awkwardly but before he could say anything his guest continued. He spoke slowly and deliberately as if he wanted to weigh each word.

'You asked me the question and you have the right to an honest answer. There is no direct evidence that the golden statue of Osiris ever existed, so we don't have anything like a photograph or even a contemporary painting to go on. I could easily say to you, therefore, that I don't believe in the story and so what you have discovered is merely a curious piece of metal. Maybe that is what I should say and let the matter relapse into obscurity. But, if I were to do that, I don't think that I would have a very easy conscience. So, take that as the official response, the sort of thing we ought to say, if we were to be asked, to the scholars from the universities and the editors of the learned journals. But there is more to it than that. The very persistence of the yarn, the fact that it turns up in a number of independent sources, and the mysterious flight of that Swede from Egypt, these add up to too much for me to dismiss the tradition as a fairy tale.

'As far as this object is concerned, it bears tool marks which would be consistent with workmanship in the Upper Nile valley prior to the Iron Age. So, to be cautious, we can say that if the golden phallus exists, this could be it and if we believe in the thing having been found by the Swede and it disappearing in Salamba, then the probability that what your boy has found is the golden phallus is overwhelming.'

'And you,' interrupted Chuck, 'without all those scholarly ifs, buts and maybes, what do you believe?'

'Personally, I have no doubt in my mind. This is the real thing.'

'Gee, that's marvellous!' Chuck enthused.

'Is it?'

'Say, Professor, what's eating you? Even with all the qualifications and reservations, you can go home and publish a paper which will shake the academic world. You will be world famous.'

'Thank you, but I consider my reputation sufficiently secure,' Halevy replied stiffly.

'So, what's the matter?'

'Have you given a thought to what should become of this object if it is accepted as the golden phallus?'

'No, I can't say that I have. I suppose it will end up in some museum. But is that our concern?'

'It might be. You have not grasped the implication of this discovery. You have been thinking of this chunk of gold in isolation. But don't you see, if it's truly the golden phallus of Osiris, then there must have been created the entire golden statue of the god?'

'And do you think that the rest of the statue still exists? Why, man, if this phallus is anything like to scale, we should be looking for a figure perhaps ten or twelve feet tall. And, solid gold? That's just preposterous! If there were such a thing, men would know about it.'

'But, my good Chuck, by the same argument, if it had been destroyed, the history of its destruction would have been preserved. We know precisely the fate of each of the seven wonders of the world and this statue would have rivalled them in its importance. Forgetting the

122

religious significance, it would have attracted plunderers for the sheer weight of its gold content.'

Chuck was puzzled. 'Let me get this straight. You believe that this is the golden phallus. Right? Then, if you are correct, there must have been an entire golden body. OK, so far? But, if it were still in existence, we would know about it and if it had been melted down, that also would be known. But there is no trace of this body, past or present.'

'It is the consideration of this problem which has kept me occupied since before lunch,' answered Halevy.

'And have you come up with a solution?'

'I can only conjecture one set of circumstances which would give a reasonable explanation.'

'And that is?'

'The worship of both Isis and Osiris was very much dominated by mystery cults – what you might call secret societies. The religion did not die out: it merely went underground. I know that there are people living today who are devotees of the Egyptian gods and many of them avoid any form of publicity. And all of them know how the body of Osiris was butchered and buried. Probably all of them also know the legend of the golden statue of Osiris.'

'Are you saying that there might be other people looking for the phallus, then?'

'Yes, Chuck, I think it is very likely, because my guess is that some of these people have already recovered other parts of the statue, perhaps all of the missing body. If I am right, it would explain how so fantastic a relic could disappear without any trace.'

'I see,' mused Chuck. 'A secret society would hold onto a hidden treasure and nobody would be any the wiser. But these worshippers of Isis or Osiris would know that the phallus was missing and would try to find it. Do you think that such people could be dangerous?'

'In my opinion,' Halevy replied solemnly, 'they would move heaven and earth to get their hands on what you have found. They would follow the trail of the Swede to Salamba, but since nobody had access to that mine until your company reopened the old workings, here the scent goes cold. That is, until such time as they learn that you have what they seek.'

'And then?'

'I am certain that some of them are sufficiently fanatical to kill you, me and anybody else who gets in their way. Now do you understand why we have to plan carefully our next move?'

'What do you think we should do with the damned thing?'

'I don't yet know the best place for it. What is undoubtedly true is that the sooner it is out of this country, the better. As long as it is here, you and that girl, Anna, are in peril. And, as a scholar, I would rather that the relic end up in the Louvre or the British Museum, the Smithsonian in Washington or the National Museum in Cairo than fall into the clutches of this gang of pirates in Ibari.'

'Will you be able to smuggle it out?'

'That would seem to be the best solution,' answered Halevy. 'However, it will take some organizing and the first essential is absolute secrecy.'

'Don't you think that you are under observation?'

'Of course I am.' Halevy's voice was scornful. 'Everybody in this police state is watched. But, if I may stay on with you for a few more days, I would take a number of trips around the country to try and confuse them and it would give us a little time to consider the most practical way of getting it past the Salamban customs.'

'Sure, Professor! You are welcome to stay on as long as you like.'

The golden phallus had been locked up for the night in the safe and they were driving back to the bungalow when Halevy remarked, 'This friend of yours, Anna; it would probably be wiser if she did not know too much of this affair.'

Chuck nodded. He agreed unhappily but without conviction: he did not underestimate Anna's persistence or her curiosity.

Sandra spent a miserable afternoon. Donald pointedly avoided her and went about with his team-mates. She began to look forward to her night out although the mere recollection of Moriba's penetrating stare brought a shiver to her spine. More to irritate Donald than to satisfy her own vanity, she took a perverse delight in making sure that she looked her best. She even found a competent hairdresser in the hotel and she was resplendent in her gown, which had almost been made by Christian Dior, when, punctually at eight, the limousine pulled up in front of the hotel. The vehicle was a custom-built Cadillac and must have been nearly as long as a couple of funeral hearses. Its bodywork was a gleaming emerald green. The Salamban flag fluttered proudly from one wing and, in her honour, the Union Jack hung from the other. The door was opened for her by a chauffeur, whose livery was more reminiscent of a coachman in the days of Louis XIV than of the driver of a modern motor car. She enjoyed a glow of triumph as she spotted Donald watching out of the corner of his eye.

They drove to the presidential palace where Asi Moriba, having ended an audience with Lomo, was waiting for them. He did not greet Sandra but he looked her up and down and it was obvious that he approved.

Without a word, the chauffeur drove off. A quarter of an hour later, they arrived outside The New Jerusalem.

Sandra gazed in astonishment at the building. It was in a modern block of dazzling chrome and glass, ablaze with neon displays. But what caught her eye were the two splendid paintings which adorned the entrance. One was a half-size portrayal of Christ on the cross: the other a four times life size portrait of Daniel Lomo, wearing a suitably biblical expression. Underneath was inscribed 'I am the Resurrection' but it was not clear to which of the two figures this statement was meant to apply. Moriba laughed sardonically.

'Our revered president suffers from an inferiority complex. Please, follow me, you will find the interior decor an improvement.'

The manager, a smiling, bowing, frightened man, led them across the wide hall and upstairs to a gallery. Here, about a dozen private rooms looked down upon the dance floor. Most of these were no more than slightly enlarged cubby holes, but that of Asi Moriba was impressive, a beautifully proportioned dining room large enough to seat a dozen people. A waiter hurried over and handed them each a cocktail. Sandra sipped hers. It was champagne-based and had a vigorous kick to it.

'May I ask what it is?'

'I haven't given it a name yet,' Moriba replied. 'Drink up, we might even call it Sandra Fizz!'

The manager ushered them to their seats and withdrew.

'Don't they bring us a menu?' Sandra asked.

'There is no need. Everything has been ordered.'

'You mean I don't have any choice?'

'You will like what you are given.'

She bristled at his conceit, but when the food arrived, she had to admit that she could find no fault with his selection or with the way the food had been prepared and presented. For some time, they ate in silence.

Then, as they were finishing some exquisite crepes suzettes, Moriba asked with studied casualness, 'What would you do if you saw Milos again?'

The question hit her like a blow in the stomach. 'I'd run as fast as my legs would carry me in the opposite direction.'

'Would you? I wonder. I rather hope that you would, that is after you had passed the word to my men.'

There was a silence during which he stared at her quizzically. It was as though he was able to burrow into her brain and read her thoughts: the man was terrifying.

'We shall take him, you know,' Moriba continued. 'And then, we shall kill him – slowly.'

'First, you will have to catch him,' Sandra ventured.

'We shall obtain enough information from his associates, the survivors of the hijack team.'

'Perhaps they won't talk.'

Moriba chuckled, 'You do not know very much about these things. Every man, and every woman too, will talk. For those who respond best to mental persuasion, there are drugs which cannot be resisted. The poor devils babble all their precious secrets, and the funny thing is that they don't even know. They remember nothing. There are others for whom a more physical approach is appropriate.'

'You mean you torture them?' She felt her guts turn to ice before his composure.

'Some would call it torture,' he agreed. 'What would be the way to break your spirit, Sandra Mitchell?'

She shuddered. 'I don't suppose that I would enjoy either.'

'Perhaps not. But I suspect that you enjoy some pain, don't you? Not too much, but enough to stimulate you.

127

How far would one have to go before the pleasure would evaporate and pain would turn to agony?'

His words were going through her, frightening her and yet giving her a thrill. With a start, she realized that this man was getting to her sexually in much the same way as Milos had done. Like a moth before a beckoning flame, she hovered, repelled by her fear and attracted by the sense of danger and the sheer overpowering potency of the giant who sat, watching her, probing her mind, playing with her as a watchful, malicious cat might torment a panic-striken mouse.

Her eyes fell to his hands, lying palms down on the table, immaculately manicured, yet huge, hands which could crush the life out of her and she found herself wondering what it would feel like to be seized by those hands, to have them possess her body. Her skin prickled, not with dread, but with vicarious anticipation.

'Maybe it would be better if you simply keep out of trouble,' Moriba said judiciously. 'Now, I expect that you could do with a strong, black coffee. And a liqueur? I recommend a Napoleon brandy: there is a local liqueur but it tends to give Europeans nightmares. And, at the same time, we can attend to our business.'

Without bothering to wait for an answer, he summoned a waiter, ordered the coffees and brandies and sent for the manager of the club.

Almost instantaneously, the worried little man was before them, wringing his hands and wide-eyed with terror.

'Was everything to your satisfaction, Excellency?' he stammered.

'The food was adequate: the service, passable.'

The manager bowed low: from Moriba, such words were a rhapsody of praise. But his relief was short lived.

'Where is my cigar?'

'Your Excellency! Ten thousand apologies, I shall bring one myself, immediately. Since you did not order one, the waiter – '

'Some things do not need to be ordered,' Moriba interrupted. 'You stay here. I want to talk to you. Send one of your boys!'

A waiter was duly despatched and the manager stood in front of Moriba, awaiting his doom.

'This young lady,' said Moriba, waving at Sandra, 'will be singing here next week. There is no need for an audition. You have my word that she is an excellent artiste. Just make sure that you have your best pianist available to accompany her. As usual, she will perform for five nights. How much are you paying your cabaret entertainers?'

'That depends, Your Excellency,' the manager answered. 'Well-known stars are paid much more than musicians who are not yet established names.'

'Don't give me any of your double talk!' roared the enraged minister. 'What is your top rate?'

'I have paid as much as five hundred lomos,' the hapless manager assured him.

'Lomos?' queried Sandra.

'Our president renamed our currency the lomo in his own honour. It's equal, more or less, to a dollar.' Turning to the manager, he commanded, 'Miss Mitchell will be paid one thousand lomos. She will instruct you tomorrow on the arrangements for publicity, meeting her accompanist and any other technicalities. You may go!'

Thankful to have escaped so lightly, the manager withdrew.

Sandra started to express her gratitude, but was cut short by Moriba.

'Don't thank me: I find it boring. Now, when you have finished your coffee, we shall be on our way.'

The entire staff of The New Jerusalem were lined up as a guard of honour when they swept out of the club. The limousine was waiting and Sandra reclined against the cushions, watching an American film on the video which had been built into the rear compartment. She relaxed and the tension drained away from her body. Then, she noticed that they were not driving back along the road which led to the hotel.

She was utterly helpless. Moriba was watching her, his face a study of scorn and amusement. He replied to her unasked question.

'Exactly! We are going back to my place for a last drink. Scared? Don't tell me that you are thinking about your boyfriend, waiting anxiously for your return.'

There was nothing that she could say that would make any difference: she hoped that she looked braver than she felt.

'Don't worry, little girl,' sneered Moriba. 'I am not going to seduce you, at least not tonight. I am very busy and I have far more important matters to occupy my time. There is something I want to show you.'

They were outside Ibari, driving through country which resembled a vast park. The road led through an avenue of tall trees to a stately stone house which might have been transplanted from the valley of the Loire. At their approach, the front door was opened and a butler welcomed his master and his guest into a spacious library. Without a word, he produced two balloon glasses, containing an aromatic brandy.

Sandra looked around her. Two walls were lined with sumptuously bound books: on the others were displayed half a dozen oil paintings, each one a gorgeous masterpiece of French impressionism. She recognized from photographs in books a Cézanne and a Renoir.

'And they, my dear Miss Mitchell,' Moriba nodded at

the pictures, 'unlike your charming gown, are originals. Remind me, before you leave Ibari, to arrange for you to pick up a dress which will suit you from Adorno of Milan. Much more your style than Dior, fresher and younger!'

'I don't remember ever hearing of him,' Sandra admitted.

'Of course not. I have only recently established him in Milan but, I promise you, in a few years, he will be the best-known couturier in Europe. Now, why have I brought you here? I want you to tell your indiscreet boyfriend the style in which, this savage lives.'

'Savage?'

'Don't play the innocent! I know everything that goes on in your hotel – and outside. Warn the young man that in Salamba, not only do the walls have ears, even the ears on the walls have their own ears. He should be more careful.'

But Moriba had not yet finished with her. He had demonstrated his culture and his manners, but there was another side to his character, a wilder, more primitive man lurked beneath the polished veneer and he was determined that she should witness it before she was released. He strode out of the room and with an imperious gesture, beckoned her to follow him. He led the way through a long corridor and up an imposing staircase at the end of which was a heavy door, behind a velvet curtain. Passing through the doorway, Sandra found herself in a spacious room of breathtaking magnificence.

The walls were hung with silk tapestries which portrayed scenes of abduction and seduction. On one wall, the Sabine women were being realistically raped while, opposite, Samson was succumbing to the wiles of Delilah. Anthony lay at the feet of Cleopatra, facing Hercules vanquished by Omphale. Leda was ravished by her swan

131

and Europa lay naked beneath the monstrous genitals of her bull.

But what commanded Sandra's attention was not the decor of the room but its occupants. For, reclining on graceful ottomans, were half a dozen of the most beautiful women she had ever set eyes on. The air was heavy with their perfume of musk, sandalwood and attar of roses and there was the merest whisper of music, as fugitive and as subtle as the aroma. The girl nearest to her was fair-skinned and golden-haired and as delicate as a Dresden shepherdess. The others were all dusky, with complexions ranging from a light gingerbread to pure ebony. Their brightly coloured robes were gossamer fine and all of them were wearing jewels, which flashed and glittered in the light of the gorgeous chandeliers. Moriba regarded them with the quiet satisfaction of a connoisseur in the presence of his own personal collection.

'There is room for a few more blondes,' he remarked, as he contemplated Sandra's flaxen hair.' But I only take the finest, the loveliest of women; I have no interest in mere numbers.'

She did not respond to the challenge. He was looking at her, daring her to commit herself in some way, but she stood there, silent and wary.

Realizing that he could not sting her into some rash reply, Moriba laughed sardonically. 'Relax, I told you that I have no plans for you tonight. As you can see, I am well able to dispense with your services. However, since we are now in my treasure trove, it would be a stupid waste of time not to taste a little honey. If you feel so inclined, choose one for yourself. Any of them could teach you more about love than you have learned in the whole of your lifetime.'

He did not wait for her to answer and she feared that if she were to accept his offer, she might find herself involved in a situation which she would not be able to control. Moriba, of course, had no compunctions. He selected the blonde and a statuesque black girl and he led them across to a vast bed at the end of the room. The other girls took no notice of the proceedings and he ignored them as he did Sandra, who was left standing to watch the show.

The sensitivity with which Moriba chose and exhibited his works of art did not extend to his behaviour as a lover. He seemed to go out of his way to humiliate his two girls, as if to demonstrate to Sandra his power over them and, by implication, over her also. Without a word, the chosen pair set about the duties with which they were obviously familiar. While the black girl carefully and tenderly removed his clothes, Moriba lay back like some oriental pasha of a bygone age. Meanwhile, the other woman walked over to a tall cupboard from which she took a slender, vicious-looking whip. She crossed to the bed, undressed and handed the whip to Moriba who was now also naked. He clearly exulted in his splendid physique and arrogantly flaunted his huge, swollen phallus before Sandra as if to challenge her to match herself against his strength and sexuality. Then, seizing the dark girl by her hair, he thrust her down roughly and she, obedient to his will, took his cock in her mouth. As he began to respond to the pressure of her lips and the caress of her tongue, his eyes half closed in pleasure. But he needed something more. The blonde was crouching, her creamy white buttocks presented before him and suddenly, with a flick of his wrist, he brought the whip snaking across her tender flesh. It was so quick and so unexpected that Sandra recoiled in shock. She gazed in disbelief at the thin, scarlet weal which had appeared as if by magic, but the victim of the blow seemed unaffected. Either she was accustomed to this treatment or she had

133

been taught that any visible reaction to pain would result in more severe punishment. Again the lash kissed her unresisting body, this time the blow was harder, the cut deeper and the sucking and licking by the black girl grew more agitated. It was as though Moriba was drawing the energy from her body through her lips and discharging it into the helpless girl who lay before him, accepting her suffering stoically.

Sandra stood very still, trembling as she watched. With something approaching panic, she realized that, just as in the presence of Milos, this man's violence frightened her, but that her fear was alloyed with an unholy excitement, and that she was sexually aroused. Moriba's sadism repelled her, but beneath the surface of her emotions, she felt powerfully attracted by it, despite herself. She gazed, hypnotized, at the game which was being played before her, unable to take her eyes off the players. The whole event could not have taken more than a few minutes, but to her it seemed an eternity before Moriba reached his brutal climax. As the movements of the girl at his crotch became more frantic, the lashes of the whip grew more savage until with a wild shout, he let the whip drop to the ground and pulled the black girl hard against him, forcing her to take the surge of sperm in her mouth.

With a shock, Sandra realized that the entire episode had not been marked by one sign of affection. Despite the blatant sensuality, all three had been stone cold. Moriba might be able to fuck, she concluded, but he surely did not know how to make love.

He rose to his feet, dressed, and silently led her out of the chamber and downstairs. She had to speak, say anything to break the evil spell which she felt was crushing her and subjugating her to the master of this gorgeous but sinister mansion.

134

'I must be getting back to the hotel,' she stammered. 'I don't want Donald sending out a search party for me.'

'Don't worry,' Moriba sneered. 'He would never be able to find you here. I shall have you driven back, but first, I think that you could do with a drink. You are quite pale. Has anything upset you?'

She did not answer, but was certainly appreciative of the stiff brandy which her host poured for her. He took one for himself and mockingly raised his glass to her in a silent toast.

When they had finished their drinks, the chauffeur was at hand to take her back to the car. Moriba dismissed her with a knowing smile. During the whole evening, he had not as much as touched her hand, but it was as though he had explored the innermost parts of her mind. She was relieved to get back to the hotel.

She rather hoped that she would find Donald in her room, but it was empty and the connecting door between her bedroom and his was locked from his side. Ah well, she thought, suit yourself! That night, her dreams were a battlefield on which stalked the images of Milos and Asi Moriba. She awoke, drenched in perspiration and in a torment of sexual frustration.

Louis Halevy also spent a disturbed night. As soon as they had arrived back at the bungalow, Chuck had proposed that the three of them should go out to dinner at one of the few really good restaurants in Ibari.

'It's no trouble to eat here,' objected Anna.

'But darling,' Chuck pointed out, 'the Professor should see what there is of life in Ibari. After all, he won't be here for long. And you deserve a break: how long is it since you had a night out?'

So, they dined out where Anna had no opportunity to question them on the results of Halevy's research and

135

they had not long been home before Halevy excused himself, saying that it had been a long day and he was tired. In reply to her enquiry, Chuck had told her that Halevy was still examining the relic and had not yet expressed any opinion on its authenticity. Anna accepted his statement with sweet good humour and did not believe it for one second.

Louis Halevy was a light sleeper and he was half awakened by the sound of his bedroom door being quietly closed. The bedclothes stirred and he became aware of a body, sliding inbetween the sheets beside him.

'Don't be alarmed,' Anna whispered, 'it's only me. I so much wanted to have a little chat with you.'

Even in his half conscious state, Halevy felt that her approach was a trifle unorthodox. When his students at the Sorbonne wanted to ask him questions on his lectures, they refrained from pursuing him into his bed. And since when was it necessary for a young lady to run her fingers provocatively around his testicles to make her point? Not that it was unpleasant: he experienced a warm glow of pleasure.

'What about Chuck?' he protested weakly. 'He will realize that you aren't there.'

'Chuck won't be any problem,' she assured him, 'I know how to take care of him.'

As Halevy was by now nursing a monstrous erection, he was in no doubt of her capacity to manage the susceptible American. He squirmed in discomfort, but her fingers tightened around his sex. His senses were drugged by the scent of her body, and her hair was brushing against his face, a silken web in which he was entrapped.

She guided his body until he was lying on his back and she eased herself above him, letting a breast just touch his lips. It was so soft, so succulent, so tantalizing: he had

136

no power to resist the sorceress. He opened his mouth and gratefully took her nipple. His gentle sucking and his hands, stroking her glorious haunches, brought a satisfied smile to Anna's face. She recognized the silent signals of submission.

Halevy moved one of his hands between her thighs until he felt her sticky, sweet-salt moisture, but she slowly pushed him away.

'Not yet,' she breathed. 'That's for you later.'

He wanted her and she played on his desire, feeling his erection growing ever harder, his balls ever tighter. His voice was hoarse. He was a man dying of thirst in a desert and she was the lushest of oases. But until she had extracted from him what she wanted to know, the richness and the ripeness of her would remain a mirage.

'I so want you to have a happy memory of your stay in Ibari,' she murmured. To emphasize what she was saying, she pushed her tongue into his ear. Her tickling, probing, massaging, and that purposeful, unrelenting coaxing of her fingers on his cock were driving him insane. He seized her firmly as if he were about to resort to rape, but she tightened her grasp inexorably, squeezing his balls until he was forced to fall back and lie still and passive, utterly at her mercy.

Her skin was satin smooth and her body was as lissome and supple as that of a serpent. Every nerve in him responded to her wordless summons. She was the temptation no man could resist, the enchantress whose spell was too powerful to be broken. Never in all his life had he met a woman so arrogantly beautiful and so unashamedly sensual.

'What is it that you want of me?' he moaned.

'I want to satisfy the needs of your body,' she purred, 'but first, you have to satisfy my curiosity.'

He realized clearly what was coming and he knew that

it would be impossible for him to hold back and prevent her from plucking the truth from him.

'You wouldn't try to lie to me, would you?' Her tone warned him against such foolishness.

'No, no, I promise.'

'Good! Very good.' She relaxed her vice-like grip and ran her fingers, light as the fluttering wings of a butterfly, around the sensitive tip of his rampant penis.

'So, tell me what you have discovered about that phallus – the other one.'

She ran her thumbnail up the length of his straining shaft to ensure that there was no misunderstanding. 'Is it the golden phallus of Osiris?'

'I believe it is,' he answered weakly.

'I was sure of it. And what are you going to do with it?'

'I haven't decided yet.'

'The truth,' she reminded him, and dug her nails savagely into the soft skin of his scrotum. 'You are going to take it out of Salamba, aren't you?'

'Yes, yes, but I am telling you the truth. I do not know how, nor have I made up my mind where it should go.'

'I shall help you.' Her voice was honey and once more her fingers were soothing him but keeping him tense yet docile. 'I know people here who have influence and when we leave together, there will be no problem.'

'Together?'

'Why not? You would like that, wouldn't you? Aren't I as classy as your friends in Paris? Would you be ashamed of me?'

'No, of course not.'

'Well, then, don't argue. I'm not prepared to spend my life in a dump like Salamba in fear of whichever lunatic happens to have seized power. I want to live! And, this golden phallus will be the key to let me out of this stinking prison of a country. We'll be a team. I can get it out and then it will be up to you to dispose of it at the best price. Do you understand?'

'Yes,' he breathed.

All the time that they were talking, she had never slackened her grip. Now, at last, she released him and he threw his arms around her, drinking in the pure intoxication of the whole of her body pressed against his own. He moved as if to mount her, but she slithered out of his grasp.

'No, my dear, this is what you really want, isn't it?'

Before he was aware of what she intended, she had raised herself above him and buried his eager tongue in the warmth of her vagina. His head reeled. Her love juices flowed over him, spicy and rich, and he savoured the tang of her body, that scent, stronger than any artificial aphrodisiac, more seductive than any perfume, which was her own. He thrust his tongue, deep, deep within her, as though he could follow and become part of the woman who so completely had possessed him.

But Anna had obtained what she wanted and saw no reason to waste more of her time. She knew that her victim was so frenzied that she could do what she willed with him. While he sucked and nuzzled, she found his rigid sex with her foot. Her toes played with him but gave him no respite.

'Now, you must come,' she commanded.

He was pressing and rubbing himself against her foot in a paroxysm of lust. He had to obey her and he felt the wild spasms of his orgasm shaking the whole of his body, as he lay there in total subjection to this marvellous creature who had so thoroughly dominated him in such a short time.

She relaxed and climbed out of the bed. 'Don't worry,' she mocked, 'the sheets will soon be dry. Now, you really must try to get some sleep. I am sure that you will have another busy day with Chuck ahead of you tomorrow.'

She had gone, closing the door behind her, before Louis Halevy had got his breath back.

5
Shoot for Goal!

The following day was the last before the Salamba versus Scotland game and there was a growing tension in the air. The visitors spent the morning in light training and when Sandra emerged from her room, Donald had already left the hotel for the stadium. She took some time deciding what she should wear for her act and which numbers to sing. Afterwards, she went out and bought a few souvenirs in the busy street market near the hotel. As she got back, the team was in the act of alighting from their special bus. Donald was one of the last to dismount and he greeted her with a brusque nod of his head.

'Are you ready for your lunch?' she asked.

'That's why we came back,' was Donald's frigid response. 'And will you be eating with us or are you away with another tribal chief?'

'Stop being childish! I'll just drop these parcels in my room and I'll join you in the dining room.'

She found him, sitting at a table for two, in a corner of the big room and she took the chair opposite him. A waiter hurried over and each of them perused a menu and ordered separately. His face was set in sullen lines of stubborn bad temper. With a sigh of resignation, Sandra attempted to break the ice.

'So how is the team shaping up?'

'Not so bad,' he admitted grudgingly.

'And you?'

'Could be worse.'

There was a silence. Donald moodily chewed an olive, remembered that he did not like them and spat it out.

'Will you be taking the trouble to come and see the match?'

She found his sarcasm heavy and irritating.

'You know damned well that I'll be along. And, what about you, Donald McFee, can I expect to see you at the cabaret?'

'I might turn up, that is, provided you are not too busy with your new friends.'

'Stop being an idiot! You know very well that I had to have dinner last night with this man, Moriba, to sign up my contract at The New Jerusalem. Nothing else happened. Can't you get that into your thick head?'

'And what sort of a time was it before you got back?'

'Hell, you sound like my mother,' Sandra cried.

'Let me guess. Did he invite you back to his flat for a cosy drink?'

'Yes, dammit, he did! And for your information, it's not a flat but a bloody great palace with antique furniture and paintings worth millions.'

'Probably looted from the homes of the white settlers,' commented Donald. 'And what's he like in bed?'

'How the hell do I know? I expect he's great, certainly better than you are. Now, is that what you wanted me to say?'

'I don't suppose it will be too long before you find out.'

'Listen, Donald,' her tone was urgent. 'That man is dangerous. He knows everything that is said or done in this hotel. Please, for your own sake, do be careful!'

'And have you been carrying tales to him? Spying on me and the lads to get into his good books so as to have him fix the guy who runs this night-club – if that is what it is?'

It was too much. Her temper had been frayed to breaking point.

'Why are you so fucking stupid?' she screamed in a

voice which could be heard all over the spacious dining room. 'And to think that I believed that I was in love with you! Listen to me, Donald McFee. You are a conceited, suspicious, ignorant, uncouth, little bastard whose brains, that is if you have any, are located in your feet. And you are thoroughly hateful and obnoxious and . . .'

She was groping for words with which to lash him when she was interrupted.

'Excuse me, Miss Mitchell?'

One of the hotel's young page boys had approached the table and was gazing at them.

'I am Miss Mitchell. What is it?'

'You are wanted on the telephone,' said the boy. He turned to Donald. 'Please, Mr McFee, may I have your autograph?'

She jumped to her feet and strode out to the foyer where she picked up a phone. Perhaps it was Moriba, ordering her to come and meet him. Or even Milos, calling to thank her for bamboozling the Ugandan police. Either would have been welcome, men of iron will who stirred her blood – anybody rather than petty-minded Donald. In fact, it turned out to be a guy called Jimmy Dash who was going to be her accompanist. She arranged to meet him that afternoon at the club to run over her numbers with him and to work out a routine for her act. When she got back to the table, Donald had disappeared.

Louis Halevy had crawled out of bed that morning feeling in worse shape than the morning after the hijack. He was not looking forward to meeting the reproachful glance of Chuck over the breakfast table but if the American had any idea of what had taken place during the night, he gave no sign of it. Anna, as was her custom, slept late and the two men had departed in the Range Rover before

143

she put in an appearance. As they had agreed, Chuck drove from one site to another and Halevy wandered about, in order to leave as many false trails as possible for any of Moriba's men who might be watching them.

When she did quit her bed, Anna was in a thoughtful mood. She had no doubt that she had wormed the truth out of their guest and that the object, reposing in the safe at the mine, was the genuine article, the golden phallus of Osiris, and that it was worth a fortune. She ought to report her discovery to Asi Moriba and come to some arrangement with him. But how could she be sure that the all-powerful Chief of Police would keep his word? If, as she had proposed to Halevy, she made a break with him, she would have to rely on the Frenchman to dispose of the relic, and although he had been subservient to her in bed, there was no guarantee that his state of mind might not change when he was back in Paris. Furthermore, double-crossing Moriba was certainly a dangerous business, but Anna was not afraid of danger provided that the reward was big enough. The best thing, she decided, was to do nothing but keep her options open as long as possible. She mooched about the bungalow until the two men returned in the early evening.

'You know, the town will be crazy tomorrow after this football match,' Chuck remarked after they had taken their drinks onto the verandah. 'If the Salambans happen to win, the entire population will celebrate and get fighting drunk.'

'And if they lose?' asked Halevy.

'Riots in the streets,' Chuck answered with a wry grin. 'What I propose is that we have a night out tonight, while the place is still calm.'

'There's nothing doing down town,' objected Anna.

'How about The New Jerusalem?'

'Come on, Chuck, we went there last month. The crematorium puts on a more lively show!'

'There's a new act, starting this evening,' Chuck retorted. 'It's a singer, a Scottish girl. They say that she's good.'

Anna sniffed her disapproval.

'I heard that she got the job on the personal order of Asi Moriba,' Chuck continued, 'so she must have something.'

This scrap of information caused Anna to reconsider. It might be as well to have a look at this latest distraction of her omnipotent lover. She was not in favour of having rivals around the place. So, after a token show of reluctance on her part, the three of them left to dine and watch the show at The New Jerusalem.

There were plenty of other men and women at the club, but one absentee was Donald. After the fracas at lunch he resolved to be a model sportsman and have an early night before making his international debut. Sandra had spent the whole of the afternoon with Jimmy Dash: there had been a lot to do, since they had time for only one rehearsal before the show. She had regretted losing her temper and had hoped fervently that Donald would relent and come to the cabaret so that they would have a chance to patch things up. As she made her way through the crowded tables to the circular platform at the back of the club which acted as a stage, his was the one face for which she looked. Her heart sank when she realized that he had not bothered to come. However, nobody would have guessed how miserable she felt: her eyes sparkled and she flashed a radiant smile at the expectant audience.

The word had got around that a girl in favour with Asi Moriba was performing and Sandra was under curious scrutiny from the moment that she made her entrance. There were women in expensive evening dresses and men

145

in dinner jackets dressed just right for Paris or London forty or fifty years ago. More of the public sported jeans and casual shirts as if in defiance of the dead traditions of another continent. Anna caught Sandra's attention. The girl was breathtakingly beautiful and she was wearing a short, flouncy dress of pure white satin which would have been fussy on a woman who lacked Anna's striking good looks: on her, it was a revelation.

There was near silence when Sandra signalled to Jimmy to start the intro to a chirpy song which she had chosen to open her act. It was a pleasant enough way of warming up and it won polite approval from the audience. Sandra had intended that it would relax her but the sensation that she was singing to an empty space where Donald ought to be sitting troubled her. It added poignancy to her big number, one of those blues which she had made her speciality. Never in her life had she sung with more of her heart and soul in those sad, lingering chords.

> 'I had a lover, now he's gone away,
> Left me feeling blue, all the long, long day.
> The house is empty, my life empty too,
> Living's just a torment, oh, tell me what to do!
> Bring back my man to me.'

She took up the melody on the saxophone and Jimmy Dash wove plaintive arabesques on his piano, underlining the melancholy loneliness of the song.

Anna was not moved by the music. She was busy assessing the singer. That kid may have a baby face, she judged, but she's not stupid. Probably tougher than she looks and good enough in bed to interest Asi Moriba. Anna's opinion was hardly flattering. All in all, Anna considered, Sandra would be better out of the way, and the sooner the better.

Sandra could not help noticing the way that this exotic

146

young woman was staring at her. She could not escape the impression of hostility and of active dislike. What sort of a personality lurked beneath the superb, sultry loveliness? She was certainly spoilt, and probably unprincipled, with a sadistic streak – not the girl to have as an enemy!

> 'Life was that easy: I thought our love so strong
> Why did we quarrel? What did I do wrong?
> Has he another woman, whose words so honey sweet
> Made him forget my love, made him want to cheat?
> Bring back my man to me.
> Oh, bring back my man to me!'

Her voice trailed away into a hopeless silence and Jimmy Dash's piano echoed her despair.

In his private dining room, Asi Moriba sat, surveying Sandra and the crowded floor beneath. He had observed Anna's frown of disapproval which had brought an amused smile to his lips. As for Sandra, while he was not the man to be melted by a sentimental love song, he responded to her charm and freshness. He relished the contrast between these women. And yet, each in her own way was proud, high-spirited and lovely. What an erotic challenge, to tame both of them and bring them to heel! So it was that Asi Moriba enjoyed his own particular spectacle and joined in the applause which the rest of the audience gave to Sandra when she came to the end of her act. She took four or five bows before she left the stage, still conscious of the void where Donald should have been, and, at the same time, the unwavering and unsmiling stare of the dark-skinned beauty in the white dress.

She decided to go straight back to the hotel without bothering to change. The quarrel had left her too miserable to want to wait for the rest of the cabaret and so she had left before the waiter, sent by Asi Moriba to summon her to his room, could catch her. And, back in the hotel, she was not surprised to find that Donald, like the night before, had gone to bed early and the door between their rooms was locked against her. Her triumphant success at The New Jerusalem could not blunt her wretchedness and disappointment. Yet, even when she missed Donald most, her dreams were still haunted by the spectres of Milos and Moriba, menacing her, yet appealing to the hidden depths of her sexuality.

She took breakfast in bed and contemplated taking her revenge on Donald by staying away from the match. Then she recalled his sheer genius on the pitch: that first game for Inverclyde seemed to be centuries in the past. She had arranged her engagements in Salamba so as to be with him when he played in his international. To stay away now because of a senseless row would be crazy. So, after a light lunch, she took a cab to the Daniel Lomo Stadium in plenty of time to arrive before kick off.

She had not seen Donald during the morning because the team had been whisked off to some secret rendezvous. There had been vague talk of a threat from the anarchists and, after the experience of the hijack, the authorities did not want to take any chances with the safety of the Scottish team.

The streets were seething with people and she had to fight the last half mile of the way through the dense crowds on foot since the roads were blocked solid with traffic. Although this was the cool season, by the time she got to the gates of the stadium she was hot and sticky. A policeman directed her to the entrance reserved for the teams where she asked for the pass which Donald had promised to leave for her. The muscular attendant on the gate shook his head.

'Nobody has left any pass for you.'

'But that's absurd. Let me talk to Mr McFee.'

148

'Nobody has left any pass,' he repeated, 'and nobody goes through this gate. If you want to speak with Donald McFee, you will have to wait until the game is over.'

She stamped her foot in rage and swore at the man with Clydeside fluency. He ignored her, aloof in his official status. She was standing outside the gate, pondering on what to do when a policeman approached her and saluted.

'Miss Mitchell?'

'That's right. Now what am I supposed to have done?'

'Minister Moriba came past and saw you waiting to get in.' The policeman was unruffled by her show of temper. 'Please follow me. You can come into the stadium through the entrance for radio and television commentators.'

He elbowed his way through the jostling crowds and she kept close behind him. They had to go halfway around the huge arena before they reached Gate No. 7 which was closed to the general public. The man on the gate was shown some sort of official card, and he let them through. They went along a long corridor, strangely quiet after the hubbub in the street outside. At the end of the corridor, they found themselves in an enclosure cluttered with radio equipment and TV cameras. They were looking out directly onto the pitch, in line with the very centre of the field. Groups of men were busy arranging their gear, testing microphones and aligning the cameras.

'This is the best place to watch the game,' commented the policeman. 'The presidential box is right above us. It's a pity you can't stay here, but the block reserved for the Scottish team supporters is in the next section.'

Sandra did not reply. She was staring at one of the men who appeared to be checking a piece of electrical apparatus. He had a livid scar on his left cheek, only partly obscured by talcum powder. His alert, grey eyes gazed back at her steadily as if challenging her to speak.

'Is something the matter?' asked the policeman.

She shook her head. 'No, for the moment, I thought that I recognized an old friend, but I was mistaken.'

'If he is in Salamba, your friend will be here this afternoon,' smiled the policeman. 'I don't know why they are bothering to televise the game since everybody is here to watch it live. I suppose it is for showing abroad.'

They went through a narrow side door which led to the next section of the stand and Sandra at last arrived at several tiers of seats halfway between the radio and TV enclosure and one of the goals.

Already the vast stadium was more than half full and people were pouring in. The place was ablaze with banners in the national colours of Salamba and there were even a few Scottish lions on display. The noise was deafening and that was merely from what passed as polite conversation. To add to the din, a couple of brass bands marched onto the pitch and the crowd burst into spontaneous song. After a selection of the latest hits in the African charts, the musicians gave a spirited, if somewhat eccentric, rendering of 'Scotland the Brave'. Finally, in order to liven up the proceedings, a veritable regiment of girls, dressed like American drum majorettes, arrived and pranced around the field, swinging their hips to the manifest delight of the men in the crowd and tossing and catching long, phallic maces. The whole display was incredibly gaudy – every colour of the rainbow was paraded in a glittering peacock-like exhibition of exuberance. Singing, dancing, shouting, strutting, the great multitude was in a fever of excitement before the teams even ran onto the field.

There was a sudden roar and Sandra saw that Daniel Lomo had arrived and was acknowledging the cheers.

The presidential box was festooned with tropical flowers and gigantic Salamban national flags. She caught a glimpse of Moriba, close behind the president, then he left the box and disappeared.

The gates had been closed: the stadium was packed to nearly twice its official capacity and at the far end of the ground, some fighting had broken out, but it was rapidly brought under control by the legions of police. Almost immediately after the president's arrival, the bands and the marching girls stamped off the pitch and the noise fell away to a dull, confused murmur of anticipation. Then the players came out and pandemonium broke loose.

Not many supporters had accompanied the Scots on their long and expensive trip but the visitors felt that some sort of response was called for in answer to the immense demonstration by the home crowd, some of whom had brought tribal drums with them on which they were performing with a skill which had been perfected during centuries of warfare. Leading the Scottish team onto the field came three pipers, resplendent in kilts with sporrans swinging, glengarries perched on their heads at a jaunty angle. For an instant, the army of spectators was struck dumb in amazement at the strident skirl of the bagpipes. Then they broke into shouts of approval, mingled with hoots of derision from one section of the crowd where obviously the tough customers had congregated.

Both teams stood to attention as the national anthems thundered out through a battery of loudspeakers. Lomo pointedly stood for the Salamban theme but sat down when, for the second time that afternoon, they were treated to 'Scotland the Brave'.

From the moment that the centre forward of the Salamban team (they persevered in the old five forward formation) kicked off, the barrage of noise was unbroken.

The Africans were fast on the ball but their passing tended to be a bit wild and they lacked the dogged persistence of the Scots. There was one wild onrush by the Salambans which had the crowd on its feet, stamping and shrieking, but it was checked by a firm tackle by the right back of the visiting team, who pushed the ball upfield to set his own men resolutely trotting down the pitch, flicking the ball from one to another. This check met with an angry outburst from the stands and, to Sandra's alarm, a volley of missiles rained down on the pitch.

The referee was blowing his whistle furiously and waving at the attackers, but a well-aimed bottle cut short his performance and the game was stopped while he received first aid. There were more savage scenes when groups of armed police attempted to restore order by maiming some of the ferocious fans. Eventually, a semblance of peace returned to the ground and the game was restarted.

Donald gave one of his virtuoso runs, dodging would-be tacklers and outstripping even the agile Salambans, but his shot went wide by inches. A foul on one of his colleagues led to the referee awarding a free kick, which the mob regarded as gross interference and once more the unfortunate referee was obliged to duck and dodge empty beer cans and some stones. Just before half-time, the Scots went ahead with an unremarkable goal, a simple header into the net when the goalkeeper was unsighted, and the crowd howled its disapproval. They had wanted their team to be the first to score but they would have been willing to applaud the Scots if they had brought off a really brilliant stroke. As it was, they felt cheated by so uninteresting a goal. Sandra's eyes had been fixed on Donald. Apart from that one virtuoso run, he had played

152

a stolid rather than an inspired game. Maybe he would rediscover that touch of magic in the second half.

The Scots were still ahead by that one goal when the teams trotted off the field to a confused medley of cheers, boos and catcalls. Sandra craned her neck to look at the adjoining stand in order to get her first glimpse of the man who was the president of Salamba.

As she gazed, the whole stand erupted into a huge rosette of yellow flame. It was as if she were watching a sequence at a movie. The entire stand disintegrated and she got the impression that the TV commentators' box, directly below that of the president, was the crater of some man-made volcano. The sound of the explosion was an insane disruption of the film set, a muffled roar from some rudely awakened god of the underworld. Only as the debris began to rain down did her senses snap out of that bizarre, slow-motion world. Thick, black, oily smoke belched out of the jagged wreckage and, amid a cloud of acrid dust, splinters and slivers of charred timber pattered and crashed onto the pitch.

Sandra could never be certain whether she did see anything of the president: possibly the lacerated flesh clinging to the shattered fragments of an arm and shoulder which she clearly discerned spinning to earth were remnants of the late Daniel Lomo.

There was confusion everywhere. Men and women were running aimlessly, screaming in panic. Sandra saw one woman clutching her child to her breast as if to protect it from some further outburst. On the other side of the ground, a small group of Scots supporters huddled together apprehensively, but they were ignored by the hysterical mob. Sandra stood still, in a state of shock.

Then the police appeared. They rushed in from the tunnel through which the two teams had left the field only a minute or two earlier. Others sealed off all the exits from the stadium. While a wailing of sirens, a convoy of ambulances sped into the arena and gradually some semblance of order was restored. A few people who had been in the TV box had miraculously survived but they were horribly mutilated and their broken, bleeding bodies were hurried away on stretchers.

Moriba was there. Sandra saw him, towering above the soldiers and policemen around him, calmly giving orders, a giant dominating his men, imposing his will, his authority, overcoming the terror and the chaos. He had got an emergency public address system working and an announcement bellowed out from the loudspeakers scattered around the ground. First in several African languages and then in English, the spectators were informed that it had been decided regretfully to abandon the rest of the game and everyone should now leave the stadium in an orderly manner. However, anybody who had witnessed something suspicious before the explosion should report to the police who were lining the corridors leading to the street.

Sandra joined the crowd who were shuffling nervously away from the scene of carnage. It seemed hours before she reached the turnstiles. Beyond the cordon of uniforms which barred the way, she could see where thousands of people were being shepherded away so as to leave a clear road for the police cars and the armoured vehicles of the army. As she reached the barrier, a coach drove past, carrying the Scottish team back to the safety of their hotel.

Perhaps she ought to have tried to tell the burly, green-uniformed police sergeant, his machine carbine held at the ready, that she had seen a known terrorist in the TV box shortly before the match started, but all she wanted was to get away and she pushed past him.

Not more than twenty paces from her stood Asi

Moriba. He stared at her, his eyes hard and hostile, and he turned to speak to an army captain, standing at his side.

She had walked about fifty yards along the road when three armed police caught up with her. Without a word, they grabbed her arms and hustled her back to a waiting car. They drove at breakneck speed through the streets of Ibari, siren screeching and lights flashing.

For the second time, Sandra found herself inside the forbidding headquarters of the Salamban police.

6

Get Thee to a Nunnery!

The news of the assassination of President Lomo was reported as a news flash on radio and TV. Halevy was sitting with Chuck and Anna in their lounge when the announcement came onto the screen.

'Now what's going to happen?' asked Halevy. 'Are we in for a reign of terror – murders, riots, looting and disorder everywhere?'

Chuck shrugged his shoulders. 'Could be. I reckon we'll simply have to wait and hope that things don't get completely out of hand.'

Anna was scornful. 'Didn't you hear? Moriba has taken charge. With him there at the centre and in power, I promise you that there will not be any disorders. Not a dog dare bark without his permission. But it might well be a reign of terror, all the same.'

'I'm not so sure,' Chuck said. 'Foreigners, especially Americans, could become targets for mobs and I would not put it past Moriba to encourage them, if he thought it could be to his advantage. I think, as a precaution, we ought to go up to the mine and stay there until things have calmed down.'

'The mine?'

'Sure, Anna. I was showing the professor, when we went there, how easily it could be defended. Not against tanks or aircraft, of course, but that's not the sort of trouble I'm afraid of. The danger would be from gangs of youngsters, not properly organized but capable of burning down isolated houses and killing for kicks. I guess that

156

here we would be very vulnerable, but they would never be able to get into the mine.'

'Sounds sensible to me,' Halevy assented.

The two men looked at Anna.

'Chuck, you drive the professor to the mine,' she said. 'I'll join you later. No, don't argue,' she continued, as Chuck was on the point of objecting. 'I have some things to attend to before I leave and, remember, I am Salamban and so not in the same danger as you are. Take the Range Rover. I know where I can lay my hands on a jeep. I'll be with you in three or four days.'

Chuck was not happy but Anna was adamant and, as usual, got her own way, so he and Halevy put a few things into their cases, loaded the Range Rover and set out.

Anna was pleased to see them depart. Until the announcement of Lomo's death, she had been seriously considering getting hold of the golden phallus and slipping out of the country with Halevy. But now that Moriba was the master of Salamba, she considered that the risk was too great. She would go to Moriba and tell him that she had been able to ascertain that the relic was genuine and that, for a share of the spoils, she could lead him to it. She realized that this might well lead to the death of both Chuck and the Frenchman but, as she cynically told herself, some sacrifices have to be made in this life.

There were other Europeans and Americans in Ibari who shared Chuck's misgivings. The manager of the touring football team had contacted the British Embassy as soon as their bus had fought its way back from the stadium to their hotel. Get the hell out of the country while the airport is still open, was the advice from the startled diplomats. Through the Embassy, the manager was able to reserve seats on the evening flight to Johannesburg and the lobby of the hotel was soon cluttered with the cases, bags and souvenirs of the Scots.

157

Donald, as soon as he arrived in the hotel, went to Sandra's room. When he could not find her there, he was told by one of the hotel clerks that she had gone to the match and had not returned.

'She'll turn up, man,' Alan Chalmers assured him. 'Didn't you see those crowds outside the stadium? We were rushed through, but even so the driver of the bus had a job to get here. She'd have to fight her way out of the ground and then get back on foot. Give her an hour and, you'll see, she'll be back, right as rain.'

But Donald was not convinced. He ran out of the hotel and tried to struggle back to the stadium through the stream of people pouring in the opposite direction. It was hopeless, like meeting a stampede head on. He was shoved and jostled, his clothes torn and he was bruised and battered back to the shelter of the hotel.

'Look lively, McFee,' called the manager as he staggered inside. 'The moment the street is reasonably clear, we're making a break for the airport.'

'But the plane doesn't leave until tonight and you have reserved our places,' he protested.

'Don't you try and teach me my job,' snarled the manager. 'We wait at the airport: that way we make sure that nobody else grabs our seats.'

'But my girl is out there somewhere. I can't go without her.'

'You are a member of the team and you will do as I tell you. She seemed a sensible sort of a lass: I expect that she will hole up in the British Embassy and join you when it has quietened down. Now, get moving!'

But Donald was by now thoroughly alarmed. 'I'm not budging from here until I have Sandra safely with me.'

'I am responsible for the team,' bellowed the enraged manager, 'and that means that I decide where and when you go. I'll call the Embassy again and ask them to watch out for the girl.'

'I am staying,' Donald shouted.

'Listen, laddie,' hissed the manager, 'unless you come with the rest of the lads, I'll have you thrown out of the side. And when that gets back to the selectors in Edinburgh, your career in professional football will be finished. Do you understand?'

'I'll save you the trouble of expelling me. I resign.' Donald prodded his thumb into the manager's chest to emphasize his words.

'Hey, man, you can't do that,' Roddy MacEwen intervened. 'You have your whole future ahead of you. You can't throw everything you have ever wanted and worked for away in a fit of temper.'

'If Sandy is in Ibari, I stay,' Donald retorted.

A stranger tapped him on the shoulder. Donald turned to face a man of about fifty with grey hair and a grizzled moustache.

'This girl you are waiting for. Is she about twenty, very pretty, with fair hair?' asked the stranger.

'Yes, that's Sandy. Do you know what has happened to her?'

'I saw her being taken away by the police as she was leaving the stadium.'

'The police!' Donald was shattered.

The other man nodded.

'Come on now,' pleaded MacEwen, 'maybe this fellow is mistaken. Perhaps they were simply checking her papers, or maybe it was another girl.'

'Listen, sonny,' the man rebuked MacEwen as if he were an erring schoolboy, 'I've been in this country for ten years and I know how things work here. That girl was being taken into custody and she will by now be at

Moriba's headquarters. As for it being somebody else, how many pretty young blondes have you seen in Ibari?'

'Who are you?' asked the manager.

'My name is Tom Blunt and I am Reuter's man here. I also represent half a dozen American and European newspapers and I report for one of the leading American TV networks.'

'Never mind who you are,' Donald interrupted. 'Since you know your way around this damned place, tell me, how do I get to this police headquarters?'

'You don't,' replied the reporter. 'There's no way that you could get in without a pass from Asi Moriba himself.'

'Then I'll go to Moriba. Where can I find him?'

'You reckon on going up to Moriba and simply asking for your girl back, just like that?' queried Blunt.

'Why not?'

'Because, my impulsive young friend, Moriba would be quite capable of having you killed on the spot. And what good would that do your girlfriend?'

'You heard what the man said, and it's obvious that you can't do any good sticking around here,' interposed the manager, 'so get your things and join the others. I understand that you were upset, so I am prepared to overlook your insubordination just now.'

'Well, try overlooking this,' said Donald, and he punched the manager with all his force, squarely on the jaw.

'You shouldn't have done that, laddie.' Roddy MacEwen was aghast.

'I'll do the same to you if you interfere,' shouted Donald.

'I don't think that would be very wise,' smiled Tom Blunt. 'He must weigh twice as much as you and he has muscles like baby oak trees. Why don't we concentrate on how to help your girl – Sandy did you call her? –

instead of littering the floor with the bodies of managers and footballers.'

'If I can't get to this Moriba, how can I help her?'

'You get somebody else who knows how to handle Moriba to see him,' was the smooth reply.

'You?'

Blunt laughed. 'No way. You need somebody a great deal more persuasive than me. Use your head, boy. How does anybody approach a tyrant, whatever his name; Moriba, Stalin, Hitler, Nero?'

Donald shook his head. He was puzzled.

'Get to him through his mistress. Remember, behind every strong man stands an even stronger woman.'

Donald shook his head impatiently. 'I've never seen Moriba himself and I certainly don't know his mistress.'

'Of course you don't,' Tom Blunt agreed. 'But I do. Anna owes me a favour: I'll see what I can do for you.'

'Anna?'

'She's as lovely as a bird of paradise and as trustworthy as a hooded cobra. But she'll help you if she thinks that it might be to her advantage. Wait here.'

Blunt walked over to the reception desk and asked for a phone. While he was engaged in earnest conversation, the manager of the Scottish team, escorted by a couple of the biggest and brawniest members of the side, walked past Donald.

'McFee,' called the manager, smug and secure under the protection of his henchmen, 'You're through! I never want to set eyes on your ugly face again.'

He swept off with an air of righteous indignation.

Roddy MacEwen sidled up to Donald. 'Leave him be,' he whispered. 'You shouldn't have socked him, you know, but he'll calm down and me and the lads will talk him round. Just keep out of his way for a day or two.'

'Can't you get it through your head, Roddy?' Donald

stressed every word. 'I am not going with you. As long as Sandy is in Salamba, I stay. And that's final!'

'I can't see what you can do to help her, but good luck anyway.'

Roddy MacEwen patted Donald on the shoulder and went off to pack his case. Donald waited in an agony of suspense. It had taken this crisis to make him realize how deeply he felt about Sandra and how ridiculous were their bickerings and quarrels of the last few days.

After an eternity, Blunt returned. He smiled encouragingly.

'So far, so good. First thing tomorrow, we drive over and you plead your cause at the feet of Madame Anna.'

'Tomorrow!' cried Donald.

'Can't be sooner. There are road blocks everywhere now and tonight there will be a curfew. Take it from me, it would be utterly impossible to get to the other side of Ibari this evening.'

'There must be something we can do now,' Donald insisted. 'What about the British Embassy?'

'Forget it,' Blunt grinned. 'They are great if you want to organize a bridge party. For a charity ball, they are splendid. But in an emergency, they are about as useful as a plateful of three-day-old porridge. Come along, I'll buy you a drink. Nothing is likely to happen to your girl tonight; things don't happen that quickly in Salamba – apart from the odd bomb and assassination, of course.'

He seized Donald by the arm and led him firmly to the bar.

At just about that time, Sandra came face to face with Asi Moriba. On her arrival at the police headquarters, she had not been taken to a cell but pushed into a kind of waiting room and the door locked behind her. It was not the most luxurious or hospitable spot. The walls were whitewashed and sturdy iron bars formed a grille in front of the tiny window. The sole furniture consisted of a dirt-encrusted wooden table and a form, the seat of which was made of three narrow planks which so cut into her buttocks that Sandra was soon reduced to standing up and walking up and down the gloomy room. It was very hot. There was no fan and she was joined by a legion of flies, which found her flesh irresistible. No sooner had she brushed away one than two more settled on her.

Time passed and nothing happened. There was absolutely nothing to do and each second dragged while she waited. Outside, she could hear the footsteps and voices but nobody took the slightest notice of her presence. Then she heard steps approaching and the sound of a key turning in the lock. She experienced a sickening sinking sensation in the pit of her stomach, the sort of thing that she had felt as she had been wheeled into the operating theatre to have her appendix removed, but much worse. The door opened and an unsmiling policeman entered. He placed a chipped enamel mug filled with strong tea in front of her on the table and walked out without saying a word. The door slammed behind him and she was again locked in. She sipped the tea. It was horrible but very, very sweet.

She wondered dully how she would manage when she wanted to go to the loo. She thought about Donald and tried to imagine what he might be doing. Had he any idea what had happened to her, and was there anything he could do about it? For one awful moment, she panicked. She was sure that she was going to be left in this tomb to rot and she was suddenly seized by an instant and terrifying claustrophobia. The moment passed, but she was sweating and trembling.

It was already dusk when, at last, she was taken from her miniature prison. This time her escorts were two soldiers in full battledress. They grasped her arms firmly and virtually dragged her along the corridor.

'Get your filthy paws off me,' she hissed, and attempted to shake them off, but they only gripped her tighter until they reached a door at the end of the passage. They pushed her through so roughly that she staggered into the large, brightly-lit room. In one corner stood a heavy desk and behind it, in a drab, olive green military uniform, sat Asi Moriba.

He glared at her and peremptorily dismissed the guards.

'Well, Miss Mitchell, you have a talent for getting into trouble,' he growled.

'I have no idea why I have been brought here,' she protested weakly.

Moriba regarded her with disdain and did not bother to reply.

'Whatever you want with me, can we get it over?' pleaded Sandra. Then she added, as if struck by a sudden inspiration. 'You know very well that I have to get ready to put on my act at The New Jerusalem soon – you got me the job; you wouldn't want me to let them down, would you?'

Moriba smiled sarcastically. 'If that is all that is worrying you, let me put your mind at rest. The club, along with every other place of entertainment, is closed. You may have noticed that our president was blown to pieces today and Salamba is observing a week of formal mourning. Not that he was much of a loss to the human race. Tell me, Miss Mitchell, when did you last see Milos?'

'Milos? The guy who led the hijack?' she floundered, as she played for time to think. 'I guess it was when he threw me out of the jeep outside Entebbe.'

'You lying little bitch,' Moriba snarled.

He leaped to his feet, strode over to where she cowered before his enormous bulk, and slapped her hard on the cheek. The force of the blow sent her reeling across his desk.

'You were with Milos this afternoon only an hour before he assassinated Lomo, weren't you?'

Her head was ringing from the great swipe she had received, but the outrage stung her to a fury. There was a heavy, brass ink stand on the desk. She grabbed it and hurled it with all her might into Moriba's face.

'How dare you lay your hands on me!' she screamed. 'Donald was right, you're a savage, a bloody savage.'

Moriba gasped and stumbled backwards under the impact. The projectile had opened up a wicked gash on his cheek and blood spurted from his nose. Sandra was delighted and exhilarated.

As there was no other weapon at hand with which she could press home her attack on her persecutor, Sandra jumped back to evade the swinging blow she anticipated.

But Moriba was too amazed at her effrontery to hit her again. It was inconceivable: the pretty little kitten had been transformed into a raging tigress. He mopped the mingled blood and ink from his face and stared at his adversary.

'No woman has ever struck me,' he roared.

Sandra ignored the menace in his voice. 'Well, it's high time that one did. It's a pity that Milos didn't blow you up with Lomo while he was about it.'

'I'll be back to deal with you in a minute,' Moriba growled, and he hurried out of the room to tend his wound and his injured pride.

Sandra waited a minute and then tried the door through which the new ruler of Salamba had retreated. It was unlocked but the two mean-faced soldiers who had been her escort were stationed outside. Hostility was etched into their wooden features and their hands went to the heavy pistols in their holsters.

'Keep calm, boys,' Sandra beamed at them. 'Just checking.'

She slid back into the room and shut the door firmly in their faces. Since escape was impossible, she retrieved the ink stand and placed it back on the desk where it would be within easy reach, although she doubted whether Moriba would be so obliging as to offer her the opportunity for a second shot. Alone in the room, she reflected on the significance of Moriba's question and his reaction to her answer. Enlightenment flashed through her mind.

Moriba returned wearing a clean uniform and with a slightly comic-looking piece of white plaster on his left cheek. The flow of blood had ceased but there was a venomous gleam in his right eye. His left eye was too puffy to do more than squint. However, before he could speak, Sandra seized the initiative.

'You knew Milos was in that TV box when you sent me through there. How did he get in without being caught? You let him in, didn't you? It was a put up job. This assassination and the murder of all those people in the stand would never have been possible without your co-operation. You did a deal with Milos to get rid of Lomo!'

The ink-stained police chief favoured her with a grim smile.

'You've got more brains than I credited you with,' he admitted grudgingly. 'But you must appreciate, little Miss Spitfire, that I cannot allow you to be at liberty and go around making such accusations.'

'You can't keep me here,' Sandra asserted. 'I would be missed and people would start asking questions.'

'I know how to deal with inquisitive nuisances,' Moriba told her with a confident grin. 'No, Miss Mitchell, you had better get used to the idea. You will never leave

166

Salamba alive. You will have plenty of time to regret the assault you made on me.'

'I'll do it again if I get the chance,' she replied.

'I enjoy women with spirit,' Moriba took evident pleasure in telling her. 'Tonight, you will be transferred to the Nunnery of the Bleeding Heart. Please forgive the unappetizing name: another of the late Daniel Lomo's quirks. Most of the inmates are prostitutes or political opponents – feminists, liberals or radicals. Lomo called any woman who disagreed with him or his policies a prostitute. However, there is one wing of the institution which houses women in whom I take a personal interest. They are constantly at my disposal: I'm sure that you understand what I have in mind. You should fit in there nicely.'

'Go to hell!'

'There is an alternative,' Moriba assured her. 'Let me show you the amenities which the fortunate residents of this building enjoy. Then, if you prefer, you can stay on here as my guest.'

He led her through a door at the back of the room. Sandra found herself on a narrow gallery overlooking a windowless space below. In one corner stood something which resembled a barbecue. Moriba explained.

'Some of our residents suffer from lapses of memory. We make sure that they don't have the misfortune to forget their names. The Nazis used to tattoo a number on people who took up residence, even if their stay was brief in their concentration camps. We don't pretend that Salamba is such an advanced country. We merely brand our women as we would any other cattle. How would you like to have your name burned onto your buttocks?'

Sandra resisted the temptation to shiver. She was damned if she would show any weakness to this brute.

'Come along,' said Moriba.

The gallery led over other torture chambers. In one, there were two harmless-looking wooden trestles, about six or seven feet apart.

'We strap a guest's arms to one and his feet to the other,' Moriba told her. 'We call it "the bridge". You can have no idea how agonizing it is to be suspended like that for a few hours. Some of my men have devised an amusing elaboration. They give the participant plenty of water to make sure that he or she has a good, full stomach. Then, from time to time, they take a little exercise by jumping on our guest's stomach while the bridge is still in place. But you may find this more to your taste.'

He pointed to a contraption like an operating table in the next room.

'It's not very original,' he apologized, 'but it is something of a classic. A man will be strapped down and an electric charge passed through his penis. In the case of a woman, we apply the electrode to a nipple. They get very brown and tend to shrivel up,' he observed. 'But there are times when rather too high a voltage is applied.' He shook his head sadly. 'Do you need to see more? For the argumentative, we tend to use hot irons on the more sensitive parts of the body. Very boring, if you follow me. There is another wing where our facilities are more chemical than physical. People there tend to have nightmares – for as long as they survive.'

'Thanks for the guided tour,' Sandra said tartly, swallowing down her revulsion and her fear.

'Well, Miss Mitchell,' Moriba gave her a friendly smile. 'I am ready to offer you all these diversions as well as a few others which we don't like to talk about, if you would rather not go quietly to the nunnery of the Bleeding Heart. Of course, there would be no difference, from my point of view, in the long run. If you stay here, your body will still be available to me whenever I want it.'

'You're bluffing,' Sandra's tone was stubborn. 'You prefer your female flesh uncooked. I don't believe that you would want to make love to a woman with a charred tit or with scars in her cunt.'

'Very intelligent of you,' Moriba said approvingly. 'Naturally, I like my women to be in good condition – at least when I start on them. But afterwards, that's another matter. Inflicting pain can be as pleasurable as making love. I intend to perform both on your body but, as you worked out so logically, I'll enjoy raping you before rendering your now desirable young body unpalatable.'

'I'll wrench off your filthy cock: I'll put something in my pussy – '

'Now you are raving,' interrupted Moriba. 'There's nothing that you can do and you know it. I have far too much to do, chasing Milos and his gang, to waste any more time on you tonight. You will be moved to the Nunnery of the Bleeding Heart immediately. A night there will give you the chance to cool off and become reasonable. After all, you never know: perhaps if you adopt a more docile attitude towards me, I might have pity on you and spare you the treatment that goes on out there.'

With a jerk of his thumb, he indicated the torture chambers beyond the door.

'What do you mean, chasing Milos?' Sandra cried scornfully. 'This whole plot has been a conspiracy between the two of you.'

'As you so shrewdly deduced,' Moriba chuckled, 'we did a deal. But I am sorry to have to inform you that I am not the sort of man who sticks to a deal. I have this bad habit of not keeping my word: Milos has been useful;

now, he can be disposed of, so I am chasing him in earnest.'

The interview was at an end and Sandra was taken back to the uncomfortable waiting room by her grim military escorts. Half an hour later, she was bundled into a truck and driven out of Ibari to the Nunnery of the Bleeding Heart.

In the morning, Tom Blunt had to force Donald to eat breakfast.

'We can't pull Anna out of her bed at the crack of dawn,' he pointed out. 'And you might have a busy morning ahead of you, so put something in your stomach while you have the chance.'

Donald grumbled and protested but eventually gave way. He had hardly been able to close his eyes all night and his nerves were strained to breaking point by the time that Blunt brought his car round to the front of the hotel.

The drive out to the bungalow was uneventful. There were road blocks everywhere but not much traffic. Inside, they had to wait almost half an hour while Anna finished her toilet and decided which of her dresses she ought to wear that day.

At last, she entered the room where the two men were awaiting her and Tom Blunt presented Donald. Anna's first reaction was that he was not her kind of man. She preferred her males big and husky and, as she did not fancy him, she was inclined not to take much notice of Donald's plea.

'If Asi Moriba has a grudge against your girl for any reason, there is absolutely nothing that I, or anybody else, can do,' she told him.

But Donald persisted and she was beginning to lose her temper when Tom Blunt intervened.

170

'Come on, Anna, you know that he listens to you,' the reporter said in honeyed tones. 'And this girl means nothing to him. What does he want with a small-time Scottish cabaret singer?'

Anna pricked up her ears. 'Cabaret singer? Is she the girl who was performing at The New Jerusalem? The one with that old-fashioned saxophone?'

Donald was about to defend the reputation of his beloved, but Blunt silenced him with a glance.

'That's the one. Nothing much to look at, is she?' smiled the reporter.

Anna recollected that she had considered that Moriba had been much too interested in that kid and how she had resolved that life would be simpler without having the baby-faced blonde about. And now, if Moriba had taken her into custody, that could only mean one thing, as Anna saw the matter.

'Perhaps I was too hasty,' she told them with gracious condescension. 'I'll talk with Moriba but I am not promising anything. You are staying on at the same hotel?' she asked Donald.

'I'm not going anywhere until I have Sandy back.'

'How romantic!' commented Anna. 'Let's hope that I can persuade Asi to let her go before your hotel bill becomes astronomical.'

They went back to wait: there was nothing else to do.

Part III

7
High Stakes

The Nunnery of the Bleeding Heart was situated in a picturesque gorge, about a dozen kilometres from Chuck's mining camp. Sandra, seated in the back of an army truck in the middle of the night, was in no position to appreciate the beauties of the landscape.

The nunnery itself was a sombre building of grey stone, decorated with incongruous mock mediaeval turrets and gothic arches. Its design was based on a blueprint which had been submitted in a competition in 1875 for a plan for the new Moabit prison in Berlin. The Prussians had rejected the plan but it had in some obscure manner come to the notice of Daniel Lomo, who felt that it possessed the solemnity which befitted a house of correction for misguided females.

The truck drove through the turreted gateway into an inner courtyard and Sandra was led into an office where her particulars were entered in a file. A woman in a plain robe of coarse, grey cloth took her into a vast kitchen where she was given a bowl of warm, watery soup. She was told that it was too late for her to be issued with her uniform. That was something for her to look forward to the following morning. Meanwhile, she was shown into a long dormitory and allotted a bed.

It was fortunate that she was tired since her bed was a rickety affair of rotting wood with stout hessian cords strung from its frame and no mattress. She was presented with two threadbare blankets and she rolled up her clothes to serve as a pillow. As she slipped out of her shirt and jeans, she looked around her and inspected her companions.

There were two lines of beds, all similar to her own, and there must have been about fifty in all, about half of them unoccupied. A few women were already sleeping, undisturbed by the noise of her arrival. Other women were sitting on their beds, some mending their clothes, others talking in subdued voices. Sandra noticed a couple of girls who were reading and who hastily stuffed their books under the blanket at the approach of Sandra's warder escort. The women who were awake stared at her without saying a word until after the guard had left them.

They were a mixed lot, perhaps half Salambans, or Africans from neighbouring countries, the rest white. With the exception of two or three middle-aged women, they were all young girls, mostly in their teens or early twenties. They regarded her suspiciously.

'Why did you hide your books?' Sandra asked in an attempt to break the ice.

One of the women laughed bitterly. 'You must be new to Salamba. Reading is forbidden in the nunneries. So is discussing politics.'

'Or religion,' added an older woman.

'Or listening to the radio,' said the girl in the next bed to Sandra. 'Of course, we are not supposed to have any radios but you would be surprised what can be smuggled in by some of the guards. My name is Marie. Who are you and what are you in here for?'

Sandra told her story briefly. None of the others appeared to be particularly shocked: such harsh, tyrannical behaviour was nothing out of the ordinary in the Salamba of Daniel Lomo.

'But you say that things can be smuggled in?' Sandra demanded.

Marie nodded. 'At a price.'

'Well, if things can be smuggled in, other things can be smuggled out. Nobody knows that I am here; I must get a letter to someone.'

Sandra rummaged in her pockets and pulled out a pen. 'Has anyone got a piece of paper?'

Most of the women ignored her. They had already lost interest in her existence. The others shook their heads.

'Just one sheet,' Sandra pleaded. 'What about those books you were reading? Couldn't you spare a blank page?'

A tall, fair girl called out, 'It'll cost you a dollar.'

'A dollar? For one lousy sheet of paper?'

'Suit yourself,' replied the blonde. 'I don't suppose anybody else will sell cheaper. Don't you understand, we desperately need money to buy food and bribe the guards.'

Sandra handed over the equivalent of a dollar and took the grubby piece of paper. She had first thought of writing to Donald, but she was not sure that he was still at the hotel, or even in Salamba. She decided to send a short note to the British embassy: they would be certain to get her released.

After all that she had been through that day, she was exhausted, and the others were not inclined to indulge in conversation. She closed her eyes and soon was asleep.

It was still dark when she was awakened by being roughly shaken. She had been dreaming of how Donald and Milos were cutting the body of Asi Moriba into countless small pieces and she was sorry to be dragged back into reality.

'What's the matter?' she asked the grey-robed woman guard.

'Out of your bed! Time to get up,' the matron boomed. 'And if you don't hurry, there won't be any water left for you to wash in.'

Sandra climbed wearily out of her bed and followed the other inmates along a tiled corridor. She entered a draughty washroom in which there were half a dozen stained washbasins. She lined up to take her turn. There was a trickle of cold water, a bar of gritty, yellow soap and a saturated roller towel.

When the morning ablutions had been completed, the women were led back to the dormitory where they made their beds.

Sandra took the chance to whisper to Marie, 'Which of the guards will take my letter out for me?'

Marie did not answer, but a few minutes later, she nudged Sandra and indicated a stocky, frizzy-haired, black girl. The young guard passed close to Sandra's bed and she was on the point of speaking to her but Marie signalled her to keep quiet. Only when the other guards had checked that the beds were tidy and had quit the dormitory did this wardress call out to the prisoners.

'Anybody want anything today?'

Sandra called her over and asked her if she would post her letter, or somehow get it delivered, to the British embassy.

The guard regarded her coolly. 'It will cost you. Ten dollars?'

Sandra nodded assent.

'Plus another five for the envelope and five for the postage stamp.'

'I don't know that I have that much on me,' Sandra said. 'But my boyfriend will pay you whatever you want, and as soon as I am out of here, I have money in my hotel.'

The guard sneered and started to walk away.

'Wait!' Sandra called. 'Take this for now.' She pulled off the one piece of jewellery which she had been wearing,

178

a heavy gold bangle. 'And here are a few British pounds – there must be about ten dollars' worth.'

The black girl inspected the bangle closely. Then, without a word, she pocketed the money, the chunky, gold ornament and the letter, and walked out of the dormitory.

Breakfast was served in a refectory, a room as cheerless as the dormitory. There was a hunk of hard unbuttered bread, a plate of maize porridge and a mug of a liquid which bore a passing resemblance to tea. However, Sandra was too famished to object and, the meal over, she was sent back to the dormitory while the other women went to work on jobs which had previously been allotted to them.

There was absolutely nothing to do and Sandra became aware that the worst feature of imprisonment is sheer boredom. She had no desire to resume her acquaintance with Asi Moriba and found consolation in the thought that, now that he was ruler of the country, he would be too busy for some days to visit the nunnery. With any luck, before that happened, the embassy would have obtained her release and she would be out of the godforsaken country.

Her reverie was interrupted by the arrival of one of the grey-robed guards who ordered her to come with her. The two women walked through the maze of corridors until Sandra found herself in a comfortable, air conditioned salon. The contrast with the rest of the building took her breath away. There were even easy chairs and a cocktail cabinet.

An imposing black woman in her late fifties looked at her with apparent distaste.

'I am the governess of the Nunnery of the Bleeding Heart,' she informed Sandra in a rich, contralto voice. 'At all times during your stay here, you will address me as Madam. As for you, your number is 598: remember it. From this moment, you have no name, only a number. You will answer to all orders given to you as number 598. Do you understand?'

'I'll be damned if I will,' Sandra retorted. 'My name is Sandra Mitchell, and if this is a nunnery shouldn't you, Madam, be Mother Superior? That would make me Sister Sandra.'

'Our late, lamented president would have approved of such names but he never got round to completing his schemes for the state nunneries. I see that you are going to be awkward and will have to be taught obedience. However, there is a more serious matter which I must deal with first.'

She produced a piece of paper and thrust it under Sandra's nose. It was her letter to the embassy.

'That was a stupid thing to do,' she commented, as one might scold a naughty animal, 'and a flagrant breach of the rules for which you must be punished.'

'How was I to know anything about your rules?'

'We'll teach you. Now listen to me, 598, and get this into your head. Even if your letter had been sent to the British embassy, it would not have done you any good. You see, an exit visa was issued in your name last night and there is a record of your having left Ibari International Airport on the night flight to Johannesburg. Officially, you are no longer in Salamba and if you have disappeared, something must have happened to you after your arrival in South Africa.'

Sandra stared at the governess in dismay. She felt a wave of hopelessness, but resolved that she would not buckle under in the forbidding presence of the other woman.

'I have been considering how you ought to be punished,' continued the governess. 'Under normal circumstances you would be whipped, but I have received an

180

instruction from Minister Moriba that nothing should be done to you which might damage your good looks until after his next visit. He clearly has in mind some special treatment of his own. But something must be done to curb your spirit. Remember,' she added, as if she recalled her own spiritual responsibilities, 'pride is a mortal sin. So, until the arrival of the minister, you will be detailed to clean the latrines of your section of the nunnery. You will find the conditions rather primitive and the chore will require all your time, so it should keep you out of mischief.'

'And if I refuse?'

'Then, number 598, you will be given enemas repeatedly until you change your mind. And they won't be merely soapy water: we have a very special preparation for stubborn cases. You will be locked in the stinking latrines and won't be able to control your bowels. After a few administrations, you will be reduced to crawling on your hands and knees because you simply won't have sufficient strength to stand erect. Lying in your own filth, you will bitterly regret that you had not cleaned the latrines. Well?'

Sandra realized that she had no choice but to submit. 'You sadistic bitch!' Sandra shouted, as she was led by two of the female guards to her appointed place of work.

The governess had been guilty of understatement when she described the sanitary facilities of the nunnery as primitive. Sandra found herself in a structure which closely resembled a cowshed and did not smell very different. President Lomo had seen no purpose in wasting good money on the basic requirements of such abject creatures as those he termed 'women steeped in sin'. The lavatories were antiquated, the pans stained a dirty brown with the grime of ages. They had been acquired cheaply as an odd lot from a dismantled railway station, thrown out by the authorities in the Sudan as too ancient for further service. There was no privacy since each toilet was separated from the next by a wooden partition which only extended up to the shoulder-level of a woman sitting on the seat. There were no cisterns and the lavatories were flushed by water from heavy enamel jugs. One of Sandra's duties was to refill these jugs after they had been used from a tap at the end of the latrine. She had also to ensure that there was adequate paper in each stall: old scraps of newspapers and even private letters which were stacked beside the water tap were used as a substitute for toilet rolls.

However, the most horrible feature was the absence of any drainage system. Beneath each seat there was a pit which had to be emptied every night with a shovel and the walls of the pit swabbed down with soapy cloths. The stench from the accumulated excreta of the day in the tropical heat was indescribable and when the pits had been cleaned out, the broken tiles of the floor and walls of the latrine had to be scrubbed. With twenty of these stalls to be kept reasonably clean and serviceable, Sandra would have plenty to keep her occupied.

Paradoxically, the punishment which had been meted out to her turned out to be Sandra's salvation. As she was permanently in the latrines, she had the opportunity to meet all the other prisoners in her wing of the nunnery. She had plenty of time to reflect on her foolishness in entrusting one of the guards with her letter. If she were to escape from this hell, her only chance would be if she had the support of her fellow prisoners and not their enemies, the guards. And where better to talk sedition than in the relaxed, though smelly, atmosphere of the loos?

Most of the girls, when they saw that Sandra was being

182

victimized and was not a police plant, were willing to talk openly with her about their 'offences'.

One of her first visitors was Marie. She showed no surprise at Sandra's plight but cocked her head on one side and gave her a quizzical look.

'That little cow turned you in, did she? I didn't think that she could be trusted, but you were so pushy about getting your precious letter out that there would have been no point in trying to stop you.'

'I've certainly learned my lesson,' Sandra replied with a wry grin. 'But I am still determined to get away from this hell. What about you? What terrible crime did you commit?'

Marie gazed steadily into Sandra's eyes. 'I am a lesbian,' she said, 'and that was enough for me to be sent here.'

'For how long?'

'For as long as it pleases the president of the fundamentalist republic of Salamba.' She laughed bitterly. 'Under Lomo that was the same thing as a life sentence. Now he's out of the way, things might become a bit easier under Moriba, but I doubt it.'

'If we could rally a few more like you, we could try to make a break-out.' Sandra ventured.

'Listen, honey, that brute of a governess has a staff of big, butch guards. You may have noticed that they have neither the manners nor the physical daintiness of sweet-tempered nannies. Of course, they work shifts, but at any one time, there are never less than a dozen on duty somewhere in the building.'

'But we could outnumber them.'

'Sure, but behind them, there are the soldiers. There is a picket on the gates, probably no more than a squad of ten or twelve men, but they are all armed. We wouldn't stand a chance: they would shoot us down without a moment's hesitation.'

'I wonder,' Sandra mused.

After Marie's departure, she was alone for about ten minutes before the arrival of Chloe, a breezy redhead of perhaps twenty-two or three.

'That's better,' she sighed. 'I thought I was going to burst before I got here.'

'Be my guest,' Sandra told her.

Chloe's situation was much the same as that of Marie, although she had been convicted of prostitution.

'I'd been on the game in England and then in Copenhagen,' she related cheerfully. 'It was pretty tough and I soon saw that those big, blond Scandinavians really went for coloured girls, and the blacker the better. I guess they thought them exotic just because they were different. So I reckoned that the opposite would also be true and that in Africa, black men would pay anything for the chance to screw a fair girl. It would have been better if I had been a blonde, more like your type, but even a redhead with freckles ought to be in demand.'

'Did it work out?'

'I wasn't doing badly until that bastard Lomo got into power, thumping his bible and lashing out at us working girls.'

When Sandra suggested that they might band together to stage a break-out, she found Chloe as diffident as Marie had been. Sandra was discouraged but decided to persist in her efforts to arouse some militancy among her fellow-inmates, at least with the next two or three of her customers.

A very pretty, slim, dark-haired girl came in from the washroom and regarded her with sympathy.

'They did not take long to get their teeth into you, did they?' she said. 'This was my job before you arrived.'

'You can have it back any time you like,' Sandra told her. 'So, what's your story?'

'I landed up here by sheer bad luck. I've knocked about in Europe quite a lot, mostly in Greece and France, and I spent some months in New York. My name, by the way, is Jennifer Maxwell and my father is Merton Maxwell, the actor.'

'Is he now,' Sandra commented approvingly. 'I've seen some of his movies. He's very famous, can't he get you out of here?'

'Maybe he could, if he knew what had happened to me, but I'm sure that Moriba will move heaven and earth to make sure that I stay in custody somewhere in Salamba. You know that Milos is the leader of the group who killed Lomo and who are working to overthrow this rotten government? Well, I am, or was, his girlfriend.'

'Is that so? Then Moriba will attempt to use you to get his hands on Milos.'

'That's right, but Milos is neither so stupid nor so soft-hearted as to fall for that.'

'Well, Jennifer, I don't pretend to understand the politics of Salamba and I'm not interested in finding out. This is my first day here and I've made up my mind that I'll get out at the very first opportunity, even if it is over the dead body of that bloody governess. So, what about it, Jennifer Maxwell? Have you got the guts to join me?'

Jennifer's eyes sparkled. 'That's what I wanted to hear,' she cried. 'I've only been here a week but I have been waiting for somebody like you to turn up. Some of the others are good types but they need a leader and they were afraid of getting mixed up with me because of my connection with Milos. I have to get back to work now but we'll get our heads together later and work out some kind of a plan.'

She gave Sandra's hand an affectionate squeeze and

hurried away. At last, Sandra thought, one other woman with the will to act. But she knew that the two of them would not be enough to crash their way out of gaol, and what Jennifer had told her about the other prisoners, along with her own experience with Marie and Chloe, did not provide her with much encouragement.

She had finished giving a couple of the stalls a desultory mopping over, when two girls came into the latrine. They made no attempt to use the toilets but walked straight up to Sandra.

'Jennifer Maxwell told us that we should talk to you.'

The speaker was a tall, loose-limbed woman with very firm, prominent breasts. Her grey eyes held Sandra in a steady gaze, and her jaw jutted aggressively below a nose which was a shade too large. She was far from ugly but her appearance was striking and interesting rather than beautiful. Nevertheless, she was the sort of woman that a man would look at twice.

'You need not know my real name but you can call me Petra,' she continued. 'I am a political activist, though not one of Milos's party. I was arrested because I was preaching feminism. The state nunneries are Salamba's response to the demand for women's rights, but we are going to change that. You want to plan a break-out? You have two accomplices here.'

Petra exuded a sort of inner strength and her words sent Sandra's pulse racing. She looked at the demure, African girl beside Petra.

'My name is Angelique and I am with you too.'

'That's great! Are you another feminist, Angelique?'

'I am a nun,' the black girl replied.

Sandra stared in disbelief. 'I know this is a nunnery, but what did you do before you were locked up here?'

'I told you, I was a nun. Don't you understand that Lomo's atrocities in the name of religion have offended

186

men and women of all faiths as well as his political opponents? Is it so strange that believing Christians should loath this so-called fundamentalism with its murders and torture? One of the first things that Lomo did was to close down the genuine nunneries and expel the sisters. I stayed on to help some of our people, got captured and stuck in here. Aren't you prepared to accept me in your resistance movement?'

'You're welcome,' Sandra assured her. 'We'll need all the assistance we can get. It was simply that you rather took me by surprise.'

By the time that the prisoners assembled for their evening meal, three more dissatisfied women had approached Sandra and promised their participation. She was in a much happier frame of mind as she spooned her ghastly soup, although she was conscious that her odour, after a day in the latrine, did not make her an ideal table companion.

The supper over, she braced herself for the worst part of her day's work, the cleaning out of the pits. As she made her way towards the grisly, evil-smelling latrine, one of the grey-robed wardresses called out to her,

'You! Number 598, come here!'

Sandra continued resolutely along the corridor as if she were deaf.

'598. Come here when you are told!'

Sandra ignored her. With a scream of rage, the wardress scampered after her and grabbed her by the arm. Sandra wheeled round and slapped the older woman hard on the face.

'My name is Sandra Mitchell,' she hissed. 'Maybe that will help you remember.'

The wardress could barely speak, so great was the surge of outrage and fury which she experienced.

'Striking an officer, that'll get you at least thirty lashes,' she howled.

'That's where you are wrong,' Sandra grinned vengefully. 'Nobody is to lay a finger on me: order of mobster Moriba in person.'

'I can wait,' the guard told her. 'After the minister has had his hour or two of pleasure with you, your immunity will be over. And I shall be there, ready for you with a cat-o'-nine-tails. Now, come with me.'

'I'm busy,' Sandra retorted. 'You must know that I have work to do.'

A second wardress had hurried up and the two of them virtually manhandled her along the corridor. They pushed her into the wash-house, past the basins, to where a rudimentary shower stood in solitary splendour. One of the wardresses took a worn towel from a cupboard and thrust it into Sandra's hand.

'Get your filthy body cleaned up,' she ordered.

Sandra was relieved to tear off her soiled clothes. Before she had started her chore, she had been issued with an old denim suit, faded and patched. On the back of the jacket, the figures 598 had been daubed in white paint. The rust-stained water which gushed out of the shower head was icy cold but as she scrubbed herself vigorously with the gritty soap, Sandra felt that it was the most enjoyable shower she had ever taken.

When she emerged, pink and fresh, she discovered that her uniform had been removed and one of the guards had brought her own clothes. She even provided Sandra with a comb so that she could tidy up her hair.

'I feel like Cinderella getting ready for the ball,' Sandra smiled cheerily.

Her escorts were not amused. When they saw that she was ready, they took her firmly by the arm and guided her along the passage which, Sandra remembered with a shudder, led to the governess's quarters. For one blissful, insane instant, the thought struck her that she was about to be discharged, as if she were in a normal prison or hospital back home.

One of the wardresses rapped on the door and, without waiting for an answer, opened it and pushed Sandra into the room. Sandra was not looking forward to another confrontation with the tough, cruel, older woman but she steeled herself for the ordeal and glared defiance.

But not at the governess. Sitting before her was the far more formidable figure of Asi Moriba. At his side was seated the most beautiful woman that Sandra had ever set eyes on; dusky and voluptuous, she attracted Sandra's startled gaze as if she were an irresistible magnet. Anna inspected her coldly and unemotionally.

'What do you think of her?' Moriba asked Anna.

'You would fuck anything,' sneered his companion. 'Look at her: she's got milk and water where you lust for hot, red blood. Go on, Asi, take her. After once or twice, you will be bored by her.'

'You may be right,' Moriba conceded, 'but we should give her a fair chance. You,' he scowled at Sandra, 'now that you have had a few hours in one of our special institutions, you had better face up to your situation. As long as I find your company amusing, your life here will be bearable. But the moment that I withdraw your privileged status, you will have to suffer the consequences of your indiscipline. In my opinion, you won't last more than a week. So, behave yourself!'

Sandra was dismayed. She had been sure that she would have a few days' respite during which she could prepare a plan to break out of the nunnery.

'Watch carefully,' Moriba instructed Sandra. 'Anna is adept at giving pleasure: she understands the sort of thing that turns me on. After she and I have made love, I shall

189

be ready for you and you had better prove yourself to be a quick learner.'

Sandra could not believe her eyes. She was left standing in front of them while Moriba and Anna stripped. Each of them, in their own way, had a magnificent body. Moriba had the physique of a giant but he was perfectly proportioned. Sandra looked, fascinated, despite his blatant exhibitionism. Anna shook herself free of her loose-fitting dress, a serpent sloughing off its skin. But Sandra's eyes were riveted on Moriba and his enormous erection. God, she thought, it's like an elephant's trunk. She tried to imagine what it would feel like to have that rampant monster inside her and she shuddered with a twinge of fear, but also with a sort of excitement which verged on pleasure.

There are many strong men who relax from their dominant role during the day by adopting a submissive attitude in bed, but that was not Moriba's way. In sex, just as in all his other activities, he was a bully and he treated his women as inferior beings, merely objects there for him to use – and abuse. Even with Anna, he was the macho male. She was a proud woman whose bed was a battlefield strewn with the bodies of the men she had vanquished, of whom Chuck Hughes and Louis Halevy were merely the most recent victims. But she knew better than attempt to challenge Asi Moriba.

At first, she took him in her mouth, kneeling before him as if she were praying before some immense idol. Moriba, eyes half-closed, lunged ferociously and the fact that Anna, her mouth crammed full, did not choke, spoke of long practice.

There was nothing the least romantic or seductive in the scene. The man just took the woman in a display of animal lust and Sandra marvelled that this was the same

190

man who collected impressionist paintings and antique furniture with such subtle and sensitive taste.

'Now,' Moriba howled.

He wrenched himself free and Anna turned round and crouched before him on her hands and knees. Sandra caught a glimpse of that great, brutal shaft, glistening from Anna's saliva, before he thrust it savagely into her waiting vagina. He took her from behind the way animals copulate, a posture in which the female is the passive receptacle; it was a fierce, loveless act of sexual aggression.

Anna grunted under the strain and Moriba let the whole of his weight press down upon her body. From where she was standing, Sandra could see his face, contorted in a wild grimace. As his thrusts became harder and faster, his eyes rolled until she could only see their whites and spittle dribbled out of the corners of his mouth. He was shouting at the top of his mouth in an African language which Sandra did not understand, but it sounded as if he were swearing and hurling insults at his partner.

It was not a protracted encounter: maybe he was holding himself back to have something in reserve for Sandra. With a gutteral cry of triumph, he exploded into Anna and the force of his paroxysm sent her sprawling onto the ground. Without saying anything, Moriba raised himself erect and strode out of the room to wash. When he was out of earshot, Anna, who had got to her feet with a contented smile on her face, gave a pitying look at Sandra.

'He'll be ready for you by the time he gets back,' she murmured. 'It's not as bad as it looks but you have to get into his rhythm and move with him, ride the punch, as it were, otherwise you'll be sore for weeks.'

Sandra said nothing. If he tries oral sex with me, she

191

thought, I'll bite it off. They'll probably kill me but it will be worth it.

Moriba came back into the room and glared in annoyance at Sandra.

'Why haven't you got your clothes off?' he demanded.

Before she had a chance to reply, he had clutched her shirt and ripped it off. Anna's hands eagerly sought the zip of Sandra's jeans and as she pulled them down, she let her fingers run lasciviously over Sandra's legs.

For a full minute, Sandra stood facing her tormentors, naked but defiant. As Anna had promised, Moriba had fully recovered from his previous exertions and he took obvious delight in flaunting his gigantic penis before her. She waited, ready to take the brunt of his onslaught.

'I don't think I will trust you with my sex in your mouth,' Moriba's smile was unfriendly. 'You have to be well broken in before we can take that sort of risk. And this time, I shall have you face to face. I want to watch you suffer. I shall read the pain, the distress, the horror, the shame in your pretty eyes.'

'Talking about eyes,' Sandra rejoined, 'that's a nasty bruise you've got on yours. Has some girl been beating you up?'

'You little bitch,' he snarled, and grabbed her.

With Anna standing by to hold her legs apart if necessary, there was no point in resisting. She was forced onto her back and Moriba lowered himself on top of her. His face was close, leering down at her and she smelt the strange, spicy aroma of his body. He was even heavier than she had anticipated but she gritted her teeth, determined not to give him the satisfaction of seeing that he had hurt her. She felt Anna tugging her legs. Then, without any pretence of foreplay, Moriba penetrated her.

He was grasping her arms so firmly that she could not shake herself free, and with Anna holding onto her legs, there was only one part of her body with which she could retaliate against the violation which she was being forced to suffer.

He was big and moving violently to and fro as, despite herself, her juices flowed and lubricated her vagina. Summoning every ounce of her strength, she squeezed. A look of annoyance came over Moriba's face.

'Relax!' he commanded.

She squeezed tighter. His movements slowed and annoyance gave way to anger.

'Behave yourself!' he bellowed.

She was hurting him. She could tell from the gasp she drew from him. His swollen sex was gripped tight and unable to move at all. She held him, entrapped, her captive.

'What's the matter?' Anna called.

'Nothing,' Moriba muttered. 'She's so tight, I think she must have been a virgin.'

Sandra was jubilant. She had found his weakness. Such was his vanity that he did not dare to lose face in front of his mistress.

'Right, you bastard,' she hissed into his ear. 'You were so keen on raping me, now I am going to show you what it is like to be raped.'

Slowly, she began to slide up and down, forcing him to comply with her movements. She would free him from the vicelike grip for an instant but reassert her command over him whenever he attempted to move freely. It was a battle of wills and such was her determination that, by degrees, she was able to force him to obey the promptings of her body. Although he lay on top of her, it was she who rode him. Her muscles ached but she was resolute and would not let up.

'Stop it,' he gurgled, 'Please!'

'Now try and hold back,' she mocked him.

She was twisting and turning, coaxing him and then frustrating him, never for a moment letting him take back the initiative. His muscles were getting tauter and he was fighting for breath. He was moaning and sobbing and Sandra sensed that he was losing the last vestige of self-control. She was concentrating so completely on his reactions and forcing him into submission, that she was hardly aware of her own sensations. His grip on her arms had slackened and she slid one hand under his thigh until she could grip his testicles. She squeezed them at the same moment as she arched her back and forced him deeper inside her.

With a strangled cry of pain and pleasure, he succumbed to the orgasm which she had forced upon him and collapsed across her body like some giant felled tree.

'Asi, are you all right?' Anna cried in alarm.

His sadistic demonstration had misfired badly and he was not capable of answering her for some seconds. Then, wearily, he lifted his body off Sandra's. Sweat was running off his face and chest in long, streaky rivulets and his hair was dishevelled. He tottered weakly to his feet and stumbled off to wash himself again and to try to regain some of his shattered composure.

'I have a headache,' he growled. 'I have been overdoing things since that fool, Lomo, got himself blown up.'

Sandra was also out of breath. At the instant that she had driven her would-be ravisher to ejaculate, she felt herself begin to pulsate uncontrollably. There was that wonderful sensation, so familiar and yet always different, and never had she experienced an orgasm so utterly unexpected. It passed and she climbed to her feet.

Anna was staring at her, amused and amazed.

'You really fucked him, didn't you?'

'I want to go and wash,' said Sandra. 'There's not

194

much I can do about it now, but I would hate to have a child by that swine.'

Anna laughed. 'That is one thing you don't have to worry about. His other women don't suspect it but Asi Moriba, that virile Tarzan, is sterile. It's quite a laugh, isn't it? That is part of the reason why he is so macho.'

Moriba returned and put his clothes on in silence. Sandra took the opportunity to slip into the adjoining bathroom and sluice herself quickly. When she returned, she found herself alone with Anna, who was also now fully dressed.

'The minister was in a hurry to get back to the affairs of state,' she said with a sly grin. 'He didn't ask me to apologize to you for his abrupt departure.'

'So, why didn't you go with him?' Sandra asked, as she pulled on her jeans.

'There are two reasons why I stayed,' Anna told her. 'First, I am supposed to explain to you how you are to behave in the future. For your information, the syllabus, if you can call it that, in the nunneries is based on two disciplines. You are taught "Retraining and Rehabilitation" – that means what your mental attitude should be to a man: you must respect and revere your lord and master. The other subject is "Physical Culture" and that deals with your physical attitude to a man. I don't think that you require much training in that respect.'

'Thanks for the lesson,' snapped Sandra. 'Now, if you will excuse me, I have a prior engagement to clean out the latrines.'

Anna was unperturbed. 'I said that there were two reasons why I waited for you. The second one is that I thought that you might be interested to know that your boyfriend, Donald, came to see me.'

'What?' Sandra could not believe her eyes.

'He must be very fond of you,' Anna continued with a

smirk, 'The rest of the team have left Salamba and he has stayed on to try and help you to escape.'

'But why did he go to see you?'

Anna explained how Donald had been advised by Tom Blunt.

'Now, I am not promising to help you in this mad rescue, but I might. It depends on the way you behave,' she told Sandra. 'I'll be seeing your Donald again: I might even take a fancy to him. And I shall be back here to see you. If you want to leave this nunnery alive, you will do exactly as I tell you. I won't tolerate any of your tantrums, and without me, there is no way that Donald can get you out of here.'

'Why should I trust you?' Sandra demanded.

'Because there is nobody else,' was the smug answer.

'So, what do you want me to do?'

'Absolutely nothing at the moment. Go back to cleaning your latrines, but when I get back, obey my instructions implicitly. Who knows, when we get you out, maybe you and I could have a session together. We could certainly give Moriba a little instruction in how to make love.'

'Where is Donald now?' Sandra asked eagerly.

'Back in Ibari. But I am seeing him tomorrow and I shall bring him to a mining camp not far from here. The manager is a special friend of mine and will help you, if I tell him to. So, remember, behave yourself.'

Anna rang a bell to summon the wardresses and flounced out of the room, bestowing on Sandra a final self-satisfied smile. Sandra was led back to the dormitory, issued with a fresh uniform and sent off to finish her day's work.

The sooner I get that cunning little creep of a singer out of Salamba, the better, Anna told herself as she was driven away from the nunnery. The way she handled Asi, she could become a menace. It would be simple enough if he were to have her killed, but if he finds that her act turns him on, I might be the one who gets confined in a nunnery – or worse.

8

Macho Men and Lusty Ladies

The following morning, Donald was pacing restlessly in the lobby of the hotel when he was called to the phone.

'You were serious about wanting to get back that washed-out, little girl of yours?' asked Anna.

'Sandy? Of course. Have you any news? Have you seen her? Is she all right?'

'Calm down,' she ordered. 'She hasn't come to any harm – well, not much anyway. I must say, I don't know what you see in her, but I suppose it must be true that love is blind. Well, if you are so eager, you had better get your arse over here and we can get moving. You remember the address?'

'I'm on my way,' Donald replied.

Twenty minutes later, he was on her doorstep, barely giving her time to slip out of her dress and into a flimsy negligée. She left him standing there while she mussed up her hair to give herself that just-out-of-bed look. By the time she opened the door, he was fuming with impatience.

'Where is she, then?' he demanded.

'A long way from here,' Anna informed him nonchalantly. 'Come in while I get ready to leave.'

Donald followed her into the house and declined her offer of tea or coffee. Anna shrugged her shoulders and made a cup of coffee for herself.

'You might as well simmer down,' she said with a yawn. 'We go when I am dressed and there is no hurry. We are not going to the convent where your wee lassie is safely locked up, but to the mining camp nearby where we have friends waiting for us.'

198

Despite his impatience, Donald had to smile at her affected Scottish accent and she noted with approval the first signs of his thawing.

Her coffee finished, Anna sauntered into her bedroom. 'Come in here,' she called. 'I shall be a little while and we can talk. I don't want to have to shout.'

'Perhaps I ought to wait until you have some clothes on,' Donald answered defensively.

'What's the matter with you? Have you never seen a woman before? Or are you afraid of what that silly little girl would say? Don't worry, you poor, timid creature, she need never know.'

With a sense of unease, Donald ventured into Anna's boudoir. She regarded him thoughtfully but made no effort to get dressed. He tried not to look at her, but her shapely body was so temptingly displayed that he could not tear his eyes away. She came close to him and favoured him with a look of mute appeal.

'You know, Donald, I am going to a lot of trouble for you and possibly some risk. Don't you think that I deserve some sort of reward?'

'Yes, of course.' Donald was covered with confusion. 'I don't have much money with me, but I shall send you whatever you want.'

'Money!' scoffed Anna. 'I never said anything about money. Look around you, stupid, do I appear to be hard up?'

'Sorry, what can I give you as a reward, then?'

By way of answer, she pulled him close, pressed her lips to his and thrust her tongue deep inside his mouth. She tasted great, but he pushed her away.

'What's the matter? Don't you find me attractive?' she pouted.

'You are very beautiful,' he admitted. His voice quavered. 'But it wouldn't be right, would it?'

'Are you still thinking about that sprig of Scotch heather?' she mocked. 'What's the harm if we don't tell her?'

Donald looking hungrily at the perfection of her breasts, peeping through the nylon, and the long, sleek legs which cried out to be touched, and he found himself imagining the bliss which lay between her thighs. He was sorely tempted. Maybe he could have resisted, or so he assured himself later, but Anna voiced the ultimate threat.

'There is no way that I am going to lead you to your Sandy until you have fucked me.'

He surrendered. And why not accept the inevitable? In fact, it was impossible not to enjoy the experience, especially now that his conscience had been assuaged. After all, with his fondling and kissing her breasts and his raptured penetration of her delicious cunt he was not being unfaithful to Sandra. It could even be said that he was doing this for her sake, although perhaps not everybody would understand this fervent demonstration of loyalty.

He had never met a woman like Anna in his life, let alone been to bed with one. Everything about her was exotic, she was sensuality incarnate and he lost himself in the sheer delight of her body. The strong, seductive scent of her inflamed his senses. The touch of her smooth skin, the moist embrace of her mouth, her hair brushing against his face, the supreme joy of being inside her aroused in him a lust which overwhelmed his reason, a sensation which, up to that moment, he did not know existed.

As for Anna, she always could enjoy sex, and it was one more scalp for her belt. She took him, savoured his energy and zest and alternately urged him on and then held back for as long as was necessary to bring him absolutely under her control. She used him mercilessly until she had enjoyed her deep, throbbing orgasm, and only then did she grant him the satisfaction which he craved. As he came, sobbing and gasping with the release of the tension, she asked slyly, if he were still thinking about another woman.

Then, before he had got his breath back, she had pushed him out of the bed and scolded him for delaying their departure. Before they left, she thought it prudent to call Chuck.

'Anna just phoned. She's on her way up. I reckon she should get here in about an hour, unless she's held up at too many road blocks,' Chuck said.

Halevy did not know whether to be pleased or not at Chuck's news. The mere mention of her name sent tiny shivers of guilt coursing through him. Chuck, on the other hand, was clearly relieved that nothing had happened to her during the past few chaotic days.

'Did she have any news?'

'She didn't say anything except that she was leaving Ibari,' Chuck replied. 'She knows that all the phones are tapped in this damned country so if there is anything that needs to be said, she would wait until we were face to face. Anyway, whatever might be happening down in the city, it's been quiet enough up here.'

The two men were sitting in the room which had served as Chuck's office at the mine. Concealed in the wall was the safe in which reclined the golden phallus of Osiris. Since the occasion when he had examined the object and had that bizarre impression of latent sexual power which appeared to emanate from the relic, Halevy had made sure that it remained securely locked away.

But although it was out of sight, the golden phallus was never out of their minds. They discussed, day and night, the burning question – how to get it out of Salamba.

As Chuck had observed, the mining camp was a natural stronghold. It dominated the rough countryside for miles around and, if it became necessary, it would be a simple matter to destroy part of the only bridge which crossed the wide river at the bottom of the valley and carried the road from Ibari.

After the assassination of Lomo, a state of emergency had been declared throughout the country by Moriba. The native workers at the mine had melted away, anxious to get back to their families or their tribes, in case rioting broke out. Chuck and Halevy carried out sporadic patrols together with the one trusted worker who had stayed behind, the camp cook. They had sufficient provisions to last for months and the accommodation, if rather basic, was adequate. Chuck's only worry had been the safety of Anna: Louis Halevy had been more concerned with the fate of the heavy chunk of gold in the safe.

The approach of his woman threw Chuck into a state of frenzied impatience. He felt a glow of pride that so beautiful a woman should be so completely loyal and devoted to him, and long before she could have possibly got there, he was pacing up and down the terrace outside the office, his binoculars trained on the winding road in the valley below. No other traffic had passed that way for days and they heard the hum of the engine before the jeep came into view around a bend in the road, the best part of a mile away.

Both men were armed and Chuck's hand dropped to the big Smith and Wesson .45 which he carried at his side.

'What's the matter?' Halevy asked.

'She's not alone. There's a man beside her in the jeep. It could be a trap.'

'But you trust Anna, don't you?'

'It could be somebody who has pulled a gun on her,' Chuck answered defensively. Actually, while he knew that he loved Anna, he had a nagging doubt as to whether he really trusted her.

The two men stationed themselves behind a low stone wall where they could observe the last hundred yards of road from under cover. Chuck slowly levelled his gun on the stretch of road. They heard the jeep's engine roar as Anna changed down to bottom gear for the steep approach to the mine entrance. As the vehicle rounded the last bend, Halevy called to Chuck to hold his fire.

'That man beside her, I recognize him. He was on the plane from London. He's one of the Scottish footballers, not a terrorist.'

'I suppose there is a difference,' Chuck agreed as he lowered his weapon.

The jeep swung through the gateway and came to a halt. The two occupants climbed out and Chuck ran across and took Anna in his arms. She kissed him passionately, as would become a faithful and chaste wife, reunited with her husband after so long an absence. She introduced Donald to Chuck and explained briefly the predicament of Sandra, immured in the nearby nunnery, and the resolve of Donald to rescue her.

'It so happens that I know that nunnery,' Anna informed them. 'A girl I was at school with got into some sort of trouble with the police and was confined there. I pleaded with the police and eventually got permission to go and visit her, so I can get a message into the place to this Scottish girl.'

'You must help me to rescue her,' Donald urged. 'As soon as we can smuggle her out of there, I'll get her on the first plane out of Salamba.'

'I wouldn't count on it,' Anna told him. 'The airport has been closed for two days.'

Donald was dismayed. 'How can that be? The rest of

the team flew out to Johannesburg the night that the president was blown up. They got out all right.'

'The airport was only closed the following day. You see, Moriba knew that it was Milos who had set off the bomb and he counted on him making a break for the airport. So he doubled up the guards there but kept the airport open, hoping to trap Milos that night. When Milos didn't show, he started looking for him inside Salamba and closed the airport,' Anna explained.

Halevy stared at her. 'How do you know all this?'

Anna was conscious that she had said too much. 'My friend in the police, the one who got me a pass to visit the nunnery, told me,' she answered lamely.

'Never mind how she found out, the important thing is that the airport is closed,' Chuck interposed hastily. 'And you wanted to leave as soon as possible, didn't you?' he said to Halevy.

Anna became alert. If Halevy were ready to leave that would mean that he would take the phallus with him. In that case, she ought to go with him. Alternatively, if she could lay her hands on the thing, she was prepared to make a break on her own and take her chance of finding some way of disposing of the relic when she got to Europe or America. But she had never been up to the mine before and she had no idea where the phallus might be concealed. Her third course was to go to Moriba and have his men storm the camp and search the place until they found the phallus, but how far could she rely on Moriba giving her a fair share of the loot once the phallus was in his possession?

'The only thing for us to do is to stay in this camp until things get back to somewhere near normal,' Halevy stated. 'And, if we can find some way of getting your girlfriend away from the so-called nunnery, this would be the best place for her to hide also.'

'You had better tell us what you know about this nunnery place,' Chuck told Anna.

They retreated into the office. Anna looked around for any obvious place of concealment for the phallus but could not see one. She described the building which housed the Nunnery of the Bleeding Heart and told them of the female wardresses and the small contingent of armed soldiers who patrolled the place intermittently.

'It is not that heavily guarded, but the walls are like those of a fortress,' she explained.

'If you got inside, is there any way that you could open the gate for us?'

Anna considered. 'No, Donald, I don't think so.'

'There must be some way that we can break in,' Donald protested. 'Don't you have dynamite in the mine for blasting,' he pleaded, turning to Chuck.

'Enough to put the convent into orbit,' Chuck replied drily, 'but I hardly think that engaging the Salamban army in a private war is a sensible course of action.'

'Leave it to me,' Anna interposed. 'I can get in and out of the convent without difficulty. I'll be able to talk to your girlfriend and we shall find some way of smuggling her out without making too much fuss and setting the troops on us.'

Donald was unhappy, but since he could not persuade his colleagues to take more drastic measures, he reluctantly assented to Anna's plan. It was agreed that Anna would visit the nunnery the following day.

Sandra had been encouraged by the news that Donald was scheming to get her out of her prison but was not very happy about the involvement of Moriba's mistress. Consequently, she pressed on with her own plot for a mass break-out and the numbers of the conspirators grew.

The nunnery latrine became virtually a rebel headquarters.

There was no time to be lost. Each day that passed and each new recruit increased the likelihood of a leak and their plans being discovered. Furthermore, in the immediate aftermath of the coup which had killed Lomo, security at the nunnery was comparatively relaxed since all the available troops were being used to scour the country for Milos and his band. The wardresses did not carry firearms, relying in the event of serious trouble on the soldiers stationed in the outer part of the building. Most of them had batons and a few of the more ostentatious bore whips, but these weapons were more for show. Sandra had two reasons of her own for wanting the rising to take place without delay. She very much wanted to be away before the next visit of Asi Moriba. She had humiliated the tyrant and she had no illusions that he would take a light-hearted view of her conduct. Also, she feared that if she worked many more days in the latrine, she would never be able to get really clean again. She felt her skin would be permanently impregnated with the filth and she would spend the rest of her days smelling like a sewer.

The day that Anna drove to the nunnery was the one for which the prisoners' uprising had been planned. During the morning there was a constant coming and going to the malodorous heart of the conspiracy. So intense was the activity that one of the guards reported to the governess a suspected outbreak of dysentery.

The coup was to take place during the midday meal since all the prisoners would be assembled in the dining hall while half of the wardresses would be off duty, having their own lunch.

The girls filed into the refectory and Jennifer and Petra took seats on either side of Sandra. Since she had started work in the latrines, Sandra found that there was not much competition among her fellow prisoners to sit next to her. Half a dozen other inmates were in the kitchen, responsible for cooking and serving the food. They brought it into the refectory in rusty iron cooking pots, and their smell blended harmoniously with Sandra's own personal bouquet. Two wardresses walked up and down between the tables while others were within easy call in nearby corridors and work rooms. It was essential for the success of the plot that these two be overpowered before they had the chance to raise the alarm.

The girls waited. Sister Angelique hurried in and found a place on the other side of the table, opposite Petra. The cooks walked slowly between the two lines of tables, solemnly ladling out dollops of a melancholy African–Irish stew. The guards sauntered along beside them, peering into the plates, as if to make sure that nobody got too much. Sandra noted with quiet satisfaction that one of the wardresses on duty was the woman who had betrayed her and given her letter to the governess. They had just doled out the slop onto Jennifer's plate when Sandra nodded to her accomplices and cried out to Angelique. The tiny nun stopped short in the middle of the grace which she was pronouncing and with amazing agility jumped onto the table and joined the others.

The wardresses had no time to react. Petra and Angelique seized one and Petra demonstrated that she had a sound working knowledge of unarmed combat. With one powerful chop from the side of her hand, she knocked the guard senseless. Meanwhile, Jennifer and Sandra had grabbed their selected victim. Without Petra's expertise, they had to have recourse to clumsier methods. While Jennifer pinioned her arms, Sandra ducked the struggling woman's head into the stew pot. Her screams were drowned in the hot, sticky mess. Holding her head in the scalding stew gave Sandra a gratifying warm glow of revenge.

'That's enough,' said Jennifer. 'You don't want to drown her.'

'I wouldn't bet on it,' Sandra retorted, and thrust the guard's head deeper.

The black girl's efforts to free herself grew feebler and she sagged into unconsciousness. Using rags from old torn-up uniforms which they had prepared, the rebels gagged and trussed up their captives. It had been so sudden: none of the other prisoners made any attempt to intervene. Now Sandra shouted to them.

'Some of us are breaking out. Any of you who want to join us are welcome, but you must take your orders from Jennifer or me. OK?'

Perhaps a dozen girls sprang to their feet, but many more remained, seated at the tables. They obviously were not prepared to gamble on the break-out being successful and they feared the reprisals which the authorities would carry out.

Petra led the way out of the refectory. In the corridors, they encountered two more groups of guards. The first of these consisted of three women who were chatting and smoking. They had no idea what had hit them. A band of new recruits, under Sandra's supervision, stowed the bodies, bound hand and foot, in the latrine. Sandra was tempted to toss them, head first, into the pits, but Jennifer restrained her.

The second group of guards put up more resistance since one of the previous batch had managed to shout a warning before being laid out by the redoubtable Petra. There were four of them and they took up a position in front of the governess's office. They were all armed with sturdy batons but, by now, so were the prisoners, who had taken weapons from their victims.

One of the wardresses landed a heavy blow on the side of Angelique's head and the diminutive nun was stunned and fell to her knees. The wardress moved in for the kill but walked straight into a vicious smash from Sandra's truncheon. The others were overwhelmed by sheer weight of numbers.

But the disturbance had alerted the governess. However, instead of locking herself in her office and summoning help, she was so sure of her own authority that she came out to confront and quell the rioters. She was a woman used to command and not the sort to be cowed by a hostile mob.

'What is the meaning of this outrage?' she thundered. 'Get back where you belong before I order the soldiers to shoot you.'

Such was the force of her personality that the wave of girls hesitated before her formidable figure. She stood with hands on hips and eyes flashing, as if she were an animal trainer confronted by some mangy, mutinous, but basically cowardly circus lions. Even Sandra felt a pang of fear, but Petra stepped boldly up to face her.

'You bloody, fascist hag,' she grated. 'I'm going to give you a taste of your own medicine.'

She spat in the governess's face. The infuriated woman aimed a blow at Petra who grabbed her wrist and twisted her arm savagely behind her back and forced her to her knees. Stamping her foot on the governess's back to get greater leverage, she jerked the arm further. There was a sharp crack as the bone snapped and the governess screamed in agony. With a cry of delight, Petra knocked her unconscious and left her to be bound and delivered to the latrines with the others.

They were now virtually in control of the inner section of the nunnery, although there were still some wardresses who had not yet been neutralized, and beyond the court-yard was the guard room with its detachment of soldiers. The most dangerous part of the exploit lay ahead. The danger was that at any minute, one of the wardresses still at liberty might come across them and give the alarm to the troops.

The ring-leaders returned to the dormitory. Marie was waiting for them. Sandra gave her a thumbs up salute.

'The next step is up to you,' she told the convicted lesbian. 'Are you sure that your friend will co-operate?'

'Lena is in love with me and has promised that, once I am free, she will desert so that we can live together.'

'You mean that one of the wardresses is a lesbian?' gasped another prisoner in astonishment.

'Why not?' Marie replied. 'It's catching.'

Lena was a guard whom Sandra had not seen before. Marie knew exactly where she could be found since the two of them often met at about that time of the day in the nunnery laundry. Marie went to fetch her. Jennifer and a couple of others took up a position where they could keep watch on the laundry door just in case Lena proved to be less tractable than Marie imagined. However, their precautions were not necessary. Lena, a Salamban with big, scared eyes and a pleasantly plump body, docilely followed Marie back to the dormitory.

When Marie told the young wardress what they wanted her to do, she shook her head in horror.

'But you must,' Marie urged. 'Don't you realize that this is our only chance of escaping? Moriba is as bad as Lomo was: he will never release me. You do want us to live together, don't you, darling?'

Lena shuddered. 'I'm terrified,' she admitted. 'Are you certain that there is no other way?'

'Please, Lena, my angel, you must do this for us. Everything depends on you.'

210

She could not resist such entreaties from her lover, but needed encouragement of the kind that only Marie could provide. The white captive led her black guardian into the dormitory.

'Leave us alone for a few minutes,' she said. 'There are some things we need to discuss in private.'

The other prisoners filed out into the corridor and Marie held Lena close to her as if she could impart her own inner strength to her lover by body contact.

'You do mean it: we shall be together always. Please, Marie, tell me that you love me,' begged Lena.

Marie responded by unbuttoning Lena's tunic and pulling off her military trousers. Their love-making was uncomplicated and had a tenderness which somehow men can never attain. Lena lay back on Marie's bed and spread her legs in sweet submission to the woman she adored: it was not only her body which was offered. Marie let her fingers play through the thick bush of wiry pubic hair before burying her face in the spicy, salt richness beneath. With gentle firmness, she parted the soft, fleshy lips of Lena's vagina. Lena sighed contentedly as she felt Marie's tongue flutter against her swollen clitoris. Her uptilted breasts were taut.

But she was not willing to be merely a passive receptacle for the affection of the other woman. She twisted round and with hardly a disruption of Marie's act of devotion brought herself into a position where she could repay Marie in kind for the thrilling homage of her darting tongue and succulent lips. Their union was perfect, each knew the other so well that she responded to the slightest tremor or the softest murmur of pleasure. There was no trace of violence in their mutual passion: it was simply a long glow of ecstasy and each felt the happiness of belonging to someone who shared completely the wonder of their love. As always, it was Marie who led, but once aroused, Lena began to seize the initiative, and, by the more agitated motion of her hands and her tongue, to accelerate their tempo as if to give expression to her own inner restlessness. As they came to their climax, it was as though they dissolved into each other; as separate persons they ceased to exist and a new being was born, not Marie, not Lena, but a miraculous fusion of them.

The tempest which had possessed their bodies passed and they lay quietly in each other's arms, scarcely daring to drift back into the world of outer reality. But their escape could not last.

Lena gave Marie a final kiss. 'Let's go,' she said. 'I'm ready now.'

A few minutes later, they had rejoined Sandra and the others and Marie reassured them with a smile that Lena was prepared to play her allotted role.

'Right, we have no time to lose. Where's Chloe?'

'I'm here, Sandra, love. Don't get excited. My girls are all ready. Now, help us get the beds nice and comfortable for our guests.'

Lena walked through the deserted corridors and crossed the courtyard to the guard room. Inside, there was a corporal and half a dozen private soldiers.

Lena fluttered her eyelashes at them.

'Say,' she murmured provocatively, 'Wouldn't you boys like to have a good time?'

The corporal stared at her in disbelief. 'What are you talking about, woman?'

'We girls get lonesome, patrolling inside the nunnery, day in and day out. A lot of us are used to a more active life, if you follow me. We figured that you must get lonesome too, patrolling outside the nunnery, so why don't you come along inside and have some fun with us?'

One of the soldiers guffawed. 'That's the best idea I've heard since I got called up into the bloody army.'

The corporal was not so easily convinced. 'What about the prisoners? Somebody has to keep watch over them.'

'The prisoners?' Lena mocked him. 'A handful of stupid women! They are all busy with their chores.'

The corporal shook his head doubtfully.

'What's the matter?' taunted Lena. 'Are you afraid? Christ, I thought that you were men.'

'Come on, corporal,' urged one of the soldiers. 'Those poor, bleeding prisoners are half-starved and have been beaten until they daren't even breathe without getting permission from the governess. What can happen if we take a few minutes off to enjoy ourselves? I don't know about the rest of the lads, but I haven't had a woman for weeks and I'm going crazy.'

The other privates shouted their agreement. The corporal was unhappy: if he did not relent, he could have a mutiny on his hands. At the same time, he had to admit that there had never been the slightest sign of unrest and he and his men were bored stiff from the inaction.

'Wait a minute,' he said. 'You can go in and see what's on offer. I wouldn't go across the road for you,' he called derisively to Lena.

'I wouldn't have you,' she sneered. 'I like men with a bit of spunk. You're not bad,' she nodded approvingly at a hefty young private. 'Or are you a pansy, like your corporal?'

'Not me, lady, I'm coming with you,' grinned the flattered soldier.

'You'll wait until you've been given permission,' the corporal cried in an attempt to reassert his authority.

'What are you on about, man?' called the soldier. 'You just said that we could go.'

'I hadn't finished, had I! You can go but one man must stay and keep watch. Any volunteers?'

Nobody spoke.

'Very well,' the corporal said. 'Private Mkimbo, you are detailed to stay behind.'

'Like hell I am,' retorted the lusty warrior who had been the subject of Lena's attentions. 'That's victimization: you're jealous because this little darling prefers me to you.'

As Private Mkimbo was considerably taller and brawnier than the corporal, the non-commissioned officer decided not to persist. He appealed again for a volunteer but his men laughed at him. Eventually, Lena returned to the inner rooms of the nunnery with the entire mini-garrison with the solitary exception of the corporal, who was left behind as the statutory sentry. Lena had hoped to leave the gate unmanned but she considered that the embattled Amazons should be able to handle the one half-hearted man.

While Lena had been busy enticing the armed guards, Chloe and her hand-picked battalion of houris had been preparing their reception. Petra had led a task force which had captured the wardresses' recreation room, taking prisoner the three guards who had been relaxing there. Chloe supervised the strewing of cushions on divans and on the floor, the dimming of lights by the simple expedient of removing half of the bulbs, and the selection of some sexy music which she put on an ancient record player. One of the wardresses had a bottle of cheap and pungent perfume and this was requisitioned as spoils of war and sprayed around the room. The result fell far short of a palace of delight, but as a sort of half-way house between a cheap bordello and an expensive abattoir, it was an admirable setting for the company which had been invited.

The girls stripped off their uniforms. Some were nude, others had laid their hands on a few pieces of lingerie which some of the guards had in their lockers. One girl

214

was attired in a bathing costume which had unexpectedly turned up, another toted a whip, taken from a guard, in case any of the men were kinky that way, as she put it.

'It's all very well for you,' a slinky black siren complained to Chloe. 'You were a professional and know the ropes. Can't you give us a few tips?'

'You're doing nicely,' Chloe grinned. 'The only thing to bear in mind is that you should keep them as long as possible so as to give Sandra and her team as much time as possible to get away. Tease them a bit: they'll enjoy it, and so should you. When we have finished with the lusty lads, we each take one of the wardresses' uniforms and make for the gate before our admirers have recovered their senses or their pants. Sandra's group should have got through by then, so there ought not to be any problem.'

There was a gentle tap on the door and Lena's voice was heard.

'Are you girls in the mood? I've brought you some congenial company.'

'In the mood and in the nude,' sang out Chloe. 'Come along inside, boys, and make yourselves at home.'

The soldiers shuffled in. Now that they had arrived at the promised land, they were assailed by shyness and, to tell the truth, were a bit scared by the prospect of the posse of pussies before them.

Lena crept away and found Sandra and Jennifer in the dormitory. She explained that the corporal was still on guard and would require special attention.

The same corporal was by then in an extremely bad temper, as he reflected on the treat he was missing. But his sense of duty was to be rewarded, because only a few minutes after his men had gone their gladsome way, a jeep drove up to the gate. The corporal, very conscious

215

of being the sole sentinel, shouldered his machine carbine and went out to challenge the driver.

'Let me in, please,' ordered Anna. 'You remember me? I was here with Minister Moriba. I want to see the governess.'

The corporal recognized her and opened the gate. He walked across to where she had parked the jeep and led her inside.

'There don't seem to be many of the wardresses about today,' Anna observed, as they walked along the deserted passages.

'They must be otherwise engaged,' answered the corporal bitterly.

Anna had come to talk to Sandra, but she calculated that if she attempted to see a prisoner without first making some excuse to the governess, she could find herself in a lot of trouble and she could not expect any help from Moriba if he suspected that she was helping his current favourite to get away.

They knocked on the governess's door but there was no answer. The door was unlocked and the corporal dared to peep inside. The room was empty.

'She must be somewhere in the nunnery,' he observed.

'That's obvious,' Anna answered scornfully. 'I am sure that I'll be able to find her: no need for me to detain you, Corporal.'

'No trouble, Miss!' The corporal was terrified that this influential woman would blunder into some room and find the whole of the nunnery guard screwing itself stupid, so he insisted on continuing to escort Anna. She was annoyed by his attentions: the last thing that she wanted was to have one of Moriba's soldiers present during her interview with Sandra but she could hardly order him to leave without arousing his suspicions.

The corporal's concerns were well founded. By this

time, Chloe and her young ladies had overcome the reticence of the men.

'What? Do it here, altogether, in front of all the rest of them?' objected Private Mkimbo.

'Why not?' Chloe retorted. 'Are you ashamed of what you've got down there? A bit undersized, are you?'

Stung by the slur on his equipment, Private Mkimbo ripped off his pants and proudly exhibited himself to the assembled gathering.

'What's wrong with that?' he roared.

There was a ripple of applause from the girls.

'All right, soldier, now let's see if you know what to do with it,' Chloe laughed.

He went to pull her onto the nearest divan, but she twisted out of his grip.

'That's no way to treat a lady,' she told him. 'Everybody knows that you can be rough: show me that you can be gentle.'

One of the other soldiers ventured to stroke the hair of the girl in the bathing suit. She turned her head and kissed him passionately on the lips.

'Come on, what are you waiting for?' cried Chloe. 'Get your pants off! What are you, men or eunuchs?'

With a joyful shout, the private soldiers of acting President Moriba's army went into action. Mindful of Chloe's instruction that their pleasure should be as protracted as possible, the girls did their best to tease and titillate their partners. There were several former hookers among them who had a shrewd idea of how to tickle and cuddle, to suck and stroke and resort to all sorts of tricks to defer fucking until their men were at the very limit of their patience. But others lacked their experience and wilted before the determined onrush of their lusty suitors. Most of the soldiers went for the girls with about as much subtlety as an express train tearing into the mouth of a

217

tunnel. In far too short a time they had shot their loads and, as if relieved of a task which, while pleasant, had absorbed all their energy, they relaxed and appeared to be on the point of leaving. Chloe sensed that this was a moment of crisis and drastic measures had to be taken. She shook herself free of the clumsy embrace of Private Mkimbo and whispered a few words to Pamela and Aurora, two of her more accomplished colleagues. They scuttled out of the room while Chloe turned to harangue the men.

'Say, what's the matter with you guys? Haven't you got any stamina? You do it once and that's you finished for the rest of the night? Why are you in such a hurry to get back to standing out in the jungle when the fun is only beginning? Or do you have other friends out there who are more sexy than we are? Are you having it off with the monkeys?'

'What do you mean, the fun is beginning?' asked a listless recruit. 'We've had what we came for.'

'Then you are an idiot,' snorted Chloe. 'Me and a couple of my girls have prepared something really special for you, a treat which you will remember for the rest of your lives, but if you would rather get back to your monkeys, don't let me detain you.'

'What sort of treat?' asked the intrigued Mkimbo.

Before Chloe could reply, the two girls returned, carrying a large basket of fruit. One of the soldiers went to take a mango, but Chloe slapped his hand.

'This fruit is only to be eaten with a very piquant sauce – a sauce with a difference.'

The mystified soldiers watched while she deftly skinned the mango and, having removed the stone, cut it into three sections. She handed a piece to Pamela and to Aurora and the three girls lay back on the divans and slid the fruit into their fannies.

'Come on,' called Chloe. 'There's a prize for the first man to finish eating his dessert. You can use fingers, but no knives and forks. You talk about juicy cunts, now find out just how delicious they are.'

There was a moment of hesitation, but Chloe winked an invitation to Mkimbo and he launched himself upon her. Not to be outdone, a couple of other men prostrated themselves before Pamela and Aurora and started to lap up the dainty dish. The other men at first merely stared: they did not know what to make of the scene. Then some of them started to shout encouragement to the contestants and to bet on who was going to win the unknown prize.

'Say, you boys,' called Frankie, a snub-nosed doll of a girl with dancing eyes and enticingly rounded hips, 'Mango isn't the only flavour in town. Who would like to share a passion fruit with me?'

She did not have to wait long for a volunteer and the other girls prepared their own brands of fruit salad which they served hot and pungent. The star turn was undoubtedly a threesome between a tall, willowy Amazon, a stubborn soldier with the tongue of an ant-eater and a very ripe banana.

The girls twisted their limbs and the diners guzzled frantically, slurping the sexy sauce all over their faces, oblivious to the passing of time. Of course, it was Mkimbo who was the first to have devoured every morsel and who claimed the prize.

'Honey, you deserve a reward for the sweet way you have cleaned up your plate,' Chloe chortled. 'And you made me a very happy girl while you were about it.'

'So what do I get?' asked the victor.

'The blow job of the century,' Chloe announced and proceeded to administer it to him.

Anna paused outside the door. She heard the sound of music and some subdued giggling. The corporal heard them too.

'Not in there,' he exclaimed. 'Some of the wardresses are having a break. The governess will almost certainly be inspecting the dormitory. Come with me, Miss!'

He clutched Anna by the arm and practically dragged her away from the makeshift brothel. Jennifer heard their approach. As the corporal led the way into the dormitory, Petra chopped him down with one mighty blow. Anna found herself seized by two other girls.

'What the hell is going on here?' she gasped.

Sandra regarded her thoughtfully. 'You tell us. What are you doing here?'

'I came to talk to you,' Anna answered calmly. 'Please, do ask your followers to unhand me.'

Sandra nodded and the girls released her.

'I came to tell you what your boyfriend was planning in order to release you,' Anna smirked at Sandra. 'Do we have to discuss this in front of everybody?'

'We don't need to discuss it at all,' Sandra told her. 'You came across us as we were on the point of leaving.'

'The question is what shall we do with you?' Petra said to Anna. 'I have seen you about with Moriba. You are too dangerous to leave at liberty.'

'I know her,' Jennifer intervened. 'She's Moriba's girlfriend.'

'And you are Milos's girlfriend,' Anna mocked.

'Why don't we take her along as a hostage?' Jennifer cried. 'After all, Moriba was prepared to dangle me in front of Milos as a bait: let's pay him back!'

Sandra recalled that not many days had passed since she had been used as a human shield by Milos: the market in hostages appeared to be booming. They had no idea what dangers they would encounter once they

220

left the camp; presumably they would be pursued by ruthless soldiers with orders to shoot. In such circumstances, Sandra thought that there was a lot to be said for their displaying Anna's succulent body as a target for the first bullet, and she said so.

If the girls expected Anna to cringe in terror at their decision, they were doomed to disappointment. She wagged her head in enthusiastic agreement.

'Of course I'll come along as a hostage. It's a splendid idea. I have a jeep outside: in less than an hour, we can all be safely inside the mining camp. Let's go!'

The dumbfounded conspirators trooped out of the dormitory and followed their compliant captive. Anna calculated that when she returned and triumphantly delivered Sandra, she would be greeted as the heroine of the hour by the camp garrison. While Chuck had seemed to be as manageable as ever, it was clear that Halevy did not trust her completely and neither man had given her any indication of where the phallus was. They would have to accept her as the liberator of Sandra and once she enjoyed their full confidence, she would somehow ferret out where the golden phallus lay hidden. On the other hand, it would do her no harm if Moriba were given the impression that she was the helpless hostage. As always, Anna planned to keep her options open.

Anna crossed the courtyard to where the jeep was parked. The others followed warily but there was no sign of life from the nunnery buildings or from the guard room. Petra found the key to the gate on the corporal's desk and, as the jeep passed under the vaulted arch onto the road beyond, they relished the clean, fresh air of freedom.

Almost within sight of the camp, Anna stopped the vehicle and all the girls, apart from Sandra, climbed out. They were going to walk back and cross the bridge.

Jennifer and Petra had plans to meet up with members of the resistance who were active in the area and join Milos. Marie, and her former gaoler-lover, Lena, intended to find some secluded village where they could ride out the political storm in safety. Sandra kissed them goodbye with the warmth and affection which comes from sharing dangers and hardships. Then she settled beside Anna for the last run up to the camp. She had taken a heavy spanner from the jeep's tool kit and she held it, ready to strike, just in case Anna tried to pull some trick.

Back in the nunnery, the discs were still spinning on the record player but none of the soldiers felt strong enough to dance. They reclined on the beds and the scattered cushions, smug, satisfied and spent. On the pretext that they needed to rinse and freshen up, Chloe's odalisques excused themselves and, in twos and threes, they slipped away, crossed the deserted courtyard and passed through the gate which Anna had left open.

Their male consorts waited for their return. Time passed.

'I wonder what the corporal is getting up to?' one of the privates said. 'Shouldn't we be getting back?'

'There's no hurry, man,' yawned Private Mkimbo. 'Remember, he volunteered for guard duty and he should do the usual stretch of two hours.'

'I don't think that I would say that he actually volunteered,' replied the first soldier.

'Don't fuss,' Mkimbo admonished. 'Let's wait for the girls to come back. I want one of them to fetch me a drink. Then, we might have time for a quickie before we go on duty.'

'They are taking a long time. Do you think that anything has happened to them?' asked another private.

'What could have happened?' Mkimbo replied. 'You

222

guys are too tense. This is the first time we get a decent break, so don't spoil things; hang loose!'

The minutes ticked away but there was no sign of the girls. Gradually, the realization dawned that their treat was over. They took their time dressing and then walked slowly back to the guard room. It was empty and the gate stood open.

'Here!' cried Private Mkimbo, 'Something funny's been going on behind our backs. Where's the corporal?'

They went in search of the missing soldier. They scoured the building from the roof to the dungeon-like cellars. The very last place they looked was the latrine of the prisoners.

9

The Turn of the Wheel

Inside the mining camp, Chuck had told the cook to prepare lunch after Anna's return. He thought it likely that she would have to stay in the nunnery for a few minutes only before getting the opportunity to pass her message to Sandra, but she was taking longer than he had expected and Chuck began to have doubts. Maybe the jeep had broken down, but it was unlikely. There were rumours that some of Milos's men were fighting a guerilla campaign in the hills close to the nunnery. He resolved to give her another half hour. If she had not got back by then, he would take the Range Rover and go in search of her.

In the office, Louis Halevy was carrying out a kind of experiment. He had borrowed the safe keys from Chuck and he took the golden phallus from the recess in the wall and held it in his hand. He had remembered the weird feeling which had come over him the last time he had handled the strange object and he had, not unnaturally, decided to test his reactions to the relic alone.

It was a wonderfully tactile thing, although it was so large that it needed both hands to grasp it properly. But it seemed to snuggle into his hands as if it were inviting him to fondle it. What a lot of nonsense, Halevy told himself, I'm just letting my imagination run away with me. And yet, the metal felt a trifle warm to his touch and his flesh tingled as though he had received a tiny electric shock. He laid it down on the desk and gazed at the inert metal. The room seemed suddenly hot and oppressive but that could have been nothing more than his becoming aware of the wretched climate. Then he looked down and realized that he had, apparently quite spontaneously, achieved a stupendous erection. Automatically, his hands dropped to his crotch and, slowly and deliberately, he began to masturbate, keeping his eyes focused on the golden phallus. It was the most eerie, yet erotic experience: an overwhelming, inner drive which he could neither explain nor suppress.

Outside, there was the noise of a car driving into the camp followed by excited voices, but Halevy heard nothing. With a supreme effort he withdrew his hands and laid them on the desk. It was as though they had a will of their own and ached to resume the gentle massaging motion.

The door burst open and Donald, clutching Sandra firmly to him, his eyes shining, cried out to him. 'Isn't she marvellous? She led a break-out!'

'And Anna drove her here,' added Chuck, as he entered with Anna by his side.

Halevy pulled himself together like a man suddenly awakened from a heavy slumber.

'Are you all right?' asked Chuck.

'Yes, fine, but do put this damned thing away.'

Anna was watching the golden phallus as a miser might gloat over his hoard of glittering coins. She felt like protesting as Chuck picked up the relic, put it in the safe, locked the door and pocketed the key. But this was not the moment to strike. She had found out where they kept the thing and she would work on Chuck when they were alone.

'Funny smell in here,' Donald remarked, wrinkling his nose.

'Can I have a shower?' Sandra asked urgently.

'What, now?' Chuck was surprised. 'Wouldn't you rather wait until after lunch?'

225

Sandra shook her head. 'If I don't get my body scrubbed straight away, I promise you, nobody will have any appetite for food if they stay within a hundred yards of me.'

Chuck shrugged his shoulders. 'I guess that there's some hot water. I'll find you a clean towel.'

Sandra went into the bathroom.

'I'll help you,' called Donald, as he followed her in.

'Who needs help in taking a shower?' asked Chuck, mystified.

Louis Halevy stared at the American in disbelief.

'Really, darling!' Anna laughed, 'you have no imagination. I'll give you a demonstration this evening. You will enjoy it.'

'Why don't you tell us what went on up at the nunnery?' Halevy demanded.

'When I got there, the girls, Sandra and a few others, had worked out a plan to overpower their guards. It would never have worked, but I was able to distract some of the wardresses and that gave them the chance to deal with the others. Then I smuggled them out in the jeep. There was nothing to it, once the girls agreed to do as I told them.'

'You are fantastic!' enthused Chuck.

Halevy was not so sure: her story sounded too smooth.

In the bathroom, Sandra gave Donald a very different account of events.

'You took Anna hostage?' Donald asked. 'But she came there to help you. Don't you understand, she's on our side.'

'Don't kid yourself,' Sandra told him. 'If you had seen her with Moriba, you would realize that she's only interested in helping herself. There's something that she wants here, otherwise she would be in Ibari with her lover.'

'Chuck believes that she is utterly devoted to him.'

'Chuck is an idiot. Nice and kind, but an idiot,' Sandra rejoined. 'He ought to be warned.'

Sandra stepped under the shower and let the hot water stream over her body. Donald rubbed the soap into a creamy lather and worked on her smooth flesh until it glowed and steamed. She sighed with pleasure, caressed by the gushing water and by the strong, sensitive hands of Donald. Through half-closed eyes, she smiled at her lover.

'The rest of the team has flown out of Salamba?'

'Aye, that's right,' he replied, a trifle gruffly.

'And you stayed behind for me?'

Donald grunted assent.

'But what about your career? I thought that I was merely a distraction.'

'Let's say that I have grown up in the past few days. As long as I have you, I don't care if I never kick a football again.'

He kissed her tenderly. Then, quickly pulling off his clothes, he joined her in the shower.

'I don't want to be the cause of your losing your chance to play for your country,' Sandra objected.

By way of answer, he kissed her again. He kissed her eyes, her nose, her lips, the delicate curve of her throat and the full richness of her breasts. He turned off the water and swathed her in the folds of the towel and let his hands roam over every inch of her body. Everything about her was as he remembered and yet was as fresh as if he were touching her for the first time; the gentle swelling of her belly and of her hips, the long tapering of her legs and the plump buttocks. He adored her and wanted to keep touching her for ever.

'Come along, darling,' Sandra smiled. 'Dry yourself

and let's get back to the others. They're probably waiting for us to have lunch.'

'Well, a few minutes more will be good for their self-control,' Donald answered. And, taking her by the hand, he led her into his bedroom.

When they made love, it was as though all the strains, the rows and quarrels, the tears and anguish that they had suffered were exorcized. The fantasy of Milos and the terror of Moriba glimmered into insignificance. All that counted was the fact that they had each other and the reverence which each felt for the other's body. Although they had little time, there was no sense of hurry as Donald entered her and his long, firm strokes both excited and soothed her at the same time. They moved together in perfect harmony, their lips pressed against each other's, their tongues savouring their warm, moist mouths. Clasped in each other's arms, they were blissfully lost to the world until the whole of creation joined in the wild, orphic dance of their joint, simultaneous orgasm. Even then, they were reluctant to separate.

'It's wonderful to think that you are safe, Sandy,' Donald exulted.

'But I'm not, darling. And neither are you as long as we are in Salamba.'

A similar sentiment was being expressed in the dining room by Halevy as the rest of the party waited impatiently to start their meal.

'I don't know anything about military tactics,' Halevy confessed, 'but shouldn't we be taking some precautions against an attack by the troops stationed at the nunnery? They might well deduce that Anna brought Sandra here: there can't be many places where they could have taken refuge. How about destroying, or at any rate blocking, that bridge?'

228

'That wouldn't help,' Chuck told him. 'The nunnery is on the same side of the river as we are. But I had already thought that we should start mounting regular guards, taking turns, and our loyal cook, now that he has prepared the food, is sitting by the gate, nursing an old Lee Enfield rifle and with orders to call us if there is any sign of activity.'

'Let's eat,' Anna urged. 'I am famished.'

Chuck looked puzzled. 'Sandra is taking a long time. I wonder what she and Donald are doing?'

'God, Chuck, you are hopeless!' Anna exploded.

Their deliberations were interrupted by the return of Sandra and Donald. When he had left the hotel at Ibari, Donald had collected Sandra's luggage so she had been able to discard her soiled clothes. Bathed, decently clothed and adored by her man, she felt that she had just rejoined the human race.

They ate a meal of canned meat and fresh vegetables and fruit. Chuck apologized for the simplicity of the fare, but after the nunnery's starvation diet, Sandra appreciated the offering more than any of the more fancy repasts she had enjoyed. Chuck explained to the newcomers that he regarded the camp as liable to come under attack at any time and that he would require them to take turns at mounting guard on the gate.

When they had finished eating, Halevy announced that he would go out and relieve the native cook. As he got to his feet, Sandra asked about the curious object she had noticed on Chuck's desk when she and Donald had arrived.

'The professor can tell you all about that,' Chuck assured them.

Donald and Sandra accompanied Halevy, and he started to tell them the strange story of the golden phallus.

Anna was left alone with Chuck. 'Let's go into your office,' she suggested.

'Why? It's more comfortable here.'

'I want to look at your precious chunk of gold.'

Chuck shook his head. 'I don't think that is a good idea. I haven't mentioned it to Halevy, but I get the strangest feelings when that thing is exposed. I shan't feel at my ease until it is safely in some museum, miles away from Salamba.'

'Well, Chuck, what about taking it ourselves? I know the frontier is supposed to be closed but I guess that if we take the Range Rover, we ought to be able to find some track through the forests to the south.'

'No, it is too dangerous. Moriba can't keep the whole country under a state of emergency much longer. He'll have to open the borders to bring in shipments of food and other essentials like medicines, vital machinery and raw materials. Then, Halevy can get out and take it with him.'

'Give it to me, Chuck. I can smuggle it out.'

'No, Anna. I would never forgive myself if you got caught and had to go through the sort of ordeal which Sandra suffered. No, darling, I am worried about that golden phallus, but I am much too fond of you to let you take that sort of risk.'

Chuck announced that he was going to take a can of beer out to Halevy and went into the kitchen. When she heard him walk out to the terrace, Anna ran into the office to see if, by any chance, Chuck had left the safe unlocked. She was out of luck and sulkily returned to the dining room to await the American's return.

When he did come back, Chuck wore an unwonted, stern expression.

Anna looked up. 'What's the matter with you?'

'Sandra told me something which I find difficult to

believe, but I can't see that she would have any reason to lie.' His voice was hard and he looked her straight in the eyes. 'Is it true, Anna? Are you the mistress of that brute, Asi Moriba? Have you been having an affair with him all the time that we have been living together? Tell me the truth.'

'I knew that stupid little cow would blurt out everything, sooner or later,' Anna spat out the words. She laughed in Chuck's face. 'Yes, I needed a man, a real man. And what were you, little Chuck? My slave, nothing more. And what are you going to do about it?'

She glared at him until he dropped his eyes: she was sure that he had not got the strength to defy her. Very calmly, she ordered him to give her the phallus.

'Go to hell!' Chuck shouted, in a flicker of truculence, but she read in his face despair and wounded pride.

'I don't want to hurt you.' Anna put on a tone of sweet reasonableness. 'I said that we could go together and I meant it. Think, Chuck, it must be worth a fortune.'

There were tears in his eyes but he shook his head stubbornly.

'Well, if you won't play along sensibly, don't blame me if you have a hard time. I'll let my strong man know the score. Think, Chuck, before it is too late. The moment I tell Moriba that both the phallus and his baby-faced blonde are in this camp, he'll be here with enough of the Salamban army to crush the life out of you and your pitiful friends. Do you really think that you could hold out here, once Moriba attacks the place?'

'You wouldn't,' Chuck cried. 'If Moriba got Sandra in his clutches again, he would kill her. She's been telling me what happened in the nunnery.'

'So let's get the hell out of here with that archaeological treasure of yours and leave them to take their chance,' she urged. 'Otherwise,' her voice grew harsher, 'don't

231

waste your tears on that silly little Scottish kitten. Asi will break your bones, one by one, until you give us the golden phallus. Well?'

Chuck turned on his heel and walked out of the room.

Anna was amazed. She'd been sure that he would have caved in either to her cajoling or to her threats. So, now she would have to come to terms with Moriba. The simplest course would be to use the phone, but when she picked it up, the line was dead. She did not know whether it was one of the frequent and regular Salamban breakdowns which had not been repaired in the state of disorder in the countryside or whether Chuck had purposely sabotaged the instrument. She strolled casually out into the yard where the Range Rover and the jeep were standing. From the disinterested way Halevy, the lone sentinel, looked at her, she was sure that Chuck had not disclosed to him what had taken place between them. It gave her grim satisfaction that she could count on his being too shamefaced to admit to the others that she had deceived him and that his touching faith in her was utterly misplaced. Chuck had removed the ignition keys of both vehicles.

She waited until Chuck was on sentry duty and then ransacked his room, but without success. She found neither the key to the safe nor those of the cars. She judged that to make a break on foot would be too dangerous: she would have to be patient, but she vowed that Chuck would suffer for his obstinacy.

Supper was a cheerless meal but Donald and Sandra were still too delighted at their reunion to notice. Chuck had coaxed their radio receiver to function and they heard a news bulletin from Ibari which told them nothing of what was going on outside and made no mention of the attack on the nunnery.

At midnight, Donald relieved Chuck on guard. Chuck's

232

watch had been uneventful but he was still wakeful when he entered his bedroom. He was taken aback to find Anna stretched out in his bed.

'What the hell are you doing here?' he demanded.

'Chuck, we always sleep together. Don't be silly, darling. We don't see eye to eye on what to do with that stupid piece of metal, but that shouldn't change the way we feel about each other.'

'And what about your strong man, Moriba?' Chuck accused.

'Oh, you are so blind. Can't you understand I had to play along with him? What would happen to a defenceless woman without anybody to turn to, if she were to refuse that man? I know I lost my temper this afternoon. It was the fault of Sandra, poisoning your mind against me. And you believed every word she said. Are you surprised that I wanted to hurt you? It was a stupid quarrel: if I had been able to tell you about Moriba myself, without that little bitch carrying exaggerated tales, none of this would have happened. Now, darling, come to bed.'

He complained and protested but without any real conviction. He wanted so badly to be with her that he told himself that he believed her, although he knew, deep down in his guts, that she had played him false and her sweet words were insincere. Inwardly cursing himself for his own weakness, he climbed into bed beside her.

She had intended to seduce him but she decided that in his present state of mind, that would be a mistake and it would only confirm his suspicions. She merely lay quietly in his arms, letting him drink in her familiar aroma. He kissed her forehead sadly and she snuggled against him.

'Darling,' she whispered, 'I'm parched. I'm going to get myself a drink. Can I bring you one?'

'I wouldn't mind a coffee, if you are making one.'

'Stay there, I'll be back in a minute.'

233

It was not long before she was back, carrying two steaming cups. They both contained coffee, but Chuck's had a little extra something added. A quarter of an hour later, he was sleeping so soundly that he would probably have remained undisturbed if the last trump had sounded that night.

Anna got up and put on her clothes. She went through Chuck's pockets. The key to the safe was not there. She looked for it feverishly but Chuck must have hidden it somewhere outside the bedroom. However, she did come across the ignition key to the jeep.

She crept through the camp building and tiptoed out to where the two vehicles were parked.

'Who's there?' called Donald.

She could see him, standing by the gate, holding a rifle with the clumsiness of unfamiliarity.

'It's all right, it's me,' Anna answered. 'Chuck has asked me to drive down as far as the bridge to check that the charges he put under the piles are in place.'

'What? At this time of night?'

'There was something on the radio,' she lied. 'There is a group of Milos's men on the other bank.'

'I'll go,' Donald offered. 'It's no job for a woman.'

Anna could not help smiling at his display of old-world chivalry.

'You are mistaken,' she called out to him. 'I know the road and you don't. Not that you would get lost, but there are treacherous potholes which you would never see in the dark. And, my gallant friend, if the worst should happen and I should run into a band of guerrillas, I can at least speak their language whereas you, a foreigner, would probably be shot out of hand. I'll be back in an hour.'

She did not wait for a reply but jumped into the driving seat of the jeep and started the engine.

'Do you have a gun?' Donald asked. He was still standing by the gate, uncertain whether he should let her pass. He remembered how Sandra had warned him against Anna, but she could have jumped to a wrong conclusion. After all, it was Anna who had brought him to the camp and made the contact with Sandra. Then again, Chuck had heard Sandra's story and yet he obviously trusted her and they were sleeping together.

Anna was ready to run him over if he did not budge but she did not want to alarm the others earlier than was necessary. So she smiled at him and waved the automatic which she had thoughtfully removed from the slumbering Chuck.

'Fire if you get into any sort of trouble and we'll come after you,' he said. And he stepped back to let her pass.

Once clear of the gate, Anna opened the throttle and made for the bridge. As the jeep rattled across, she was happily unaware that Chuck had actually laid explosive charges under the two middle spans in case it became necessary to defend the camp. Across the river, she swung the jeep onto the road to Ibari.

An hour later, when she had not returned, Donald was uneasy. He decided to give her another half hour but when that had elapsed without sight or sound of her, he went inside and aroused Halevy.

'Is it my turn on watch already?' asked the drowsy scholar.

'Not for another twenty minutes,' Donald replied. 'But I think that we might have a problem.'

He explained the circumstances of Anna's nocturnal excursion and the two men went to confirm her story with Chuck.

Their host was lying strangely motionless in his bed and when Halevy shook him, he made no response.

'Good God, is he dead?' gasped Donald.

235

Halevy bent close over Chuck's face. 'No,' he pronounced, 'but I think that he has been administered a Michael something, do you know what I mean?'

'A Mickey Finn!' exclaimed Donald. 'That bitch, Anna! What can we do?'

'Just wait, I guess. When he comes round, he'll have a hangover as if he had been wearing the Eiffel Tower as a hat. We can pour black coffee into him then but for now, let him sleep it off.'

'And Anna?'

'My dear young friend, what can we do? She has obviously got away and even if we were to chase after her, she has nearly two hours' start.'

It was eleven in the morning before Chuck began to stir. He felt terrible and was sure that if he were to die and be condemned to hell, he would rejoice in the improvement in his condition. When he had recovered sufficiently for Anna's flight to register, he told the others of how obsessed she had been about getting her hands on the golden phallus and of her threat to go to Moriba.

'We could be in for a full-scale attack by the army and, if that happens, we won't stand a chance.'

They kept a sharp look out for any sign of life on the road up from the bridge, but for the time being, everything was quiet. Then they heard the news bulletin from Ibari Radio. For the first time, the Nunnery of the Bleeding Heart was mentioned. The announcement reported that an attack had been mounted on the nunnery but beaten off. Among the inmates, it was stated, was a British girl, Sandra Mitchell, an accomplice of the bandit, Milos. The girl, Mitchell, was undergoing a course of education and civic training.

'What's that all about?' Sandra wanted to know. 'Moriba must have found out by now that we got away.

236

After all, his goons would have been released from the latrine when the new guard arrived to relieve them.'

'I don't know,' Chuck answered, 'but if something is going on at the nunnery, it could take the pressure off us, at least for a time.'

Driving back to the capital, Anna had been stopped at three road blocks. Her papers were in order and, at the first two, she was allowed to proceed after the soldiers had satisfied themselves that she did not have anybody concealed in the jeep. At the third, however, she encountered a swaggering sergeant, proud of his three stripes and his macho moustache.

'What do you think that you are doing out at this time?' he blustered. 'Don't you know that there is a curfew in Ibari?'

'But I am not in Ibari,' Anna answered in an even, controlled voice.

'Don't argue with me, woman!' roared the sergeant, 'You are heading for Ibari, aren't you?'

'And when I get there, I shall explain what I am doing to the police who are responsible for the city. Now, may I go on my way?'

'You may not. Out!'

Anna climbed down from the jeep and pulled a piece of paper from her pocket. She thrust it under the nose of the self-important soldier.

'You had better read this,' she ordered him, 'that is if you know how to read.'

The sergeant snatched the paper and perused it in the light of the jeep's headlights. It was an authorization for Anna to be allowed to pass wherever she wanted and it was signed by Moriba. The sergeant seemed to shrink and crumple. He saluted smartly, handed Anna back her pass and went to help her remount the jeep.

'I beg your pardon, Miss. Very sorry to have troubled you, but we have been ordered to be on the look out for this bandit, Milos.'

'Do I look like a man?'

The sergeant saluted again and started to repeat his abject apology, but Anna cut him short.

'I have no time to waste on you. Tell me your name and number: you will be reported to Minister Moriba.'

She had originally intended to go to the bungalow but she changed her mind and stayed instead at a motel on the outskirts of Ibari. She did not expect Chuck to pursue her, but if he did, the obvious place to look was the home which they had shared. She snatched a few hours' rest and, after breakfast, set out for the police head-quarters building. She guessed that, as long as Milos was at large in Salamba, Moriba would continue to use his old office and resist the temptation to move into the presidential palace.

Her hunch proved to be right. After showing her pass at the door, Anna was escorted to a waiting room. Then, after dismissing his secretary, Moriba had her brought to the room where he sat, waiting for her behind his vast desk.

'So you have finally turned up,' he greeted her with a sardonic smile.

'I was at that nunnery,' she told him.

'I know.'

'When the women revolted, they seized me. I was a hostage.'

Moriba's smile broadened. 'Indeed? You don't appear to be any the worse for the experience.'

'Asi, I can help you. Your little girl, the singer, she is at the mining camp.'

'Of course she is,' assented the police chief. 'Where else could she have gone without running into one of our

238

patrols or a road block? I didn't need you to tell me anything so obvious.'

That was not the response on which Anna had counted. 'I was taken there but I escaped.'

'You mean that you deceived that poor American boy yet once more? You are a most unfaithful woman, Anna.'

'Asi, you know that you are the only man in my life. What do I care about Chuck? He's a puppy, still wet behind the ears! But at the mining camp, there are only three men, the girl and a Salamban cook who would run for his life if there were any fighting. Aren't you going to attack it?'

Moriba shook his head. 'Now, I wonder why you are so eager to have that camp stormed. It can't simply be to push another girl into my arms. I have troops in the area but they are deployed to cover the nunnery and that's where they will remain.'

'The nunnery? But why? Nobody who matters is there. God knows how many of the girls got away, so what are your men hoping to achieve?'

'You know that, but Milos, somewhere in the bush, doesn't. He has heard that his English girlfriend is in the nunnery.'

'Jennifer Maxwell?'

'That's right. Now, it is being announced on the radio that Sandra, the Scots singer, is also imprisoned in the nunnery. Milos, although an anarchist, is a gentleman – in a manner of speaking. Twice Sandra helped to save his life. Do you think that he will be so heartless as to leave her to rot in the nunnery, undergoing an intensive course of what we euphemistically call retraining? And with Jennifer there as well, he must attack the place and try to rescue them.'

'But Jennifer escaped. How do you know that she hasn't already got to him and told him what happened?'

239

'Because we have traced her to a hotel in town and my men are bringing her in at this very minute.'

'Asi, you must capture the mining camp. Please, do it for me.'

'There's something that you are not telling me, isn't there?' he mocked.

There was nothing for it: she was obliged to confess. 'It's the golden phallus. I've seen it there. I must have it – I mean we must have it, of course. Think, Asi, the Frenchman has told me that it is genuine. It must be priceless. And it's there for the taking. How many men would it take to rush the place? There is only Chuck, who has the remotest idea how to use a gun. I am sure that neither the French professor nor the Scottish footballer have ever handled one. And as for his girlfriend, she would probably break her arm if she tried to fire one.'

'You have become obsessed by this phallus,' laughed Moriba. 'I always thought that you were a nymphomaniac, but you are making yourself ridiculous. And, while we are on the subject, how did the Scottish footballer get to the camp? I had a report that you took him there.'

'Never mind him; he is of no importance. Won't you help me get the golden phallus?'

'No, my dear Anna, I shall not. My men stay, covering the nunnery. Once we have Milos, I shall deal with the fools in the camp in my own way. Be patient and I might give you a reward when it's all over. Now, excuse me, I am going to the nunnery to take charge of the operation in person.'

He strode out, leaving her to find her own way to the door. She was furious. If only there were some way to divert him from the nunnery or to abort the operation, she was sure that she could persuade him to smash his way into the camp. What he had said was true: her quest for the golden phallus had become the one all-absorbing passion of her life.

She had reached the lobby when she saw, in the street outside, the great, golden Rolls Royce which had once been the pride of Daniel Lomo, sweep past with Moriba reclining in the back seat. She stood perfectly still in the hall for several minutes, letting the fierce waves of her anger rush through her.

She was on the point of leaving when a police car drew up and three policemen dragged a struggling, handcuffed girl into the headquarters. It was Jennifer Maxwell. Her face was bruised and her lip was bleeding. She recognized Anna and shot a glance at her, charged with disgust and hatred.

But Anna saw her arrival as a promise of deliverance. She confronted the policemen and flashed before them the pass which Moriba had given her and which carried the force of law for his fearful subordinates. But the sergeant had already recognized her as the companion of his boss and he saluted her with obvious respect.

'Your prisoner,' Anna rapped out. 'Is she the English girl, Maxwell?'

'Yes, Madam,' replied the sergeant.

'I've been waiting for you,' Anna told him. 'She is to be taken to Minister Moriba immediately, for interrogation.'

'We're taking her upstairs now.'

'Idiot! The minister left for the Nunnery of the Bleeding Heart and asked me to bring her to him. Put her in my jeep; I'll drive her myself.'

The sergeant was not happy at such an unusual procedure but he was afraid of disobeying the woman who enjoyed the favours of the ruthless minister.

'Shall we come along as escort?'

'What for?' Anna sneered. 'Have you nothing else to do?'

'For security – '

'Security!' she interrupted. 'She's handcuffed, isn't she? What can she do? Come along now, look lively, I haven't got all day. Get her into the jeep.'

The policemen obeyed. They saluted again and were about to leave when Anna snapped her fingers.

'They key!' she demanded. 'Give me the key to the handcuffs.'

One of the men handed her a key. She did not thank him, simply dismissed him with a haughty nod of her head and drove off.

They went for about half a mile in silence. Then Anna pulled off into a side street and drew up outside a shabby, deserted café.

'You are not very good at keeping out of trouble, are you?' she said sadly to Jennifer. 'Would you like a cup of tea or coffee?'

Jennifer stared at her in disbelief.

'There's no catch,' Anna assured her. 'I have a proposition to put to you and I would rather that we sat and talked like civilized people. Let me set your mind at rest: I have no intention of taking you to Moriba. After our chat, I shall drive you out of town and set you free. You were stupid to come into Ibari in the first place. You should have made straight for Milos, wherever he may be, and that's where you are going as soon as I have finished with you. Now, if I remove those absurd bracelets which you are wearing, will you give me your word to sit nice and quietly while we have our talk?'

Jennifer shrugged her shoulders. 'I trust you about as much as I would a rattlesnake, but I don't see what I have to lose. OK, you have my word.'

Anna released her from the handcuffs and handed her

a comb and a tissue to freshen up her face. When she was
satisfied with Jennifer's appearance, she led the way into
the café, ordered a couple of cups of coffee from a sleepy-
eyed, native girl, and settled herself beside Jennifer at a
table near the door from which she could keep an eye on
the jeep. She waited until the waitress had shuffled across
and placed the coffees in front of them on the stained
tablecloth. Only then, when they were alone, did Anna
speak.

'Just in case you are still labouring under any delusions,
let me tell you that Asi Moriba will kill Milos if he
catches him. There won't be any nonsense, like giving
him a fair trial; Moriba will shoot him down like a dog.'

'He'll have to catch him first,' Jennifer pointed out.

'That's right. And for reasons of my own, I don't want
Milos to be caught. Not yet, anyway,' Anna added,
with unusual honesty. 'So you are to go to your rebel
sweetheart and warn him that Moriba is setting a trap for
him.'

'What sort of a trap?' Jennifer asked suspiciously.

'Moriba is telling everybody that you and Sandra Mitchell, who might turn out to be your rival for Milos's
favours, are both in the Nunnery of the Bleeding Heart.
Whatever he does, Milos should avoid going anywhere
near the nunnery; the whole area is teeming with soldiers
waiting for him. Moriba himself is on his way there, just
as I told those cops back at headquarters.'

There was a pause while Jennifer digested this information. They sipped their coffee.

'How do I know that this isn't some plot against Milos
which Moriba has put you up to?' Jennifer asked.

'You don't, but use your head. I am not telling Milos
where to go, only to avoid one particular spot. And if
you get to him, he will realize that there is no sense in

rushing off to rescue two girls, both of whom are at liberty. You will be able to find Milos, won't you?'

'Perhaps.' Jennifer was not giving anything away.

'Right,' said Anna. 'That's all I have to say. Finish your coffee and let's get on our way. I have to go and join Moriba at the nunnery, otherwise he will suspect that I am up to something. Where shall I drop you?'

'Anywhere on the outskirts of town,' Jennifer replied.

'Suit yourself. I have no desire to know which direction you take to meet up with Milos.'

They got back into the jeep and Anna rejoined the main road. After a mile or so, they had cleared the built-up area of Ibari and Jennifer stopped Anna at a cross roads.

'It will be fine here,' she said.

The jeep came to a halt and Jennifer jumped out.

'Perhaps I ought to thank you,' she said, 'I really don't know.'

She waited by the roadside until Anna had driven off and the jeep had disappeared into the distance. Only then, when Anna could not see which road she took, Jennifer turned and started walking back into town.

Anna took her time. She stopped for a snack and it was the middle of the afternoon when she crossed the familiar stone bridge. She was reasonably sure that she would not be intercepted by Chuck or his friends. There were not enough of them in the camp to indulge in reconnaissance patrols as far as the bridge. Once across the river, she followed the other road at the fork, the road which led up to the nunnery.

Long before Anna found Moriba, Jennifer had joined Milos in his hide-out in the heart of Ibari, within sight of the presidential palace. He greeted her with an affectionate bear hug.

244

'I was told that those pigs of Moriba had picked you up. I am so glad that you got away before they could do much to you.'

'It wasn't very pleasant,' Jennifer protested.

'No, of course not, my dearest. But you are all right, aren't you?'

Jennifer reassured him and then went on to relay Anna's message. Milos grinned and nodded happily.

'You don't seem to be surprised,' Jennifer complained. 'I thought that I was bringing you important information.'

'So you were,' Milos agreed. 'But I had already worked it out for myself.'

'You knew that Sandra and I were out of the nunnery? How?'

'I was told by someone who got here before you.'

He went to the door and called. Petra came into the room.

'Jennifer,' she cried, 'what the hell happened to you?'

Jennifer was astonished. 'Petra, you never told me that you were working with Milos!'

'Of course not. I was in enough trouble in that nunnery without running the risk of being overheard by some spy or informer in the place.'

'You see,' Milos told her, 'once Petra had got here and I heard Moriba's broadcast that you and Sandra were still being held in the nunnery and being given the treatment, it was obvious what his game was. He's a great brute of a bully but when it comes to strategy, he is playing scrabble when the game is chess.'

'Milos,' Jennifer's tone was serious. 'If we really had been up there at the nunnery, would you have come to save us?'

His eyes were steady as they met hers. 'No,' he answered. 'I could not allow anything to interfere with a more important operation.'

245

'What could be more important? Do you know they were torturing us?' Jennifer was indignant at their suffering being dismissed as a side issue.

'Of course they were,' Milos agreed. 'You will have the answer to your question tomorrow morning. Now, why don't you go with Petra and get something to eat? I am sure that it is ages since you had a proper meal. I am busy, but I shall join you in a little while.'

She followed Petra. She could not suppress her disappointment. Milos was his old warm self but he had other things on his mind and she felt deflated. Perhaps, that night, it would be better when she and Milos could be alone together.

There seemed to be people swarming all over the house, scurrying about with a great sense of purpose and suppressed excitement. Jennifer even noticed that some of the men wore military uniforms.

'I thought that Milos was in hiding,' she remarked to Petra. 'It looks more as if he were organizing a charity jumble sale or running for president.'

'Something like that,' Petra agreed. 'He hinted with all the subtlety of a charging rhinoceros that he would appreciate it if I stayed out of his way today. So I am working in the kitchen. With all these people about, most of them hungry, there's plenty to do. After you've had a meal yourself, why don't you come and help me?'

Jennifer consented readily. She was glad of Petra's company. Nobody else, including Milos, gave her the impression that they wanted to be bothered with her, and in the kitchen she felt that she was at least being helpful.

During the evening, Milos emerged to bolt down a sandwich and a cup of scalding coffee. Then, when she was least expecting it, he led Jennifer to his bedroom.

'Tonight, you sleep here,' he pronounced. 'It's not the

246

height of luxury but it must be an improvement on your last establishment.'

The dimensions of the bed were such that it could accommodate comfortably one quite fat person or two very skinny ones. Milos was well built: it would be a tight fit. Jennifer stretched out on the bed and waited. Milos rummaged in a cupboard, brought out a battle dress tunic and trousers into which he changed. Then he bent over Jennifer, kissed her lips and, with a sweet smile, walked out of the room. Sullenly, she went back to her work in the kitchen.

As night fell, the activity in the house grew more feverish. Shortly after eleven, Jennifer told Petra that she was tired and went off to bed. She took a quick shower, climbed into the narrow bed and settled down to wait for Milos. She knew that in his arms all her worries and frustration would be soothed away.

She must have dozed off and she awoke with a start in the early hours of the morning. With dismay, she realized that she was alone. There could be only one reason for his total neglect of her. Milos was an attractive man; hadn't Sandra got herself emotionally entangled with him? There must have been dozens of good looking young girls among the hordes who had seethed round the house all day. Or perhaps she did not have to look so far; Petra was noticeably at ease with him. She was his type, a committed revolutionary with the sort of strong, forceful personality which would appeal to him. She burned with jealousy, resentment and shame at the way she was being treated.

If Jennifer suffered from a lack of sexual activity, Anna might have complained of an excess. About a mile from the nunnery, she had run into a strong detachment of regular soldiers and they had led her into the forbidding

247

building. The governess, her arm in a plaster cast, had greeted her frostily. She noted with amusement that nests of machine guns had been placed in the turrets where they could repulse the attack which Anna knew would never come. There were plenty of troops in and around the great stone prison, more than enough to crush the occupants of the mining camp when Moriba grew tired of sitting in ambush and came to his senses.

Asi Moriba was in a remarkably good mood. His earlier cynicism had vanished; he was even affectionate towards her. The unfortunate governess had been turned out of her office which Moriba had converted into a communications room and he and Anna spent the night in her requisitioned bedroom.

Patrols came in to report. One of them had made contact with a group of armed men, presumably guerrillas, but they had no way of establishing whether they were the main force of the rebels, since Moriba had ordered his men not to engage the enemy so as not to prevent them from launching their attack on the nunnery. Then came a breakthrough.

Moriba and Anna were eating a carefully prepared dinner when an officer entered with a radio message which they had intercepted. Moriba read it and chuckled with delight.

'It's from Milos. An order to his men: they attack at dawn tomorrow. What a fool the man must be, sending such a message over the air, uncoded!'

'He won't come, Asi.'

'Don't be silly, woman. I knew all the time that he would be tempted with those two girls as bait.'

'I'll bet you that he doesn't attack and that the message is a blind.'

'What do you bet?' asked Moriba truculently.

'The winner takes the golden phallus,' Anna ventured.

Moriba roared with laughter. 'You and that thing! Very well, I accept.'

Anna was exultant. She had got him to commit himself to storming the camp and soon the relic would be hers – and hers alone, provided he kept his word.

At the same time that Jennifer had gone to bed to wait for Milos, Moriba led Anna into the governess's boudoir.

'Tonight is going to be something special,' he gloated.

'Shouldn't you stay awake, ready for Milos?'

'Plenty of time,' Moriba grinned. 'I have told my aide to wake me half an hour before daybreak. I shall receive our impetuous visitor in full dress uniform and wear my medals. I wouldn't like him to feel that he had been treated with any lack of respect. Then I'll shoot him.'

Anna sighed. She genuinely did have a headache, but she knew that if she told Moriba, she would have to undergo even rougher handling. Why did she have to find herself a lover with the stamina of a bull?

However, such was his good temper that he was quite gentle with her, at any rate by his standards. He lay back, taking his ease like a pasha in the decadent days of the Ottoman Empire, while she took him in her mouth; an immense, black lollipop.

'You know, you are a beautiful woman,' Moriba murmured, as he stroked her hair.

What a funny thing to say when he can only see the top of my head, Anna thought. But she showed her gratitude with a special lick, the one he found most satisfying. However, it was not Moriba's way to rest passively for long. He jerked her up and turned her round so that he could seize her by the ankles and pull her legs over his shoulders. Anna, her head thrown back, fondled her own breasts, as her lover drove into her so powerfully and so fluently.

'Why do you want a golden phallus when you can enjoy this one?' Moriba demanded.

'Don't stop,' she moaned.

It was bliss. The whole of her body was throbbing with pleasure, her juices bathing that remorseless piston which brought her such cruel delight. But at the moment that she wanted it most, he held back, delaying his orgasm as long as possible, like a little boy sucking his sweet carefully and slowly to make it last. He never waited for her to come: that was not Asi Moriba's way. But she was so attuned to his rhythm that her body responded to his and the governess's chaste bed almost fell apart at such brutal violence.

He gave her no respite. It was as though he were some implacable machine created by a sex-mad scientist who had discovered how to achieve perpetual motion and inexhaustible energy. She was still moaning, but no longer from pleasure. She was sore from his remorseless pounding and her head was splitting. If only the gods had fitted this fantastic sex engine with a brake!

Anna lost track of time and she had no recollection of how many times he had come but his penis remained as stiff as a ramrod. What a way to die, she complained to herself. Then, when all hope had vanished, Moriba leaped from her with a startled howl.

'Asi, what's the matter?'

'I've been stung. Look, a mosquito!'

He pointed to the tiny speck, buzzing triumphantly round the room.

'So what's the big deal?'

'Don't you understand, woman, there's a lot of malaria in this part of the country.'

He ruefully massaged his punctured buttock and his eyes rolled in distress and alarm. It was so incongruous, the panic which that diminutive insect had inspired in the huge hulk of a man, that Anna could not help laughing. He resented her amusement and turned out the light in a sulk. He climbed into bed and Anna gratefully settled down to sleep.

Up in the mining camp, the course of true love was running into rough waters.

Sandra confronted Chuck. 'It's not good enough,' she protested. 'Donald is away for four hours, watching for non-existent intruders and simply falls asleep as soon as he gets back. We aren't even married and I am already contemplating divorce.'

Chuck was sympathetic. 'It is only for the duration of the emergency,' he assured her.

'And how long is that likely to be?'

He shrugged his shoulders in a gesture of hopelessness. 'How do I know?'

When dawn broke, Sandra was standing by the gate, holding a rifle and scanning the horizon for the enemy who never came.

Asi Moriba, attired in his ceremonial uniform and gleaming medals, was doing much the same thing. The attack was overdue: the forest below the nunnery was deathly quiet. Moriba swore at the inefficiency of the rebels who couldn't get their act together on time and subjected him to the inconvenience of waiting for them. That damned Milos has no consideration for other people, he told himself. He was still in a bad temper when he heard over the radio the first news of the attack. Milos had captured the radio station.

Because of the desertion of many of the troops who had been left in Ibari, there was little fighting in the capital. By ten that morning, Petra was preparing breakfast in the presidential palace, much to Jennifer's bewilderment. The absence of Moriba and the élite corps of the army, ensconced in and around the Nunnery of the Bleeding Heart, greatly simplified Milos's seizure of power.

The sequestered garrison of the mining camp also learned of the coup from the radio. The same bulletin mentioned the presence of Moriba and his men at the nearby nunnery.

'They are too close to us for comfort,' Chuck pronounced. 'Everybody get packed. Somehow we'll all squeeze into the Range Rover.'

'Where shall we go?' asked Halevy.

'Ibari, of course. If Milos's men are in command there, we shall be safe from Moriba. Now, hurry, we have no time to lose.'

In a very few minutes they were on the road, the golden phallus hidden among their possessions. If they had delayed another ten minutes, they would have run into the vanguard of Moriba's men. Moriba had learned that, in addition to the radio station, the rebels had taken the airfield, the post office, the presidential palace and, vital for morale, the Daniel Lomo Stadium. Hand to hand fighting was going on in police headquarters but the city was virtually in Milos's grasp. But there were small bodies of troops stationed in various parts of Salamba who had not been involved in the seizure of power. Moriba calculated that if he could get to these forces before they were infected by the anarchists' propaganda or contacted by men from Ibari, he could still rally enough support to launch a successful counter-attack. He abandoned the nunnery, much to the relief of the governess, who did not take kindly to having to sleep in a dormitory, and assembled his men. He left with the first detachment, a light armoured column, capable of moving rapidly across the country.

Nobody had disturbed Anna with the news, but the

252

hubbub outside woke her up. Bleary eyed, she went to the window in time to see Moriba, still in his ceremonial uniform, seated in a scout car being driven hell for leather through the gate, followed by a line of armoured cars.

A couple of minutes after their departure, the nunnery was shaken by the shock of a distant explosion. Moriba's scout car had reached the fork below the mining camp. It roared along the road down to the river valley, flinging stones from the broken surface.

At the river bank, the car screeched to a halt and the rest of the column stopped behind it. In impotent fury, Asi Moriba gazed at the wreckage of the middle spans of the bridge which Chuck had thoughtfully blown up after his party had reached the far side.

10
Away Match

The delay at the wrecked bridge proved fatal to Moriba's hopes. In his absence, whole units of the army defected and the discontent spread rapidly to the force which had occupied the nunnery. Unable to rely even on his own bodyguard, Moriba, no longer in full ceremonial dress but wearing the inconspicuous combat suit of a simple private soldier, stole away under cover of night. He followed rough tracks through scrub and forest. By the time that Milos's men had rounded up the last of the disaffected warriors of the Salamban army, Moriba had found his way to safety across the border. He had been obliged to travel light and abandon all unnecessary baggage, in which category he included Anna.

By contrast, Chuck had an easy and relatively comfortable drive into Ibari. He went straight to the bungalow and his first act was to collect all of Anna's clothes and possessions and pack them into a wooden crate.

'I reckon she won't be coming back for them,' he commented. 'I'll give them to Oxfam.'

Sandra had been looking forward to her first night alone with Donald, undisturbed by guard duties and free from the nightmare of the Nunnery of the Bleeding Heart. However, the sleeping arrangements were far from ideal. Chuck might have surrendered his bedroom to them now that Anna had departed but his mind did not work like that. There was only one other bedroom which was cluttered up with Halevy's reference books. They considered the servants' quarters but they were full, not only of servants but also other Salambans, real or spurious relatives of the servants, who had taken refuge in the bungalow during the past crisis-ridden days. Donald wanted to go with her to their old hotel but Chuck dissuaded them since by then it was already dark.

'It's far too dangerous to go out now. There will be a curfew and it would be crazy if, having got away from Moriba's hoods, you got snuffed out by Milos and the good guys. Make do here tonight: tomorrow you can go and see if the hotel is still functioning.'

'I wonder,' mused Halevy.

'What do you wonder?' asked Sandra.

'Whether Milos and his men will turn out to be good guys, now that they are in power.'

'With Moriba out of the way, everything will be fine,' Sandra proclaimed airily.

'I wonder,' Halevy repeated.

So Donald and Sandra spent the night on a couch and a makeshift bed consisting of a couple of cane armchairs pushed together. Perhaps she was not being strictly rational, but the arrangements spoiled things for Sandra. There was an atmosphere which ruined her mood and, to the disappointment of Donald, she insisted on their not making love until they were installed in a proper bed in a room of their own in the hotel.

Anna had to make do with much worse sleeping conditions. After Moriba's departure from the nunnery like an avenging eagle whose nest had been invaded by small boys, she had dressed, looted the nunnery kitchen for food for the journey and set out to make her own way back to Ibari. She took her jeep and drove out of the nunnery compound. She managed to cover about two hundred yards before she ran into the rear of the massed vehicles of Moriba's armoured column, halted before the

255

demolished bridge, blocking the road for a mile. Progress was impossible, and the drivers of the armoured cars were content to sit by the roadside and wait for something to happen. Abandoning the jeep, Anna fought her way on foot through the knots of men, smoking and chatting, and the trucks, scout cars and light tanks which obstructed the road as far as the eye could see. They stood, motionless, with the muzzles of their guns pointing ineffectually in the direction of their victorious foes.

Eventually, she reached the approach to the bridge. Moriba was nowhere to be seen so she left the road and started to walk along the bank of the broad, sluggish river. She had stopped to eat some of her food and was wondering where she might have to spend the night when she came across a tiny village. There could not have been more than half a dozen miserable mud huts but what attracted Anna's attention was not the dwellings but the two log rafts, moored alongside the bank. She roused a man who was snoozing in one of the huts and, by offering him the rest of her food, persuaded him to ferry her across the river.

Once across, she made her way back along the far bank until she reached the road leading to Ibari from the stone bridge. Many of the armoured vehicles were still stranded, facing the river, but others had retreated to the nunnery. None had crossed the river. She started walking along the dusty, empty road.

The sun was beating down on her and she was covered with the white powder which blew into her eyes and caked her hair like talcum. She must have trudged for two hours before her luck turned.

She heard the truck coming up behind her and turned to face it, lifting her thumb imploringly. It was an ancient Ford which had been bought or stolen from the American army, probably decades ago. There were two men in the cab and they were carrying a load of peppers to the market. She stood in the middle of the road to make sure that they would stop. With a screech of brakes, the truck shuddered to a halt.

'I must get to Ibari,' Anna cried. 'How far are you going?'

The driver looked at his mate and gave a knowing smile. The two men regarded Anna from head to toe.

'You know, she wouldn't be a bad looking bit, if she were given a good scrubbing. What do you think?'

The other man answered the driver with an approving nod.

'All right,' said the driver. 'We can take you all the way. Mind you, we were not going to Ibari, so we would expect something for our trouble.'

'I have some money,' Anna replied.

'That's not the way we want to get paid.'

She contemplated the two men without enthusiasm. The driver was in his twenties and there was a mad gleam in his dark eyes. His appearance was not improved by pock marks, giving him a cratered look. His companion was a smaller, morose man with a moth-eaten moustache. In Anna's opinion, neither of them would have qualified as a male model in a magazine for the blind. While they were talking, they had climbed down from the cab and now the driver grabbed her by the arm.

She took a swipe at him but his mate caught her wrist and she was dragged, screaming and scratching, to the back of the truck.

The road was deserted. There was nobody to come to her assistance and struggle as she might, she stood no chance against two brutal and determined men. The driver held her securely while the other man tore off her clothes. Then they hurled her bodily into the back of the truck. She had heard it rumoured that peppers possessed

257

aphrodisiac qualities but never expected that they would be administered externally.

There was nothing refined about their love-making. One after the other, they lay on top of her and fucked with hard, remorseless piston strokes, ripping into her until she was sore. They were stained red from the squashed vegetables and they stank of stale sweat. Bruised, mauled and humiliated, she wiped herself on a grubby rag to remove the worst of the pepper juice and, fighting down her nausea, put on her tattered clothes and took her place in the cab beside the two men. She feared that having violated her, they would not trouble to take her to Ibari, but they seemed to be prepared to keep their side of the bargain which they had imposed on her. She loathed going with them, but she had to get to the capital and there was no alternative.

'We've just about got time for another go,' proposed the driver with a villainous smirk as they approached the outskirts of Ibari.

But the truck was held up at a railway crossing and Anna took the opportunity to open the door and leap out before they realized that she was escaping. She ran wildly across the railway tracks and dodged into a side road. After a few minutes of panic, she realized that she was not being pursued and she stopped to get her breath back before making her way in to Ibari.

It was dusk when she entered the town and Anna looked for somewhere to spend the night. She avoided the smarter streets in the centre of Ibari from prudence and also because she did not have much money on her. Since the capital of Salamba did not enjoy a thriving tourist industry, there was no great choice of smaller hotels and pensions but Anna found a run-down establishment which catered, in the main, for commercial travellers who were not fortunate enough to have expense accounts.

She was filthy from her eventful journey and she took a tepid bath before going down for a meal in the dining room. The food was abominable and so was the company. A white man who had been too long in Africa, a sort of land-locked beachcomber, cast lustful glances at her. She scowled discouragingly at him and bent her head over her unsavoury soup. As soon as she had finished eating, she rose from the table and went straight to her room. With a sigh of thanksgiving that she had survived the hideous day, she climbed into the torn sheets and the bed springs twanged a welcome.

She had only been in bed five minutes when the door was opened and the unappetizing man from the dining room stole inside. It was too much.

'Get out!' she shrieked. 'I have been fucked by one deposed dictator and two filthy truckers. That's more than enough for today.'

To emphasize that he was unwelcome, she hurled an ashtray at him. The man fled.

Anna left in the morning. She had no idea what she ought to do, but the lure of the golden phallus was as strong as ever. She was walking close to the presidential palace when she caught sight of a familiar figure. Anna was at heart a gambler and she did not hesitate. She called out and Jennifer turned in amazement.

'You owe me a cup of coffee,' Anna said.

'I thought that you would be with Moriba,' Jennifer exclaimed.

'Skip the coffee. You know that if I had not got you away from those thugs, you would have been beaten up and possibly killed before Milos or anyone else could have got to you.'

'Well?' Jennifer's gaze was unfriendly.

'So now, you do me a good turn to make it quits.'

'Do you want me to smuggle you out of the country?'

Anna laughed. 'Nothing so complicated. Take me to Milos.'

'What? Are you insane?'

'I have something to say to him.'

'But you will be risking your life. And don't think that I have enough influence to save you.'

'Thanks for the consideration, but I know what I am doing and I am prepared to take the chance. Now, will you do it?'

'Are you armed?'

'Of course not, you can have me searched before ushering me into the presence of our new master.'

Jennifer was profoundly unhappy. She detested Anna and was secretly rather afraid of her, even in her present distressed state. But she knew that what she had said was true: she was under an obligation to Anna. So, reluctantly, she agreed.

Milos had moved his battle command post into the police headquarters which had been stormed the previous evening. Anna smiled humourlessly at the reversal of their roles as Jennifer led her into the building. Their way was barred by two girls wearing arm bands in place of uniforms and carrying automatic pistols. Anna could not place them but they looked familiar.

'You should remember them,' Jennifer told her. 'They were in the nunnery. Petra has organized a corps of those who broke out with us: she calls them her Lesbian Legion.'

Anna waited while Sandra got one of the sentries to pass a message to Milos. It was Petra who came down to find out what Jennifer wanted. It took five minutes of urgent entreaties by Jennifer before Petra consented to ask Milos whether he would be willing to see Anna.

About an hour later, having been thoroughly searched,

Anna was escorted by Petra and Jennifer into the presence of Milos. She had never before seen the notorious anarchist leader and she found him unexpectedly attractive. He had the same sort of quick intelligence as Asi Moriba but his self-confidence had not deteriorated into arrogance; perhaps he had not yet enjoyed sufficient power to be corrupted. He watched her with apparent indifference.

'I have no idea what you can want to discuss with me and I am only seeing you as a favour to Jennifer, who believes that you helped her to get away from your boyfriend's toughs. I am busy. You have five minutes.'

Anna tossed her head in the direction of Petra and Jennifer. 'I want to talk to you alone.'

'You cannot lay down conditions. Now, speak.'

She started to tell him the story of the golden phallus and the myth of Osiris. As she went on, she could see that she had captured his interest. She had long exceeded her allotted five minutes before she got to the end of her account.

'And you say that his man, Halevy, is an expert and that he is convinced that the thing is genuine?' Milos asked.

Anna confirmed the details of what she had related and Milos cross-examined her minutely.

'You say that this relic is worth a fortune and this Frenchman is intent on smuggling it out of the country?'

'Chuck Hughes, an American mining engineer, is helping him. I am pretty sure that the two of them are up at Hughes's bungalow now.'

'Alone?'

'They have a slip of a girl and one of the Scottish footballers with them. That's all.'

'The girl,' Milos spoke sharply. 'She is the one who was with me at Entebbe, isn't she?'

261

'Of course it is,' cried Jennifer. 'She's talking about Sandra.'

Milos ignored her. 'What do you propose?' he asked Anna.

'Send a detachment of your troops to the bungalow. I can show them the way and seize the golden phallus.'

'And give it to you?' he asked ironically.

'We'll share,' she replied. 'I can take it abroad and find a buyer. It's fair; without my information you wouldn't know anything about the phallus.'

Her fervour was electrifying. Milos looked thoughtful.

'You can't take her seriously,' Petra broke out. 'If this relic is there, it should be treated as a national treasure. It belongs to the people of Salamba: how can you consider selling it?'

'I shall send a squad of armed police tomorrow. They can't be spared today while we are mopping up the last pockets of Moriba's men. You had better go with them since you can recognize the phallus.'

'But, Milos,' cried Jennifer, 'Sandra is there. If there is fighting – '

'Then she had better keep out of the way, hadn't she? She should have learned how to behave after her experience at Entebbe.'

Petra and Jennifer stared at him in amazement but Anna was exultant. This was a man with whom she could do business.

'You had better stay here for the night,' Milos told Anna. 'See that she is properly looked after,' he ordered Jennifer. 'Now, leave me!'

The three women withdrew. Jennifer took Anna to the canteen in the basement of the building. They did not speak. Jennifer felt as if she had been betrayed. But the shock had not been the behaviour of Anna. She could not believe that her Milos, the idealist who had devoted his life to the overthrow of tyranny, could ally himself with a woman like Anna. Petra's resentment burned in her eyes and she left the others without a word.

Donald awoke with a crick in his neck, an aching back and a general impression that he had attained the age of seventy during the night. He had to convince Sandra that she was only suffering from cramp and not paralysis. Louis Halevy, sprightly and refreshed, sauntered into the room.

'Sleep well?' he enquired.

'Aye, well, now that it's morning, we'll be away to the hotel to get some rest,' Donald informed him.

'Wait a few minutes and have some breakfast before you go,' said Chuck, entering the room.

Sandra's only contribution to the conversation was a prolonged groan which Chuck took to signify consent.

'Will you be going to Johannesburg now to start on your South African tour?' Chuck asked Sandra.

'That depends on how soon they reopen the airport,' she replied. 'I must say, I don't feel much like singing the blues in some night club: I could do with a holiday. By the way, Donald, darling, did you pick up my saxophone when you collected my things from the hotel?'

'How could I forget it?' he smiled. 'I put it in the cupboard where Chuck keeps his guns, safely under lock and key.' Turning to Halevy, he said, 'And I suppose that you will be away back to Paris?'

'As soon as it is safe to leave with the golden phallus,' he answered.

They were interrupted by one of Chuck's men, who told him that a young lady had called to see him.

'I've no idea who that can be: tell her to come in.' His heart missed a beat in case it was Anna, although he told himself that was impossible.

Petra did not wait to be summoned. She pushed her way into the room, nodded curtly at Sandra and spoke with urgency. 'I've come to warn you: there's a squad of police on their way here to seize the golden phallus. Milos sent them.' She spat the words out in disgust.

'Milos? What does he know about the golden phallus?'

'Everything. Anna got to him and told him that it is worth a fortune. She's done a deal with him.'

'Milos!' Sandra gasped. 'I can't believe it. I thought that he was the dedicated revolutionary, incorruptible.'

'So he was,' Petra said bitterly, 'but that was before he got to the presidential palace. It's easy to be good when you don't have the chance to be wicked.'

'Yes, but Milos!' Sandra objected. 'How could he?'

'You wouldn't understand. After years on the run, living in the bush like a hunted animal, a man gets tired and wants to quit. It's more comfortable to be President of Salamba – and better paid,' retorted Petra.

'Judging by the record of the last two residents of the palace, the chance of keeping the job long enough to draw a pension is remote,' Halevy observed.

'Never mind Milos now. You have no time for philosophical discussions,' Petra told them. 'I see that there are quite a few black servants and their families about the house. Will they fight if there is trouble?'

'They'll disappear at the speed of light,' replied Chuck.

'I thought that might be the case, so I've brought along a few of the girls to help defend the house. Not that I think that you have any right to this relic. It belongs to the people of Salamba, but I'm damned if I am going to let Anna and Milos steal it.' Petra was bristling with indignation.

'It does not belong to anyone in Salamba,' Halevy pronounced decisively. 'It was stolen from Egypt by a Swede who brought it here and then vanished.'

'Vanished?'

'It is my opinion,' Halevy continued, 'that he was done to death by people who were seeking this golden phallus.'

When Petra stated that the police posse was on its way, she was anticipating events slightly. The sergeant and seven policemen were at the headquarters, being addressed by Milos. He pointed to Anna.

'You are to accompany this lady to a house on the outskirts of the town: she knows the exact locality. The occupants are holding a part of a statue which belongs to the nation. You are to retrieve this stolen property and bring it back here. Is that understood?'

'What if they offer resistance?' asked the sergeant.

'Shoot them!' Anna told them.

'You will not shoot them,' Milos contradicted. 'The owner of the house is the manager of an American-owned mine. That mine is vital for Salamba's prosperity and the Americans are not likely to keep it going if we make a habit of killing their managers. You will use only sufficient force as may be necessary to recover the relic. Nobody is going to make a fuss about a bleeding nose or one or two broken bones since the object has been stolen. You have batons: keep your hands off your guns. And that's an order,' he added, with a defiant glare at Anna.

However, when they arrived at the bungalow, their way was blocked by a solid phalanx of the Lesbian Legion. The sergeant demanded, in the name of the law, the handing over of an object which Anna would identify. One of the deployed damsels delivered the dignified reply.

'Go fuck yourself,' she called.

The sergeant was nonplussed. That sort of attitude could not be tolerated among women whose place was among the cooking pots. But there were a lot of them.

'Come on, sarge,' urged one of the more impulsive policemen. 'We're not going to run away from a bunch of bleeding women, are we?'

Before he could respond, Anna had pushed her way forward. She was shaking with anger and frustration.

'Give it to me,' she shrieked. 'It's mine. It belonged to my father.'

Halevy was standing with the others in the porch. He turned to Chuck. 'Was Anna's father Swedish, by any chance?'

'I guess so. She did not talk much about her family, but I do seem to remember her saying once that he was an archaeologist from Stockholm. I'd never given it a moment's thought until now.'

The sergeant, egged on by the aggressive policeman, judged that the moment had arrived for him to exercise his authority. Squaring his shoulders, he strode forward and announced that he was going to force his way into the bungalow. His men advanced behind him.

Petra stepped forward. 'Oh no you are not,' she cried.

The sergeant raised his baton and went to strike her. This proved to be a mistake. Petra carried out a carbon copy of her riposte to the governess, stamping on the man's back to ensure that she broke his arm. His men gazed in stunned horror, which gave her time to get in with a vicious chop to the face of the overeager young cop which drew blood and sent him reeling and stunned. The other girls screamed a wild war cry and charged. Before this onslaught, the policemen did what they had learned from years of rigorous training. They took to their heels, leaving their casualties to fend for themselves.

'They'll be back,' Chuck commented, as he watched the helter-skelter flight of the forces of law and order.

'I think we should reconsider our plans,' Halevy remarked.

Back at the police headquarters, an infuriated Anna confronted Milos.

'I told you that we should have shot them,' she shouted.

Milos shook his head irritably. 'Can't you get it into your head that we are not in a position to offend the United States? If they close down that mine, Salamba will be ruined. And if that were to happen,' he added, 'I don't think that I would be as lucky as your friend, Moriba. I'd be lynched before I could get out of the country.'

'They are not all Americans,' Anna objected.

'That's true. But the Frenchman is a world authority on the ancient civilization of Egypt. If anything were to happen to him, it would provoke an international incident and with the revolution two days old, we cannot afford that kind of publicity abroad. As for the Scotsman, he's a footballer, and in Salamba that means that his person is sacrosanct. If I had been a first class wing forward or a great goalkeeper, I could have taken over this country years ago.'

'That leaves the girl,' Anna pointed out.

'Yes, my adoring Sandra Mitchell,' he mused, 'you may have a point. Perhaps we have been going about this the wrong way. Suppose we grab the girl. You know these people; would they trade the golden phallus to get her back?'

'Sure they would,' Anna replied, 'but first we have to get her out of that bungalow and away from the wild women. That's going to be difficult.'

As it happened, there was no problem. Shortly after noon, Sandra and Donald returned to the hotel. Sandra went upstairs to unpack and Donald drifted into the bar.

'I am glad to see you are still alive. What will you have to drink?'

'Tom Blunt!' exclaimed Donald. 'Fancy meeting you here.'

'There's nothing miraculous about that,' smiled the reporter. 'If there is a breath of a scandal in this country, it gets to this hotel in minutes; that is if it did not start here. I am here practically every day, and where else but in the bar?'

Donald ordered a drink and recounted his exploits to Blunt.

'That will make a good story,' Blunt said, 'but I shan't let a word be printed until you and your girl are safely out of the country. This Milos seems to be as vicious a brute as Moriba was and every bit as artful. However, I have a scrap of good news for you. The buzz is that the airport will be reopened tomorrow.'

'We'll be on the first plane out,' Donald vowed fervently.

Tom Blunt had been in Ibari throughout the uprising and Donald listened to his account of events. Two whiskies later, he glanced at his watch and frowned.

'Sandy's taking a hell of a long time unpacking one small suitcase. I thought that she'd be down to join us by now. Excuse me for a minute while I go up and see if everything is under control. I'll be back in ten minutes.'

He took the lift and went to their room and knocked on the door.

'Come in,' called Sandra. 'It's unlocked.'

He found her, lying in the king-size bed. She looked up at him in blissful contentment.

'Darling, do you know what this thing is called? It is a bed – a real one and it is so long since we had one to ourselves that I thought you might have forgotten. It's lovely, come in and try it!'

'Tom Blunt's downstairs and I promised to go back.'

'Off you go then, if you would rather sit boozing with an ageing English gossip than come to bed with me.'

'That's a difficult choice and requires a lot of consideration,' answered Donald, as he climbed in beside her.

They cuddled close to each other. Neither of them could remember the last time that they had been able to relax in such sybaritic ease. Sandra leaned across and nibbled his ear.

'Darling, do you really love me?'

'Uh huh, you know I do, so why do you ask?'

'It's just that I like to hear you say so sometimes.'

'Actions speak louder than words,' he replied, kissing her and clasping her close to him.

She felt her nipples grow taut as he fondled her breasts and then his lips follow where his hands had gone before. She wanted him more than she had ever wanted any man – or that's how it felt.

'Show me,' she invited.

Her flesh was firm beneath his touch, yet as soft as down. He let his fingers play along that tiny line of golden hair which ran down from her navel to merge into the soft fuzz of her pubic triangle. She grasped his hot, eager penis and stroked it before pulling it to her. She rubbed herself against it.

'Do you like that?' she asked.

'Don't stop, I'll tell you later,' he breathed.

'I thought that you wanted to go down to the bar to join your pal, Tom Blunt,' she reminded him, a minute later, as they became more closely united in a loving embrace.

'Who?' Donald replied.

Their limbs were intertwined, their mouths joined and they made love in a wonderful act of mutual adoration. Romeo and Juliet, Anthony and Cleopatra, all the lovers who had ever lived in fact or fiction were brought back to the world, incarnate in the glory of their bodies. When they came in a supreme orgasm and separated, it was only an intermission before coming together again with even greater ardour.

'Were you serious about our getting married, Sandy?' Donald queried, as they took a rest.

'I don't think that we shall be able to spare the time out of bed,' Sandra answered. 'Unless we can get a clergyman to come to our bedroom.'

'I don't think that's likely with the Church of Scotland. I suppose we shall simply have to live in sin until we are about ninety and cool off.'

'You talk too much,' Sandra complained. 'Do you realize that every time you say something, you could have been kissing me?'

Donald kissed her in a wordless apology.

They were lying in perfect peace with the world when the telephone beside the bed shrilled out.

Donald picked it up and answered. It was Tom Blunt.

'I thought that you might conceivably be interested to learn that there has just been a newsflash on the radio,' he announced with deceptive good humour. 'It seems that our good friend, Milos, has denounced your bonny wee lassie, if that is what you Scots say, as an enemy of the Salamban people.'

'You can't be serious!'

'I wouldn't consider it to be a suitable subject for light-hearted banter. Milos says that your Sandy is a spy for Moriba. I don't think that you should hang about here for long.'

'Hold on, I'll be with you in a flash.' Donald slammed the phone down.

'Something wrong, darling?' Sandra asked.

'Hurry up and get dressed or you'll be late for gaol!' he informed her.

A couple of minutes was all that it took for the two of them to join Tom Blunt in the bar. However, in that time, Donald had done a spot of rapid thinking.

'The first thing we must do is to hide Sandy for the moment,' he stated. 'Have you any idea where she might be able to keep out of the police's way for a day or two?'

'Sure,' Blunt answered without hesitation. 'She can stay at my apartment.'

'Will you take her there now and then come back here?' asked Donald.

'I'll bring the car round to the entrance. Be ready to make a dash for it.'

'I'm surprised that the gestapo hasn't arrived already,' complained Sandra. 'Christ, to have the pleasure of their company twice in the same day!'

'I don't think that they spotted us leaving the bunga-low,' Donald said thoughtfully. 'With the sort of reception they are likely to get up there, I think we may have a bit more time in hand.

His diagnosis was correct. A task force, stronger than the original squad, had been despatched by Milos to Chuck's house to bring Sandra in. Their way was blocked by the indomitable Lesbian Legion and they might have stayed outside the house indefinitely had they not intercepted one of the servants who informed them of the departure of the lady with the fair hair and the strange English accent.

Donald waited with restrained impatience for the return of Tom Blunt. He was not treated with any hostility by the hotel staff and he concluded that they either had not heard the newsflash or they considered him to be in some way a being apart from Sandra. That gave him food for thought.

Blunt strolled into the bar, patting his moustache and

apparently without a care in the world. However, Donald noted that he downed his scotch in record time.

'Well, she's nice and comfortable,' he confided. 'Nobody made any fuss: I think we got away without being spotted by any of the usual gang of informers.'

'Tell me,' Donald said, 'do you have much influence around here?'

'My dear fellow, nobody has any influence yet with Milos, it's too soon. Apart from Anna, of course,' he added ruefully. 'It didn't take her long, did it?'

'I'm not interested in Milos. What about with the media – radio, TV, newspapers?'

'That's different. As I am the link with the biggest news agency and some of the most influential networks and papers in the world, I am everybody's friend.'

'Can you get me a spot on TV? Tonight?'

Blunt blinked. 'That's a hell of a tall order. All the programmes will have been scheduled long ago. It is important?'

'Life and death,' Donald assured him.

'Leave it to me. Exclusive interview by young, Scottish international footballer – how does that grab you?'

'I don't give a damn what you say or how you fix it, just get me air time.'

It took time, but Blunt had not boasted idly about his connections. He monopolized the phone for an hour. He urged, he wheeled, he threatened, he pleaded. He refused to be fobbed off onto secretaries or assistants. He interrupted conferences, he dragged one programme director out of a meeting with the newly-appointed minister of propaganda, another out of a meeting with his mistress and, most serious of all, a third out of his tea break. But, at the end of his efforts, he was able to tell Donald that a camera crew and a journalist would be at the hotel to broadcast the interview live at seven that evening.

'Is that a good time?' Donald asked.

'Good God, man, it's peak viewing, five minutes before the latest instalment in our local soap opera and directly after the news bulletin.'

Donald had intended to spend some time preparing for his TV appearance, but he was distracted by the arrival of a group of uniformed police, seeking Sandra.

Donald was helpful. 'She was here but she went out.'

'Where did she go?'

Donald wrinkled his nose in concentration. 'Well, to tell you the truth, I wasn't listening too carefully. She said something about buying a few souvenirs for the folk back home. Why don't you go and have a look for her in the market? Or she might be buying records; Sandy is very fond of music, you know.'

'She will be coming back here?'

'I suppose so. Unless she goes somewhere else,' Donald added by way of clarification.

'It's hot to go traipsing around that damned market in the sun,' one of the police complained. 'If we phone headquarters, they can send some other men while we wait for her here. That way, we are sure to catch her.'

It seemed a good idea and the police, after marching up and down the lobby to scare anybody with a guilty conscience, gravitated to the bar where Donald welcomed them with great cordiality.

'Let me buy you boys a drink.'

A sergeant, who was in charge, sadly shook his head. 'Thank you very much, Sir, but we are not allowed to drink when we are on duty.'

'Of course, I quite understand.' Donald's affability was positively infectious. 'But you came here to arrest Miss Mitchell, didn't you?'

'That's right, Sir. She must be a very dangerous woman.'

273

'Absolutely lethal,' Donald agreed. 'Especially in bed. But the way I see it, you are only on duty when you are actually arresting this fugitive from justice.'

The sergeant was puzzled. 'We are waiting for her.'

'That's right. But when you are waiting, you are not strictly on duty, are you? When she turns up, you will be on duty again. As you say, now you are only waiting. Have a drink.'

The sergeant suspected that there was a flaw somewhere in Donald's logic, but he could not put his finger on it. He was uncomfortably aware of the growing discontent of his thirsty men.

'Very well, Sir,' he conceded. 'I don't see that it can do any harm. We'll have beers, thank you, Sir, small ones.'

'Make that large whiskies,' Donald ordered the barman. 'These poor guys have had a hard day. Heroes, that's what they are, keeping us all safe from blood-thirsty terrorists.'

With such praise being bestowed on them, it would have been churlish for them to refuse the substitution of scotch for native beer. Nor could they in conscience decline to partake of a second whisky when it was offered expressly to drink a toast to Milos, their noble leader. The third round was in honour of international football and the fourth was a mark of respect to their benefactor (although it went onto his bill). By the time that the TV crew arrived, the guardians of the law were all past caring about such trivial matters as tracking down the enemies of the people. They regarded their surroundings with owlish good humour and several of them were singing lustily, if not very tunefully, some much-loved, dirty ditties.

Tom Blunt nodded in approval at the rollicking cops.

'You've done a good job on that lot,' he congratulated Donald. 'I don't see them making any trouble.'

274

The two men went into the hotel manager's office which Blunt had arranged should be taken over for the TV interview. There was the inevitable clutter of cameras, microphones and bright lights with cables snaking everywhere ready to be tripped over. Donald was introduced to a voluble man in his fifties, wearing a slick, American suit of the latest fashion (or at any rate, the latest to have hit the Salamban market) and with an accent to match. However, his manner of speaking was derived from Chelsea rather than Manhattan.

'Now, don't be nervous, will you, sweetie!' he chirped encouragingly. 'We have a ten-minute slot and, if you dry up, I'll be right there beside you to prompt you with the sort of questions you can answer standing on your head. You know the sort of thing – what was it like growing up in an English industrial town – '

'It was a Scottish village,' Donald interposed.

'Same thing,' sniggered the interviewer. 'Do you think that any of that lot out there will know the difference?'

'Five minutes,' warned a harassed technician who was staggering under the weight of an enormous set of headphones.

An intense young woman pushed her way forward.

'Meet Chaka,' said Donald's self-appointed mentor. 'She will be making a simultaneous translation of the interview into Salamban.'

'And I'll keep an ear on what she is saying,' Blunt growled, 'just to make sure that none of your words get twisted.'

'Mr Blunt!' protested the interviewer. 'How could you suggest that we would do such a thing? You and I are in the same business, aren't we? Integrity, that's what it is all about.'

'Delighted to hear it,' Blunt replied acidly. Then he

spoke to the young woman in the native language to make sure that they realized that he was fluent in it.

'Two minutes,' called the bearer of the headphones.

They took up their positions with Donald sitting in a chair opposite the interviewer who settled himself behind the manager's desk.

'Are you sure that you aren't nervous?'

'I'm just fine,' Donald assured him.

'Most people are a bit nervous the first time,' the interviewer pointed out hopefully.

Donald shook his head irritably.

'You'll be seen all over Salamba.'

'Ten seconds.'

'Don't panic,' urged the interviewer. Then he set his features into a smile fit for a toothpaste commercial and beamed inanely at the camera. On a signal from the man in the embrace of the headphones, he launched into his introduction of Donald to the population of Salamba.

One of the viewers, now comfortably installed in the presidential palace, was Anna. She stared in disbelief at the earnest face of Donald on the screen. Picking up an internal telephone, she called the president's private study, where Milos was working.

'There's something coming over the television now which you ought to see,' she told him.

Within seconds, Milos bustled into the room. Donald was just getting into his stride.

'Who the hell put that kid on the box?' roared Milos.

'Take it easy!' Anna rebuked him. 'Why are you so alarmed by a moron who keeps his brains in his boots?'

'That's what worries me,' Milos rejoined. 'We'd better watch what he is up to. By the time I could get the programme suppressed, he would have finished his spot. And cutting him off would probably do more harm than letting him ramble on.'

Donald had made short work of narrating how he had joined Inverclyde, been signed up on the spot for Glasgow Rangers and catapulted into the Scottish side to tour Africa. Before the interviewer could trot out some other anodyne topic, Donald addressed the nation.

'You have been told who I am, one of the team which came to play against your national side. What you are probably wondering is why I have remained behind in Salamba when the rest of the Scottish team have left to continue their tour.

'I shall tell you. I stayed to right a fearful injustice and to make sure that Salamba stays one of the great fraternity of sporting nations whose footballers will be welcome wherever they go throughout the world, a country which teams from Europe and Latin America will be proud to visit.'

The interviewer had no idea what Donald was driving at but while the Scotsman confined his remarks to the national sport, the interviewer nodded enthusiastically. He tried to interrupt the flow of Donald's rhetoric and regain control of the programme, but Donald ignored him.

'As soon as your airport at Ibari is reopened,' Donald continued, 'I want to go home, but with the intention of returning with my team mates so that we can play to a finish the game which was so tragically cut short. That is, if I am included in the side,' he added, as he recalled the circumstances of his parting from the team manager. 'But I shall not leave Salamba alone.

'My fiancée is being denied her freedom.' In view of the peculiar attitude to morality of the previous Salamban administration, Donald thought it prudent to formalize his relationship with Sandra. 'As a footballer, I appeal to you, the people of Salamba, to ensure the safety of Sandra Mitchell. Hounded by Moriba, threatened with

277

torture, she is again being persecuted. And she has committed no crime: she bears no ill will to the Salamban people. Now, that is not the way sportsmen behave towards each other.'

The interviewer was frantically waving at the girl who was translating Donald's speech. She nodded, but after a few words, Tom Blunt snatched the microphone from her and took over rendering Donald's oration into Salamban, accurately and without censorship.

'If you want Salamba in future to be host to the best known sides of the world, you must let me leave your country a free man. But I shall not go without my woman. What sort of sportsman would I be, if I were to run out on her now?

'We wish your country well. Whatever our differences in politics or religion, football unites us. So, let us go home in peace. Otherwise, if we are detained against our will, how can you expect the great teams, which you want to see, to come and play here? I challenge Milos, as your leader: are you prepared to face the consequences of holding us as prisoners? Put right this injustice and the lads will be back soon in that splendid stadium, playing with your own team, before your marvellous crowd.'

'That's all we have time for today,' screamed the apoplectic interviewer who had visions of his body suffering the same fate as that of Osiris. 'Thank you, Donald McFee. We return you to the studio.'

Donald slumped back in his seat, exhausted by the passion he had put into his speech. He mopped his brow and looked at Blunt.

'How did I do?'

'Fine! That was the most skilful combination of flattery and blackmail I've heard for many a long year. If you change your mind and decide to stay, you could be the next president of Salamba,' Blunt replied jocularly.

278

The TV crew dismantled their gear in fearful silence; they shared a presentiment that retribution would not long be delayed. The door burst open and a flushed police sergeant stumbled into the room. He glared at his unhappy fellow countrymen bul let his gaze settle on Donald.

'Have a drink,' he invited.

Sandra had watched Donald's performance in her refuge at Tom Blunt's apartment. She felt tremendously proud of Donald. Moriba and Milos had impressed her as strong men but each of them had the reassurance of the gun at his side. Donald had stood up, alone and fearless, and defied the dictator with all his police and soldiers. And he had done it for her.

Chuck, Halevy and Petra had also seen the programme.

'That took immense courage,' Chuck commented.

'Will Milos have him liquidated?' Halevy asked.

'I don't know,' Chuck admitted. 'Who can be sure of anything in this screwy country?'

Milos entertained no doubts. He switched off the set and spoke to Anna with quiet, concentrated anger.

'You have a task to carry out. It is your responsibility to see that Donald McFee, together with this accursed woman of his, are on the first flight out of Ibari tomorrow morning.'

Anna shook her head in bewilderment. 'What are you talking about? The airport is still closed.'

'It reopens tomorrow. We urgently need to bring in freighters. I have given the necessary orders. The first plane leaves Ibari in the morning.'

'But what about the golden phallus?' Anna howled. 'We have to get hold of that girl to swap her.'

Milos shook his head impatiently. 'Can't you understand? You have lived in Salamba all your life; you ought to know the mentality of your people. McFee will be a hero, a popular idol. If he is molested in any way, after that broadcast, there will be a riot. Every hour that he stays in Salamba we are at risk of serious trouble starting. Get him out!'

'But, you heard, he won't go without Sandra.'

'So get her out too!'

'But, Milos,' Anna cajoled, 'I don't know where she is.'

'Don't play with me, woman!' he shouted. 'McFee knows where she is hiding. Go and talk to him before he does any more damage.'

'And the phallus?'

'You will have to wait,' he told her. 'What I'll do is increase the force which is surrounding the bungalow. Sooner or later, the American will have to come out or the Frenchman will make a break with the phallus. Now, you can take the Rolls and the chauffeur, but move!'

Anna was not happy, but she had no alternative but to comply. As she got to the door, she turned and asked, 'Where do you want them flown to?'

'Anywhere!' Milos cried in exasperation. 'Just put them on the first flight. I don't care if it's to Moscow, Miami or Manchester, just as long as it is some place outside Salamba, and the farther the better.'

In the bar at the hotel, Donald and Tom Blunt found that their police escort was unwilling to leave.

'We are waiting here to apprehend somebody,' burbled the sergeant. 'Can anybody remember who we are supposed to arrest?'

His men considered the problem. They had a hazy recollection it was some woman or other. Their eyes lit up when Anna hurried into the hotel and went over to Donald.

'You're under arrest,' the sergeant informed her.

'What the hell are you talking about?' she demanded.

'You had better come quietly,' one of the policemen advised her. 'Otherwise, you'll get done for resisting arrest as well.'

'Who do you think I am?'

'You are the woman we are supposed to take back to police headquarters,' the sergeant informed her. 'What your name is, that's of no importance.'

Donald had no objection to Anna being carted off to the gaol but while the policemen were struggling to their feet, Tom Blunt managed to exchange a few words with her and learned of her mission.

'Hold it, boys,' he called. 'This is the wrong lady. The one you are after has been found and is at headquarters.'

'That's what you say,' retorted the sergeant. 'How do we know that is the truth?'

'Go back and see for yourself.'

The sergeant considered this suggestion and discussed it with his men. They decided to take a chance.

'How about one for the road?' proposed the sergeant.

But there was nobody to take him up. During their befuddled consultations, Anna and the two men had slipped away to Donald's room where they could talk in peace.

Donald was suspicious that Anna's offer was merely a trick by Milos to capture Sandra. Anna assured him that she was being sincere, but Donald insisted on taking his own precautions.

At eight the next morning, the golden Rolls Royce, flying the presidential standard, drew up outside the departure hall of Ibari International Airport. It was surrounded by an escort of the Lesbian Legion, fully armed and determined that there should be no treachery.

Donald, Sandra and Anna descended from their stately conveyance and went into the VIP lounge. Anna looked after the arrangements and brought them two first class tickets.

'You're on Africavia 102 to London,' she announced.

'First class,' Donald observed. 'That's very generous of Milos.'

'Tourist class was full,' Anna explained.

She accompanied them through passport control after their luggage had been registered and saw them into the customs hall.

'What have you got there?' The customs officer pointed to the odd case which Sandra was carrying.

'It's my saxophone,' she told him, and opened the case so that he could see the instrument. 'It would get broken if I let them put it in the hold.'

He waved her through with the scornful sneer of a confirmed music hater.

Anna watched them board the plane and she waited at the airport until it took off.

Seated in the first class cabin, Donald and Sandra were celebrating their freedom with a bottle of champagne.

'Do you remember that first bottle of champagne I bought for you?' Donald asked.

'At The Blue Siren,' Sandra smiled. 'It seems a hundred years ago.'

'I know that we are lucky to get away, but I am sorry about your South African tour,' Donald told her. 'It could have been a big chance for you.'

'I doubt it,' Sandra replied. 'I am sure that Mr van der Bejl found an acceptable substitute. No, the one regret is your getting thrown out of the Scottish team.'

'Maybe I can get back again,' Donald said. 'The African

282

tour is over now and I expect that Roddy MacEwen and the rest of the lads will be able to talk the manager round now that he has had a chance to cool off.'

There was a confused noise behind them and, pushing aside a vainly protesting air hostess, Jennifer Maxwell walked in from the tourist cabin.

'I had to come and wish you both the best of luck,' she said.

'Jennifer!' Sandra was flabbergasted. 'What on earth are you doing here?' She kissed her, sat her down and gave her a glass of champagne, much to the annoyance of the air hostess.

'When Milos made that deal with Anna, I decided to quit. He's not the same man as the one I fell in love with. So I'm going back home, and I'll see what Fate turns up next.' She turned to Donald. 'You were fantastic on TV yesterday.'

'It seemed the only thing to do,' he replied modestly. Then, refilling their glasses, he lifted his in a toast. 'Let's drink to absent friends.'

'Yes,' Jennifer was serious. 'Poor Chuck and Louis, cooped up in that bungalow. Milos is going to starve them out until they let him have the golden phallus.'

'They are going to have a long wait,' commented Sandra. 'Tell me, do you think that we are clear of Salamban territory yet?'

'Sure, long ago.'

'Good. I have something to show you.'

Sandra got to her feet and took down the shabby case from the rack and opened it.

'Are you going to give us a tune, then?' asked Jennifer, puzzled and amused.

Sandra didn't answer. She took the old saxophone from its case, put her hand into the wide bell of the instrument and drew out from its hiding place the golden phallus of Osiris.